Wicked Words 5

D1256685

Other Black Lace short story collections:

WICKED WORDS
MORE WICKED WORDS
WICKED WORDS 3
WICKED WORDS 4

Coming in June 2002

WICKED WORDS 6

Wicked Words 5

A Black Lace short-story collection

EDITED BY KERRI SHARP

Black Lace novels are sexual fantasies.
In real life, make sure you practise safe sex.

First published in 2001 by
Black Lace
Thames Wharf Studios,
Rainville Road, London W6 9HA

Strawberry Sunday ©Maria Eppie
Cinderella ©Ruth Fox
The Celibate ©Barbie Scott
Playing With Fire ©Kimberly Dean
Keeping Company With Chameleons ©Saskia Walker
The Last Deduction ©Alison Tyler
Sci-Fi cliché #10 ©Astrid Fox
Bad Girl ©Mini Lee
Opening the Veins of Jade ©Renée M. Charles
Two-Timer ©Louise Demartigny
Dorina Gray Never Did This ©Maria Lloyd
The Pillory ©Mathilde Madden
Frustration ©Lois Pheonix
Teen Spirit ©Louise James
The Lesson ©Catherine Miller
A Matter of Interest ©Rosetta Stone
Erotica? ©Leah Baroque

Typeset by SetSystems Ltd, Saffron Walden, Essex
Printed and bound by Mackays of Chatham PLC

ISBN 0 352 33642 0

All characters in this publication are fictitious and any resemblance to real persons, living or dead, is purely coincidental.

This book is sold subject to the condition that it shall not, by way of trade or otherwise, be lent, resold, hired out or otherwise circulated without the publisher's prior written consent in any form of binding or cover other than that in which it is published and without a similar condition including this condition being imposed on the subsequent purchaser.

Contents

Introduction and Newsletter

At the risk of sounding overblown, I think that Black Lace short-story collections are an interesting yardstick with which to measure the changes that are constantly occurring in the sexual arena. Language and gender dynamics are perpetually evolving, shifting and being tweaked as we soak up the influences that assault us from a variety of media. As the advertising industry hoovers-up all that was once considered 'underground' (i.e. fetishism, S&M, body modification) and uses it to sell luxury items (cars, perfume, alcohol etc.), we need to look in new places for our sexual inspiration. In the past couple of years it seems the mainstream media has become obsessed with the minutiae of our sex lives. Not a week goes by without one of the many TV channels we can now choose from running a documentary about female sexuality. This is, overall, a positive step forward. Who would have thought even 10 years ago that we would be seeing magazine-format programmes where subjects road-test vibrators and presenters run through the mechanics of how best to give yourself an orgasm . . . without there being any complaints? The real viewers and listeners, it has been proven, are not offended by explicit sex; it's violence and swearing that gets up their wotsits.

The British sexual consumer has never had it so good. We now have erotica exhibitions, sex shops opening on provincial high streets and genital piercing salons in every town (although we still have some of the toughest censorship laws in Europe regarding adult entertainment on video and DVD). The potential drawback to sexuality having all this media attention is that the excitement of 'doing something naughty' risks becoming commodified and commonplace to the extent that buying a vibrator will be no more thrilling and than purchasing a toothbrush.

And that's where Black Lace books aim to keep the wow! factor in effect. As ever, the sexual imaginations of our authors have been working to full capacity to bring you 17 new stories of weird and wild behaviour that's guaranteed to have you turning the pages. We've never been shy of pushing the envelope when it comes to our short-story collections and this one is no exception. The pub garden scene in *The Pillory* is wonderfully dirty and deviant, while the stalker's letters in *Playing with Fire* send a frisson of danger through the arousal factor.

Curiously there are no less than four cross-dressing stories this time – three of them male to female. I could have included even more than this but it may have seemed like overkill on the gender-fuck! Does this mean that many of you like chicks with dicks? Conversely, there are quite a few laaads as well: we have a brawny horny building-site worker (*Frustration*), some 'avin' it large, lovin' it festival goers (*Strawberry Sunday*); and the obnoxiously dirty but sexy Simon and Harry in *Two-Timer*.

We've got loads of bad girls, too (not least in *Bad Girl*), some blue-skinned, sex-mad aliens (*Sci-Fi Cliché #10*) and some beautiful time-travelling creatures full of eastern promise who happen to like the occasional tattoo (*Opening the Veins of Jade*). So, hopefully, there will be something in this eclectic mix to suit everyone's tastes. For those of you who wonder if Black Lace books are 'hardcore erotica' or 'softcore pornography' you must read the final story in this collection called – not surprisingly – *Erotica?*. I'm none the wiser myself and my last word on the subject is that I think the naming is in the cultural conditioning!

That's it for this anthology. For those of you who have been following Black Lace books since the early days, keep an eye out for our series of reprints of earlier titles that have been out of print for some time. Forthcoming reissues include such classics as *The Gift of Shame, Odalisque, The Captive Flesh* and *Elena's Conquest*. Remember: gotta catch 'em all!

If you want to keep up with all the latest news and find out more about our forthcoming titles, check out our website at www.blacklace-books.co.uk

Wicked Words 6 is due for publication in June 2002. Until then, be sexy, be strong, behave!

Kerri Sharp
July 2001

I'm always keen to see stories from women who write from the heart and the groin. Women who aren't afraid to be bad girls, and who want to translate their most outrageous fantasies into top-notch erotica stories. If you think you could write for us, send a large S.A.E. to

Black Lace Guidelines
Virgin Publishing Ltd
Thames Wharf Studios
Rainville Road
London W6 9HA

A first-class stamp is sufficient. If you are writing from abroad, remember that you need to include a British postage stamp or an International Reply coupon.

Strawberry Sunday

Maria Eppie

Strawberry Sunday

Glastonbury, the year it didn't rain. Me and the two Michelles – Meesh and Shell. Me, skinny and tall, tanned and red haired. Shell, short and dark and a bit clever. And Meesh, one hundred per cent blonde babe. Three girls in a tent. Not on the pull or anything. Quite the opposite. We had an agreement: no skanking, just three girls out for a laugh. Supposedly.

We were so crap we couldn't get the tent up (some complicated geodesic affair). The boys on the neighbouring pitch (dark-haired moptops affecting Manchester accents of the mad-fer-it, livin'-it-laaarge, Gallagher brothers variety) asked us if we needed a hand. Shell, who fancied herself as Riot Grrrl, went right into one, so they told us to fook off and look up equality in't dictionary then. That didn't solve the tent problem and I was contemplating sleeping in the car when finally Meesh batted her baby blues. The Gallaghers relented and started slotting poles together manfully. Turned out that they were nice boys (northern posh) called Damien and Jeremy.

Once we'd got them organised, we stretched out on the shady side of the tent, happily enjoying a smoke. The idea was to shelter from the sun but as soon as the Gallaghers finished banging in pegs, Meesh instructed Jeremy to begin rubbing sun oil into her creamy-white skin. (Not being a bronzed Nordic blonde, her hair came out of a bottle.) He kept shooting smug little looks at Damien, who was trying on statements like, 'I'm a feminist, actually!' in his real voice now (minor public school) to ingratiate himself with the still glowering Shell. I contributed to the fun by unhitching my bikini top so I was down to cut-offs, and tantalising them as I sprawled on my tummy and toasted myself. Then I tuned out and took in the view. It was burning hot; all the grass had turned to dust. A shanty town of tents sprawled away, as far as the eye could see. And everywhere boys.

I don't know if they'd been specially bussed in, but they were all over the place – gorgeous and scantily clad. Most of them wandering round in shorts and headscarves in a choice of styles – pirate or PLO were favoured. Shades were de rigeur. Sunbathing gets me horny anyway but remembering our No Skanking pledge I fought the urge to think lascivious thoughts about what exactly well-trained young men might do with suntan oil and over-heated young women. I made do with haphazardly squirting factor 10 over my shoulders while surreptitiously grinding myself into the baked hard earth. Don't know why I bothered cos Shell immediately ordered Damien to get her sun-protected too.

We hung around the tent till the sun went down and the boys lit us a campfire. It was all getting way too cosy, but they had a bottle of brandy and the Michelles were making puppy-dog-please noises so eventually I had to relent and let them play Truth or Dare. Which is fine when you're interested in copping off but not when you've got a definite agreement that this would be a girly holiday. No lads, that was the deal. Didn't seem to bother the Michelles though.

The evening turned into a predictable pairing-off pre-fuck flirt fest with me the gooseberry fool in the middle. I was bored (the lads were definitely not my type) but, as we'd arrived early to get a good pitch and the festival hadn't officially got going yet, there was nowhere I could go to escape from them. I turned in early, stuffed my glowstick under a rucksack and crawled gratefully into my sleeping bag.

Sometime later, the rip of velcro woke me as the Michelles came crashing into the tent, nearly dismantling it in the process. I was pissed off with them for reneging on our deal so early, so I played dead as they bumped around getting undressed and mumbling and giggling at each other. It took some time before I realised that one of the voices was definitely a lower register than either of the girls'. Shell had dragged Damien back with her, on the first night too. What had happened to Riot Grrrl? And the no-boys agreement? I made my feelings plain by doing a big production of tossing and turning before trying to get back to sleep.

Needless to say, to no effect. After a period of subdued muttering and murmuring and general rustling, I became aware of the static crackle caused when man-made fibres are rubbed vigorously against each other. Something was kicking and churning around by my face. Whatever it was had managed to knock my sack and the six-hour glowstick I'd snapped five hours earlier was partially exposed. A sulphurous, crepuscular glow dimly lit the tent. A few feet from my nose, Damien's bare buttocks were rising and falling, framed by Shell's ankles dangling midair. Somehow, they'd managed to reverse their alignment in the tent; their heads by my feet, and vice versa. And they were, to quote a phrase, bang at it.

I was about to give it my best, 'Oi, copulation? No!' when the thought struck me that I could have a bit of fun and not compromise my own morally superior kept-the-pledge status. Shell and Damien were probably way too pissed and/or stoned to realise that they were illuminated, albeit faintly. They could be my personal floorshow for the evening. Now, I'm no innocent, but I'd never actually watched people fucking before, certainly not from such close quarters. I have to admit that, aggrieved as I was at their selfish behaviour, the spectacle was interesting.

So, I relaxed and watched as Damien's rather scrawny cock slithered and bashed inexpertly around Shell's fluffy-haired, spreadeagled crotch, while Shell issued a continuous stream of instructions and comments, largely concerned with the rigidity of Damien's performance. It was not all that it should be. Maybe it was the brandy, maybe the occasion, but Damien was increasingly wilting, while Shell was getting increasingly pissed off. I could see this going on all night. Someone needed to take the matter in hand.

I had an idea. I quietly squirmed deeper into my sleeping bag, surreptitiously pulling my zip down with me so that I could maintain eye contact. After I'd slithered down about a foot, I was level with the action, or lack of it. Tentatively, I reached out and took hold of Damien's semi-flaccid penis by the base and applied pressure. Gradually, the member increased in girth and length till it was at least semi-respectable. Then, I aligned it with Shell's slippery hole and, plop, it was sucked straight in. Now, the performers, who seemed oblivious of my assistance, were able to get down to it properly. Damien spread his knees and started ramming Shell with a degree of vigour that surprised me. I watched, fascinated, as the bulging prick slapped and pushed against Shell's pussy which, maintaining full-on receptiveness when the cock was withdrawn, remained hungrily, urgently gaping for its return. Sometimes Damien's aim was true and he slipped straight in, sometimes he missed and slithered up Shell's gleaming slit or down into the crevice between her buttocks.

Much as I didn't really fancy him, I couldn't help

picturing Damien's cock slithering in and out of my own hole. I was so slick with juice, I knew I'd just engulf it whole in seconds. I knew, because I'd just swallowed three of my fingers with ease. Soon, I was rocking them in and out of my own orifice while my thumb worked against my anxious clit. The problem was, I was far more expert than Damien and got myself sorted while he was still thrashing at an increasingly noisy Shell. I wanted sleep now, so I snaked a hand beneath Damien once again and managed to cup his balls with it. Then I squeezed gently. Immediately, his cock stiffened and lurched. With a moan, he forced himself deep into Shell's pussy, trapping my wrist between their bodies as he did. Automatically, Shell curved her spine to receive him and I could feel her pussy tighten round his pumping cock.

Honestly, I'd never touched a pussy other than my own before and I don't know if my brain got confused or what but my fingers sort of circled the slippy entrance to her hole and, as my own pussy began to spasm again, I automatically slipped a finger in. Then I got annoyed that I'd allowed myself to get so turned on. I yanked my hand away quickly, not caring if they realised I'd been there, and sealed myself back inside my sleeping bag for the rest of the night.

Next day, I was tired and irritable. I tried guilt-tripping the Michelles, reminding them of our agreement. They laughed at me and Meesh said, 'You're just sulking cos you didn't cop.' I played my morally superior card and said I didn't give a toss who they wanted to shag as long as I didn't have to spend the night listening to them trying to do it. They laughed harder and called me a prude. I was seething, partly cos I did feel a prude. Then Shell said, 'Maybe you could swap tents with the boys?' I was in such a nark that I snapped back, 'Fine, it's every girl for herself, then, is it?' and moved my stuff into the boys' tent there and then. So, for the next 48 hours, I sulked around on my own while the Michelles and the

Gallaghers played at being engaged or something like that. I could have hung round with them or copped off myself if I'd wanted to, but I'd gone right off the idea of boys.

On the Sunday, there was a dance act I wanted to see, Hyperhyper. I was determined that the entire weekend was not going to be a complete blow-out and insisted that the Michelles accompany me. They must have been feeling guilty and maybe they were wearying of the Gallaghers' attentions, cos they agreed. I insisted on going down early to get a good spec even though Hyperhyper wouldn't be on for hours. We hung out by the dance tent but the temperature was too suicidal to venture in. It was only mid-afternoon but the ravers were dropping like flies, completely cabbaged. I made do with dancing outside, enjoying the attention I was getting cos I am a fucking good dancer.

Then a big flatbed truck, full of security, came thundering through. They weren't coming to assist the whacked-out punters or anything as useful as that. They were doing it simply to show that they weren't punters. See, festivals operate within their own universe, with their own hierarchies. Punters at the bottom. Stallholders and crew and performers have their allotted places. Security are a breed apart. As few vehicles have access on to the main site, those that do flaunt it as showily as possible. The flatbed was no exception. It hurtled past, air horns blasting, scattering assorted ravers and hippies, then wheeled round in a huge cloud of dust.

The security guys were sat all over the cab roof and crammed into the back, bursting the seams of the wagon like Keystone Kops. The truck passed right by us and, as it passed, two guys leaned out and scooped up little Meesh into the back. Shell ran alongside, yelling and screaming at the occupants to release her friend. Next thing, she too was hauled on to the wagon. My heart zinged. At last, some excitement. I hollered, 'What about me?' The wagon did a loop, came back and a giant of a man reached down and hauled me on board.

I sat on the roof of the cab with the big bloke who'd lifted me in holding me tight round my waist. I waved at Damien and Jeremy, who looked distinctly nonplussed at the hijacking of their girlfriends. The Michelles themselves were shocked into silence as the wagon took off once more through the crowd.

Floyd, who had lifted me into the wagon, was like the captain. He told me he was a boxer. A heavyweight, natch. I thought, right, I'm with Floyd. I wasn't scared because, though Floyd was massive, he was quite sweet and polite. He'd just grabbed us for a laugh. He was going to drop us off but the sight of Damien and Jeremy doing their concerned boyfriends routine had sparked a revolt inside me. Weren't we supposed to be having some girlfun, not pairing off? These guys looked like they knew how to give a girl a good time.

'Keep on truckin',' I said to Floyd.

'Anything you say,' he said.

The wagon bounced off and into Bouncertown. This was the place where the security guys camped out. They'd been there a fortnight. Without women. When we arrived, it felt like the stagecoach bearing whores arriving in the Klondike. Three girls and about a hundred, decidedly non-boyish, men. The Michelles were visibly panicking, but not me. Bouncertown sounded a decidedly civilised place. Floyd had told me it had its own shower block and everything. Seeing as the Michelles had decided it was an every-girl-for-herself weekend, I couldn't see a reason to change now. I called out cheerily, 'Enjoy yourselves,' before turning to Floyd and adding, 'That ride's left me so dirty. Howzabout you show me those showers?'

Now, I was expecting to have to fight Floyd off but he just handed me some shower gel and said to yell if I needed anything else. Well, I did, and I thought Floyd was just the man to provide it (as I said, boys aren't really my style). 'Wanna scrub my back?' I asked matily.

He suddenly looked all bashful and said, 'It's not that you're not a very attractive girl or anything but I'm engaged.' I was lost for words. Oh fuck, I thought. Haven't I been here once already this weekend?

So I stood under the jet, alone, and indulged in hot water heaven. After a couple of minutes I realised that the place was filling out with guys coming off shift and piling into the other cubicles. They were moaning about the job and about being stuck with all the other guys. One even said it was worse than being inside, cos at least inside, you weren't confronted with thousands of half-naked babes prancing around in front of you day after day. They all agreed that it was a bummer and I could see their point.

I waited until they had gone and was about to leave when I realised that there was still somebody in the next shower. The stalls were only divided by makeshift partitions with a gap next to the wall. It dawned on me that whoever was there could have spied on my cubicle from his. I was worried about what might happen if he knew that a naked babe was only inches away from him, alone. I decided the situation needed checking out. I squinted through the gap and was rather surprised to discover he was far too preoccupied to be thinking about me.

He was leaning, braced one handed against the back wall of the shower. A big man – not as big as Floyd maybe, but big enough – with a really muscular body and dark, silky skin. He had a broad chest, with tight little whorls of hair, and an arse like a Grand National winner. And a cock to match. About the biggest I'd seen in my life. It was big because his other hand was wrapped firmly round it, lazily pulling along its length.

I held my breath. I knew I shouldn't watch but I was riveted. I had never seen a man really do this. Sure, I'd had boyfriends wank themselves in front of me, but I always felt they were acting. This man wasn't. He obviously needed what he was doing and it obviously felt good. Soon, he was leaning back against the partition opposite me. His right hand was stroking his cock from base to tip, deliberately teasing it, while his left fondled his balls. His head was thrown back and his eyes were closed in concentration. I had to watch now. I knew he'd want me to, if he'd known I was there. (Well, if he'd known I was there, I think he'd have probably come right through that flimsy partition, but you know what I mean.) What he was doing was sorta private but it was better shared. He had his hand cupped under his balls, which didn't look like they needed much supporting, and he was really getting into it now, running his hand all over his cock, squeezing it, feeling the shape, enjoying the swollen plumpness, unashamedly fondling himself. He was completely gone. Suddenly, he looked down. His cock bulged and a spurt of white shot out the end, then another and another, as his come cascaded on to the shower floor.

I pulled back from the gap, trying to control my breathing so I wouldn't give the game away. I had a desperate urge to indulge myself, to do to myself exactly what that guy had done to himself, while I pictured him jerking furiously at his handsome, heavy member. More than anything, I wanted some cock, but I was scared. Then his shower was turned off and I heard him moving outside my door. He banged on it and shouted, 'Come on, wanker. I know what you're doing!' I held my breath in terror. Then I realised that, of course, he assumed I was another bloke. So that's what guys get up to in the showers!

When I was sure he was gone, I yelled for Floyd and asked him if he had a clean T I could borrow. 'Sure thing,' he growled and padded off, returning to toss a T-shirt over the door. It had 'Behave' emblazoned across its front and was big enough to wear as a dress. I pulled it over my head and fished my thong from inside my shorts. Floyd discreetly turned away while I hoicked it up my legs, which was a disappointment. The T-shirt came down lower than my crotch (just), so I decided to abandon my disgustingly crusty cut-offs. I stood up on tiptoe and tapped Floyd on the shoulder.

'It's OK, I'm ready now.'

Floyd said, 'Not quite.' I thought he was implying I wasn't properly decent but he merely fished something out of his pocket and clamped it around my wrist. At festivals, everyone is issued with a plastic bracelet, like in hospital. Different status, different colours, for instance, red for punters, blue for press. My new one was gold. The Holy Grail; an Access All Areas wristband. 'You're female security now. Right?' Floyd said.

'Cool,' I said. 'A bounceress.'

'Ms Bounce!' he corrected me.

Floyd led me through the campervans of Bouncertown into Showbiztown, where the trailers were beautiful aluminium Winnebagos and the tents were marquees kitted out with real furniture. One was all minimalist silver inflatables and white flowers and giant bubble lights. Another was a Bedouin tent with carpets and cushions and tables laden with fruit and big hubbly-bubbly pipes. Rock and roll, heh? They even had proper toilets.

Floyd said he'd make sure I got back to my tent when I wanted, then got off, saying that he had work to do. I wondered round a bit but the initial excitement of seeing musos in the flesh soon wore off. All they were doing was moaning about the catering and asking each other where they were staying. I was contemplating going back to the girls when I saw Todd disappearing into the Bedouin tent. Todd is one half of the famous Hyperhyper. I, of course, attached myself to the rear of the entourage and followed on in.

A harassed young woman clutching a clipboard and a walkie-talkie came panting in behind me. She hissed at a tall, languid black girl flopped on a cushion next to me, 'Gina, Chloe's ankle is fucked. Definitely broken. She won't be doing any dancing tonight.'

Gina rolled her eyes and said, 'So who've we got instead?' Harassed Girl shrugged her shoulders. Gina popped the gum she was chewing. 'Are you gonna tell him or am I?' Todd was turning out to be a total fuckwit. He was like a sulky little boy, ordering people to fetch things for him then, when they produced what he wanted, tossing things aside, saying they were the wrong colour, shape, size. The guy was a prick. I could see the girls' problem.

Then Gina noticed me. She looked me up and down, scrutinising my T-shirt especially, then asked, 'Girlfriend, who are you?'

I smiled my biggest, dippiest smile. 'Ms Bounce!'

'And do you?' she asked.

'Definitely,' I replied. I didn't have to expand further because Todd noticed there was something going on that did not revolve around him.

'Oi, Sophie, where the fuck's that silly bitch Chloe?'

Gina and Sophie looked at each other, then Gina said, 'Change of plan, Todd. This is, err, Ms Bounce.'

Todd looked me up and down before saying in a bored voice, 'She'll do.'

Well, I'm not a dancer, really. But I look like one. And I can keep a mean rhythm and can wiggle my arse to any danceable beat. And, truth was, at that point I was up for just about anything. I'd been revving up ever since I climbed on that wagon and I was all set for take-off. I'd seen Hyperhyper more than a few times and I knew what the girl dancers had to do. Not much, really, apart from look good. Let's face it, two nerdy boys behind a bank of keyboards and computers isn't the most visually challenging experience you're gonna get, is it? So, a couple of females wiggling arse downstage makes all the difference.

Gina considered me through narrowed lids then

drawled, 'All right, sister, if you're gonna dance with me, I wanna see what you can do.' She led me off to a little area between a herd of grazing Winnebagos and said, 'First thing first. Let's see your body.'

Now, I'm not shy about getting my kit off, as you know, but I wasn't sure I liked Gina's tone. 'Why?' I demanded.

Gina clicked her tongue. 'Because, girlfriend, if you can't shake your arse at me, how're you gonna shake it at our adoring public?'

I pulled a face at her and hauled Floyd's T-shirt over my head. I could see her appraising my body quite openly. Good job I was fit. After the Michelles had pissed me off, I'd traded a good wedge of our food kitty for whizz, figuring, with nothing to go to bed for, I could stay up and lose weight too. I knew I looked good.

'OK, turn round,' she said eventually. I did a neat pirouette and smirked at her. 'Fine for ballet school, but it ain't hip hop,' she drawled.

'Well, put some fucking music on, OK?' I snapped.

Gina raised her eyebrows and clambered up the steps into one of the trailers, reappearing with a portable CD player. She sat down on the step and hit play. A solidly phat beat boomed out. I grinned and went for it. As a finale, I slipped my string so I was completely naked then turned my back on her, arched my spine and shook my arse so it bounced and shimmied. I thought I'd let Gina know I could live up to my new name.

I heard her laughing hysterically. 'For a skinny bitch, that's a fine bootie! OK, hon, you'll do.'

So that was it; I was in. Gina played Hyperhyper's set and we worked up an act. She'd do a move, then I'd add something to it and throw it back and so on. Like a competition. Gina, who was built like me, except a tad more African in the bootie department, found me something more clubby to wear on stage than an outsized T-shirt. Then we had a few smokes and hung out together for the rest of the day. She was cool; I liked her.

I started off in ultra-baggy combats and a waistee over bikini top and batty riders. Gina was wearing a sarong and loose-fitting cotton top over same. The idea was that, as we danced and got hotter, and our dancing got hotter, and as we started competing with each other, we'd strip down to a tiny bra and shorts. It didn't quite work out like that. We got into some pretty dirty moves, holding on to each other and sliding around in each other's arms, and my bikini just sort of rode up my tits. The crowd loved that, so I hauled it off and flung it at them. Not to be outdone, Gina unfastened hers. Lovely tits, impressively pert nipples. Back to me now, so I unzipped my shorts and I left it so they were resting on my hips. I turned my back on Gina and shook my bootie at her, like I did back at camp.

Next thing, she'd spooned in behind me and held me tight with her arms round my tummy so we were dancing coupled together. Her satiny skin was sliding over mine, our sweat acting like a lubricant. I could feel her breasts in my back and her hard nipples against my skin. It all really happened at once from that point. Gina yanked down my batty riders and I was completely bare-arsed naked in front of two thousand people. Just as that happened, down below me, I saw two familiar faces. Two mop-headed Gallagher faces staring up at me, agog. It was brilliant. I dived on Gina and wrestled off her satin boxers to reveal her gleaming, dusky arse. We finished the set *au naturelle*, to massive applause.

Immediately afterwards, we fled to the Hyperhyper Winnebago and got stuck into Todd's supply of charlie before any of the liggers could come piling in. As we'd just been shaking our respective booties in front of thousands, it seemed pointless to go all bashful on each other now, so Gina and me barricaded the door and flopped naked on the cushions.

'Girlfriend, you are fun.' She grinned at me. 'Wanna do that again sometime?'

I giggled and was about to say, 'Like when?' when there was a knock at the door and a familiar Brummy voice enquired, 'Everything OK?'

'It's Floyd.' I said, unlocking the door and letting him in. Gina looked quizzical. 'We're safe with Floyd – he's engaged,' I added sarcastically as he stepped into the trailer, visibly startled at so much naked female flesh.

Gina considered him appraisingly. 'Is he now,' she purred before carefully relocking the door.

Poor Floyd didn't stand a chance. We sat him between us and Gina asked him to tell us all about his fiancée. He started mumbling away, while Gina selected a huge strawberry from the obligatory platter of fruit on the table and began sucking it thoughtfully. When she leaned across him and pushed it into my mouth with her tongue, he started to stammer.

'Floyd!' Gina teased wickedly. 'You're supposed to be telling us about your fiancée!'

Floyd swallowed. 'What about her?'

Gina smiled mischievously. 'Well, for instance, what does she like you to do to her?' Floyd didn't reply. 'Jo,' she said, 'pass me a strawberry.' I did as I was told. Gina drawled, 'Floyd, you've gone quiet!'

She swivelled to face him on the cushioned seat, exposing her pussy to his gaze. Then she rubbed the strawberry at the entrance to her cunt before mashing the glistening fruit between her pink pussy lips and rubbing the pulp around her clit. The juicy gash looked shocking and violent against her chocolatey skin. Then she lifted the squished mess up to Floyd's lips and smeared it over his mouth. Leaning against Floyd as I was, I could feel his heart pounding against his rib cage almost as hard as my own. 'Perhaps she likes that?' Gina smirked. Floyd was beginning to sweat.

'Well, would you like it if she did it to you?' asked

Gina, and deftly unfastened his fly. 'Jo, get another,' she instructed, 'and rub it along his cock.' Floyd let out a great gasp of air. I tentatively pushed the strawberry through the gap so it squashed against Floyd's taut, trapped cock while I stared at Gina with a big silly grin all over my face. She smiled coolly back. 'Girlfriend, we're safe with Floyd. He's engaged!'

I fumbled around and eventually uncoiled Floyd's erection so it sprang free from his flies. I said he was a heavyweight. There were absolutely no surprises in the cock department. I rubbed and squished the fruit along the underside of his handsome prick till the strawberry turned to mush in my hands and as much juice was coating his cock as was flowing down my fanny.

'Floyd, honey, I think you'd better take your clothes off now, before you get in any more of a mess,' Gina suggested. Floyd stripped and stood naked before us, his swollen cock sticky and gorgeously rigid. 'Now,' Gina said to him, 'you get a strawberry – and rub it into Jo's cunt.'

Floyd looked at her for a second, then, kneeling between my legs, he inserted its tip tenderly between my pussy lips. I held my breath. 'Relax, Jo,' encouraged Gina, moving to kneel beside me. She lifted my thigh out so my own pink pussy was open and exposed and said, 'Come on, Floyd, she's waiting.' Floyd put the fruit against my hole and I yielded so easily that I almost swallowed it. 'Not there, Floyd,' said Gina. 'Higher up. Watch.' Then she took the strawberry out of Floyd's hand and mashed the fruit into my pussy, pulping it against my clit until the juices ran in a sweet sticky mess all over my inner thighs and seeped down the cleft between my buttocks.

'Oh, Floyd, we've made a mess of this girl,' Gina tutted. 'Better start cleaning her up.' She pushed me over on my back and began licking the inside of my thighs, her own gorgeous arse high in the air. I looked down at her and up at Floyd, his cock bulging urgently. Gina's darting tongue reached the skin between my pussy and my arse. I'd never been licked by a girl before and my brain was spinning with 'Do I, don't I?' thoughts. But, when she suddenly stopped, I could have screamed. Floyd stood panting and shaking, on the edge of self-control. He was staring at my exposed cunt like he wanted to take me there and then. I would not have objected.

'Now what,' said Gina smoothly, 'is the most practical way of doing this?' Floyd and me were staring at each other hungrily. 'Floyd, do you want to fuck Jo?' asked Gina. Floyd winced, but his cock tightened in assent. 'I think you do,' she said. 'But what about me? I'm filthy. Look!' she added, and, kneeling in front of us, she parted her pussy lips before squishing another luscious fruit on to her exposed clit. Then she began to finger herself. We both watched, hypnotised, as Gina shamelessly rubbed herself, her eyes closed like the man in the shower stall, till she was trembling with excitement too. I expected her to come but she stopped and, in a voice hoarse with sex, asked, 'Floyd, what would your fiancée say about you getting two girls so dirty? You're a bad, baaad boy. I think you've got to clean your act up *now*!'

Then Gina told me to lick Floyd's cock clean. I kneeled before him and tried to take the swollen, plum-like end in my mouth, while Gina pushed me over to my side and finished cleaning me. Her long, slender tongue began retrieving the strawberry from inside me. Then, while I slurped on Floyd, she moved up to my clit. So this was what it was like with a girl; I remember thinking, I like this. But when she suddenly stopped and gently pulled me away from eating Floyd, I groaned, cos my cunt was aching to be finished off.

'I can't help thinking this isn't fair on Floyd's fiancée,' she said teasingly. 'I mean, what's in it for her? Floyd, you're getting all the fun. It's payback time now. Lie on the floor.'

Floyd stared at Gina intently for maybe a couple of

seconds, then did as he was bid, his cock raised like a flagpole. I kneeled beside him and began sucking again while I cupped his balls, just as the man had done in the shower stall. Gina straddled his other end, lowering herself on to Floyd's mouth and working against him urgently. 'Go ahead, sugar, if you want,' Gina groaned, nodding at his erection. I manoeuvred his penis up to my swollen, juicy entrance. The head was so fat, I could hardly work it in, but, with help from Gina's agile fingers, we eventually eased it up my lubricated sheath and I immediately began riding it vigorously. At last! Three days of watching cocks and finally I'd got one inside me, and a fine one too.

Gina and me were face to face now; rocking, grinning, panting pretty much in unison. I threw my arms round her and kissed her joyfully. I said 'Thank you,' though I didn't know why, but I meant it. She returned my kiss and soon we were snogging and stroking each other's backs and caressing each other's tits while we both hammered down on poor old Floyd, prone and trapped beneath us. 'What about his fiancée?' I panted in her ear.

'She'll be OK,' she murmured, slipping a finger down to feel Floyd's flesh tightly filling my cunt mouth.

'She's one horny bitch. She'll do anything to get her man to eat her out.'

It was three hours before knobhead Todd got his trailer back. By then, there wasn't much left in the fruit bowl. Both Gina and me had given Floyd an extended seminar in the art of eating fruit, while alternately having our respective pussies thoroughly attended to by his heavyweight cock. That man had stamina.

When we'd done, Floyd was as good as his word and returned me to my tent. I was received with stupefied acclaim by the Gallaghers and sheepish grins by the Michelles, who, incidentally, seemed to have lost all interest in nice boys.

I keep the gold pass above my bed as a little reminder

of my best fest ever. Oh yes, and I'm going up to Brum next week, dancing with Gina. Ms Bounce and Gina G. We're staying with Floyd and his fiancée. Or should that be Gina and her fiancé? Either way, it'll be healthy. They eat loads of fruit, apparently.

Cinderella

Ruth Fox

Cinderella

It was the classic love scene. She was kneeling on the stage picking up sticks as the script instructed, totally oblivious to everything around her. My lines called for me to walk up behind her and cough discreetly to attract her attention, but all I could do was stare.

We were both members of CADS – Castle Amateur Dramatic Society – and this was the first night of the yearly production, this year we were putting on *Cinderella*. I had only met Jessica – sorry, Cinders – for the first time earlier in the year, when she was dragged along with a group of the dancing chorus and turned out to be perfect for the unfilled part of Cinderella. We bullied her into staying if only for that one season. She agreed.

I couldn't stop staring. My lines had completely gone from my head and as the prompt desperately tried to rescue me I felt like a lovesick teenager. She looked absolutely exquisite; her long blonde hair, which was usually tucked up under a very unattractive baseball cap worn backwards, transformed her. The jeans and baggy sweatshirts that were uniform to all our dancers had kept her secret well.

She was costumed in a tapestry dress with a medieval

bodice that thrust her breasts upward until they threatened to spill over the front of the dress and her gloriously shiny blonde hair hung down in soft waves to her waist. The spotlight danced across this apparition as I leaned towards her, nervously clearing my throat.

The audience gasped as she leaped to her feet startled, turned towards me and, gazing up at me shyly through her fringe, blushed – she actually blushed. She recited her line perfectly: 'Forgive me, sire, you startled me.' Next came the line I had dreaded through every rehearsal. We had giggled and made fun of it right from the initial read-through. Every time I recited it in front of the rest of the cast it had received wolf whistles and mocking laughter. Suddenly that same line took on a whole new meaning; it called for me to stand close to Cinderella and, as an 'aside' to the audience, say in smitten voice, 'Oh me, oh my, I truly believe I have fallen in love. What vision stands before me, what charm, what grace, what beauty?'

We went on to talk of Royal Balls and dancing, with me pretending not to be Prince Charming and Cinders pretending not to guess that I was really the Prince even though I had only changed hats with Dandini, my aide. That's panto. Illusion. Halfway through the scene I had to take her in my arms to teach her to dance, ready for the ball. She was soft and trembling as I held her to me. Even though every thespian knows to only look at the audience at all times and not the character you are playing the scene with, Cinderella gazed into my eyes as we danced. We were in a world of our own, the gentle strains of the waltz filled the auditorium and not giving a damn what it looked like, I crushed her to me.

When the music ended and we waltzed into the wings breathless and flushed, she kept hold of my hand and tugged me into a dark corner behind the static curtain. 'You look wonderful,' she whispered, 'so dominant, sort of a cross between a man and a woman. I wish our costumes had arrived in time for the dress rehearsal yesterday – then I might have been prepared for the sight of you towering above me in those amazing boots. Where on earth did you get them?'

I looked down at my costume, seeing it through her eyes. To me it was just a costume; I could just as easily have been cast to play a witch or the ugly sisters' mother, Baroness Hardup. My high-heeled shiny black-leather boots with the gold buckles up the sides took on a new meaning, with fishnet tights and the tight-fitting black-velvet jacket with its frothy white lace jabot at the neck: a textbook principal boy.

I realised with a jolt that Cinderella was still holding my hand and didn't seem to mind a bit. I couldn't believe this was happening: my breasts were aching within the confines of the jacket – or was it the nearness of this sweetly perfumed maiden? I found it impossible to snap out of character, so I knew I had to break the moment or go crazy. I stepped back into the classic stance of principal boy, with feet astride and hands on hips and in my best Prince Charming voice I joked, 'Goodness, maid, would you spoil the script and rob me of my chance to seduce you in the ballroom scene?'

She dropped a deep curtsy and very demurely, through fluttering eyelashes, coyly said the words that devastated me: 'Sire, I will of course allow you the chance to seduce me as you will in the ballroom scene.' Then in a mock-up of my 'aside' earlier, she added, 'Oh, that it were a bedroom scene.' With that she skipped between the curtains and prepared herself for her next entrance.

My next two scenes with Dandini and other courtiers went by in a blur, with lots of help from the prompt. I had no time to dwell on what had happened or to decide how I felt. I tried to tell myself that it was the excitement of first night – the hype and the applause. So why, when I did my quick change into my red-satin embroidered ballroom costume that called for court shoes, did I wish I could keep on the boots, and why was the tight satin crotch of my costume prickly and damp? I had no time to ponder this question, as the callboy broke through my thoughts and called me into position for the ballroom scene. My heart pounded.

I stood with Dandini at the side of the ballroom, greeting the guests and awaiting the arrival of my Princess. My legs turned to jelly as I recited my other lines like an automaton. Finally, there she was at the top of the sweeping makeshift staircase. She floated down in a cloud of golden lace on the arm of a footman in all his glorious livery, her eyes never leaving mine for a second. I realised that it didn't matter that we were both women; I wanted her like I had never wanted anyone in my life before. I wanted her in my arms; I wanted to bury my face in her flesh and taste her essence from deep within her cunt.

'My Princess Crystal, now I have found you I will never let you go.'

We danced again and I felt as if I were on a first date as she whispered in my ear, 'I am going to hold you to that, my Prince.'

In the finale I led her downstage and, bowing deeply, kissed her hand, but instead of kissing the back I turned it over in mine and tickled the delicate palm with the tip of my tongue. She moaned softly but the audience was oblivious to anything but the happy ending. She dropped to the floor in a sweeping curtsy with her head bowed until I raised her to her feet again. The audience loved us. They screamed and cheered through three bows then, just before we backed into the rest of the cast, and quite unscripted, she stood on tiptoe, kissed me on the cheek and whispered, 'Come to my dressing room.'

When the last curtain call had finished everyone strolled back to their respective dressing rooms, exhausted but happy at the standing ovations we had received. I busied myself while everyone changed and removed their make-up, then hung up their costumes ready for the following night, shouted goodbye and left.

I changed back into my original costume with the boots and nervously walked down the dimly lit corridor to her room. I fully expected her to have gone and had convinced myself in the half-hour since the final curtain that I had imagined it all. I tapped on her door.

'Come in, my Prince.'

Keeping up the pretence I opened the door. I walked into the room and over to the chair where she sat. Like me, she had felt the need to keep on her costume. I bowed courteously.

'My Princess, now you have consented in front of thousands of witnesses to be my bride, would you allow me to sample the delights of your flesh? Perchance I could stroke the alabaster flesh of your breasts that has tormented me all evening. Never before have I tasted the pleasures of a woman's body but if you would consent to this honour, I would, I am sure, live happily ever after.'

'My Lord, my Prince, how could I deny you anything? Take my lips, they are yours. Take my breasts that ache for your touch, but please be gentle for I am but an innocent maid.'

I took her face in my hands and kissed those soft lips that had driven me wild. She relaxed into my arms as my tongue probed her mouth and my shaking fingers started the long process of undoing the forty pearl buttons that held up her golden dress. As I slipped the dress from her shoulders and revealed the creamy-white globes of her breasts she moaned softly, deep in her throat. The buds of her dark-pink nipples were hard and crinkled as I took each one in my mouth in turn and sucked deeply, nibbling and licking until she was gasping and shaking like me.

It felt so strange to be taking the lead like a man but I felt totally in control of the situation as I swept her half-naked body into my arms and carried her over to the couch in the corner of the room.

I laid her down, watching her breasts heave with

arousal, and part of me wanted to strip her completely, but I was scared to break the spell, so I raised her pretty petticoats one by one, carefully exposing first her dainty, slippered feet and then her white-stockinged legs. I couldn't believe it when I reached the top of her thighs: she had on authentic garters of lace with small gold-ribboned bows, topped by white cotton pantaloons with a split crotch – straight out of a Dickens novel.

I groaned my approval as I kneeled on one knee, for all the world like an arrogant prince. She took hold of my ponytailed hair in her hands, took off the wide black ribbon that held it in place, and as I shook out the length, she gently pulled my face to her breast and cradled it there.

I couldn't wait any longer to taste her and ran my nervous fingers up her thighs into the dark mysterious depths of her undergarments.

With my head still resting on her chest, I pulled aside the damp crossover gusset of her pantaloons to reveal the sweet pink invitation of her innocent young pussy. Tiny petal-like lips surrounded by wisps of curly blonde hair parted at my gaze, creating a new wanton image as they oozed with her copious juices.

I moved down the couch until I sat between her spread legs and lowered my head for the taste I craved. She tasted like the woman she was, musky and aroused. I devoured her like a cat with a toy, worrying her lips and nibbling softly. She wriggled and arched her hips off the couch, greedily trying to fit her whole pussy into my mouth, but I teased and tormented her with my teeth and tongue, nibbling and sucking until I thought she could take no more.

All pretence of innocent maidens and gallant princes was forgotten as I spread her lips wide with my fingers and jabbed my tongue deep within her. Then, without a pause, I ran it up the groove of her sex to her hard dainty clitoris and caught it gently between my teeth, swirled my tongue around it once or twice and again returned to her pussy, fucking it hard with my tongue.

Her frantic writhing told me she was close to coming, so I removed my stabbing tongue and replaced it with two fingers that I slid knuckle deep inside her, scissoring gently to and fro, while my mouth, already slick with her wetness, latched on to her bud. My tongue started flicking relentlessly.

She exploded, filling my mouth with her response and clutching my head between those creamy, pantalooned thighs.

Princess Crystal lay cradled in my arms like a child and drifted off to sleep with a smug satisfied look on her sweet innocent face.

Just as she closed her eyes she murmured, 'My Prince, tomorrow I will do the seducing.'

I too drifted to sleep with visions of my Princess, with her golden head nestled between my booted thighs.

As the curtain rose on the second night my heart was thumping in my tight jacket and already I was finding it difficult to concentrate on anything but Jessica. I towered over her as she picked up her sticks, very conscious of my high boots that elevated my height to over six foot. We recited our lines and danced, once again oblivious to the audience, but it wasn't until, as we had the night before, we danced off the stage into the wings and our dark little corner that Jessica showed her feelings.

As soon as we were out of sight of the rest of the cast she stretched up on tiptoe, put her arms round my neck and whispered in my ear, 'Oh, Princey, you haven't a clue what you did to me last night, have you?' With that she nipped my ear lobe with her teeth and giggled.

I was bent over with my face buried into her sweet-smelling hair, and my arms, incapable of staying by my sides, wrapped themselves round her and swept her off her feet. 'Jesus, you horny little bitch. I can't stop thinking about your taste. I was so excited yesterday, what with the build-up on the stage and your amazing underwear with the split crotch showing just a peep. I hope you are going to stick to your promise after the final curtain,' I queried hopefully.

She squirmed out of my arms and skipped away. She must have kept one ear on the dialogue on the stage because she ran on stage just in time to deliver her lines and I wandered back to my dressing room wondering if she was just teasing me.

Eventually we arrived at the ballroom scene and again I stood at the bottom of the stairs with Dandini. She rounded the staircase with her footman and, avoiding my gaze, swept down the long staircase into my arms. As we waltzed across the stage I thought my plans were doomed. But then, just before the last strains of music and just at the moment when we turned and her back was to the audience, with my height protecting her from the sight of the rest of the cast behind me, she looked into my eyes, grinned and stuck her tongue out at me, wiggling it very provocatively. My stomach lurched.

Right at the very last moment of the show, when all the rest of the cast had done their walk-down and there was just Cinderella and me waiting in the wings, she shocked the life out of me. The script called for us, as the principals of the pantomime, to start our walk-down from opposite sides of the stage. We stood right at the back in the wings, facing each other across the expanse of the stage and waiting for our cue to join together in the middle, turn and walk down to the front, bow, and back into the rest of the cast. We only had a split second from when Dandini entered before we had to make our entrance. In that split second, as I stared at her across the bright lights of the stage, waiting for her nod, my horny little Princess pulled down the bodice of her golden gown, exposing her beautiful breasts. She cupped them in her hands and tipped one up to her mouth to lick the nipple.

I gasped at her brazenness but thrilled at the image that filled my thoughts, and completely put me off my cue. Jessica, without a pause, replaced her dress, ran to centre stage and stood looking at me with her hand outstretched. Before I had a chance to join her she laughed out loud and delighted the audience by saying, completely unscripted, 'Come, my Prince, would you abandon me now?' The audience loved it. They cheered and whistled as I joined her on stage, swept her up in my arms and strode to the front for our bow. She was wiggling her legs and squealing with delight and the crowds loved it even more.

I knew we would be in trouble from the director but I didn't care; I knew then that, for tonight at least, Cinders would be mine.

When John, the director, called us over afterwards we tried to keep straight faces as we waited while he finished what he was doing. It was obvious he was making us stew as he flapped about moving bits and pieces of scenery and discussing in length some lighting that he felt wasn't quite right. When he eventually spoke to us he surprised us both.

'I don't know quite what has come over you two because in rehearsals you were so wooden together that I despaired of ever getting a decent role out of you, but you have really come good and I am proud of you. I know the end there was not part of the script and I should be angry with you, but the audience knows best, so keep it in. Go on then, go home. What are you waiting for? The others have gone already. I'm afraid I can't wait while you get changed. Can you make sure everyone has gone and slip the catch on the door when you leave? See you tomorrow.'

With that he left and we stood there on the stage, silently looking down to the front two rows of the auditorium with its tiered, plush, scarlet seating and the high vaulted ceiling. The footlights were still blazing, turning the stage into an oasis in the dark of the theatre.

I bent down to Jessica and asked if she was still game. 'Are you kidding?' she replied. 'I haven't been able to think of anything else. I didn't even dare look at you on stage because I knew I would forget what I was supposed to do.' She paused for a second or two, obviously thinking, then added, 'Will you go and put your other costume on for me? I love the fishnets and short jacket and those boots destroy me. I will check that everyone has gone and meet you back here in a minute or two.'

I rushed to my dressing room and quickly changed into the provocative costume of the classic principal boy then returned to the stage. I couldn't believe my eyes. The lights were still on and Jessica had dragged a pink-velvet chaise longue into the centre of the stage and was reclining on it with her dress raised to her thighs and her legs spread open, revealing her pantaloons and garter. I groaned with arousal at the brief glimpse of her sex.

I strode across the stage, ready to drop at her feet and worship her as I had the night before – but she beat me to it. As I got close she jumped up and, in a parody of an innocent maid, she dropped a curtsy and, demurely lowering her eyes, begged, 'Please, sire, would you take my place on the chaise? I would beg for the honour of pleasuring you.'

What could I do but comply? My legs had turned to jelly and my cunt was throbbing, shamefully soaking the crotch of my satin costume pants. I sat on the edge of the chaise but tonight my ravishing Princess was in a much more daring mood. She pushed me back into the cushions and, still on her knees, lifted one of my feet up on to the chaise and spread my legs, encased in their black fishnets, until I was open and available. She raked a nail down the damp crotch of my pants and tutted. 'Oh you naughty Prince, how wet you are.'

I groaned loudly and tried to sit up to respond to her,

but she just pushed me back down. She grasped the back of my pants and pulled and tugged them until she had removed them from my feet; then she spread my legs again. I was totally transfixed by her, until five minutes before, even after our games of the night before, I had believed her to be like me, a novice to the charms of other women, but this was a revelation. She knew exactly what she was doing. Out of the volumes of her skirt she produced a small pair of gold scissors with which she proceeded to snip away at the crotch of my fishnet tights.

'This is such a rude sight. I can see your wet cunt poking through the mesh of your tights.'

I was shocked. In my head I thought of her sex as a cunt but it hadn't occurred to me that she would use the word that I found so erotic. As she continued speaking, telling me in no uncertain terms how debauched I looked with my inner lips squashed through the net, she touched the exposed bits, sending a thrill through my mind with her words and through my body with her inquisitive fingers.

A twinge of pain shivered through me as I felt her snip one more link then pull my lip through the hole left by her devious scissors. Then she did the same with the other lip and pulled it through until my sex was tight against the crotch of my tights and dripping shamelessly. It was such an amazing experience to be staked out on the brilliantly lit stage like that, as if this were all part of a performance, with a very adventurous girl thinking up devious things to do to me under the spotlight. I wallowed in the feelings that flooded over me and just let myself enjoy.

My lips were beginning to chill, but Jessica had just the answer. She lowered her mouth and first breathed hard on my stretched pussy; her breath burned my flesh. Then she sucked each lip harder through the holes in the material until the nylon mesh acted like a tourniquet, cutting off the blood. Just as I started to wriggle in discomfort she played and tugged and manoeuvred until my lips were back behind the tight crotch and my clit was pushed through a slightly larger hole. The tightness of the gap pushed back the flesh that protected my erect bud and exposed the pink shiny skin that usually hid itself away.

I couldn't believe what she was doing. She was playing with my cunt as if I was a toy. She was experimenting with my reactions and gauging my responses like no one had ever attempted before, not even me really, but she read me so right. I loved it. I loved the way I felt helpless to argue and the way she made me feel that I didn't have to reciprocate; I could just let her play me.

I was so excited that I wanted to stop her for fear of something exploding in me, but she was relentless. She manipulated me until I was almost screeching with delight, but just as I thought I would come she would stop and go back to gentle sucking. She played me like a virtuoso, knowing exactly when to push me, and when to stop. As I lay back on the velvet, with my hands clutching frantically at her hair, I realised that she had already taken me to heights of arousal that I hadn't dreamed possible.

She leaned back then and began to cut more of the crotch away. I could feel my whole pussy bulge as she snipped away at each tiny thread, allowing a little more of me to protrude with each snip. I wanted to share with her what I was feeling so, just as I felt the whole of my sex almost pop through the tight elastic mesh, I clutched at her body with both hands and pulled her towards me. I wanted her over me. She tried to resist as she bent to devour me again, but this time I was not to be cheated. I leaned up and grabbed her rear end and pulled her until she was lying on top of me with her head buried between my thigh boots and her skirt and all her petticoats between her bottom and me.

I wriggled us both down until I was almost flat and

then pulled up her skirts until I had exposed her pantaloons. It was so difficult concentrating on what I was doing, with her sweet mouth burying itself into my crotch and sucking furiously. I was determined. I pulled her leg over until she was kneeling astride me and then flicked her skirt and petticoats up and over her haunches until the only garment between my prize and me was the white cotton pantaloons. Gone was the delicacy of my lovemaking yesterday; gone was the need to be gentle with her and explore the folds of material. I grabbed the elastic waistband and pulled them down as far as I could, exposing her round bottom and the soft oozing flesh between her thighs. I ran my finger down her cleft from the crease where her buttocks divided, through the soggy fluff and her wet lips and down to her tiny clit. She groaned and wriggled her pleasure.

I pressed my fingers into her and explored until I felt a hard nub that throbbed under my finger and I rubbed it. Jessica arched her back and pushed her bottom backwards and down, forcing my hand in deeper until I had to flex my arm to keep up the pressure she obviously required. Her mouth was still performing miracles on me, nipping my lips and sucking my whole pussy as far into her mouth as she could. I could feel my flesh being wrenched through the hole in my tights, throbbing in spasms.

We both climbed towards relief, Jessica pounding herself up and down on my hand and me forcing myself into her mouth, both with our thighs spread to their limits.

The noises that filled the auditorium rose loudly, using the acoustics to their full potential and resounding in the rafters.

We were oblivious to our unseen audience.

By the time we peaked, with Jessica's screams muffled by my thighs and my uncontrollable moans bouncing off the walls of the theatre, the man in the back row was standing and clapping quietly. As we began to relax, he gradually clapped louder, the sound of his clapping rising as our groans faded into whimpers and snuffles of pleasure.

He started to walk down the sloped aisle towards the stage, cheering and clapping his appreciation, but it was seconds before I realised that the noises weren't ours. Still with my fingers buried to the hilt in my Princess and my thumb searching for her clit, I turned my head towards the sound and was completely mesmerised by our audience. I felt Jessica's breathing quicken again. She had turned her head too. We both stared at the handsome young man that had entered the glow of the lights and reached the rail surrounding the orchestra pit. He continued his walk without taking his eyes from the tableau before him, making his way through the discarded instruments towards the front of the stage, still clapping rhythmically. Fuelled by his encouragement we carried on enthusiastically as he kept up his clapping and said, 'Please don't stop for me; this is better than the panto. In fact it is better than anything I have ever seen. Jessica, you naughty girl. I come all this way to watch you as the innocent Cinderella and what do I find? My very rude young wife in the arms – or should I say in between the legs of – another man.' He laughed, obviously delighted by finding his 'very rude young wife' between my legs.

At that, Jessica groaned one word, 'James', then buried her head back where it belonged. I followed her lead, shocked to find that our audience was Jessica's husband but excited by her renewed arousal, obviously inspired by her husband's encouragement. He watched hypnotised as we again, this time rapidly, brought each other to blazing orgasms, me with my hand buried inside her, surrounded by her pantaloons and petticoats, and her with her face buried in between my booted thighs.

James cheered and clapped furiously at our enthusiastic performance, shouting 'Encore! Encore!'

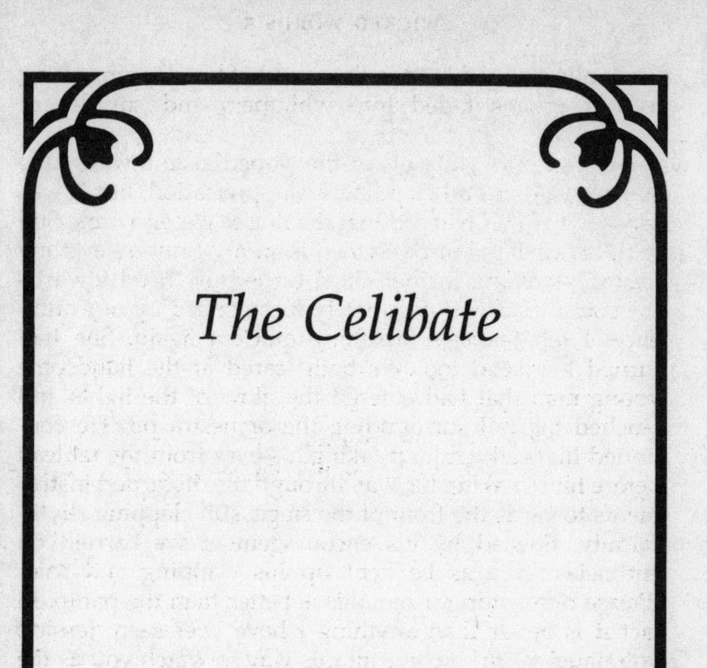

The Celibate

Barbie Scott

The Celibate

It was a voluntary decision. OK, I'd just broken up with Vinnie and didn't have a lover, but that wasn't the reason. We hadn't had sex in ages anyway. I could have gone looking for someone else right off – that's what I usually do when things come to a sticky (or in this case, decidedly unsticky) end. But I didn't want to. I'd had it with men. I'd had it with women too, more than once, but that's another story. I needed a break. To be in my own space for a time. To be alone and free and clean. I needed to *find* myself. They say it takes months, sometimes years, to clear a sexual partner's energy from your aura. I didn't want anybody else's bad vibrations cluttering up my psychic space for a good while yet.

So I did without.

Friends pitied me. *You'll find someone. Give it time.* I didn't bother replying. Sometimes it's impossible to make people understand. 'I'm fine on my own,' sounds like rationalisation. *Oh yeah. Until the next one comes along.*

I'd heard about Tantra at the meditation centre I go to now and then. Don't get me wrong. I'm not one of your holy molies. Sin has always had its little claws firmly embedded in my heart. But I try. Now and again. I try.

Anyway, I find meditation soothing. You should try it. Don't knock anything till you've had a go yourself, that's what I always say. After that you can knock away as much as you like.

Tantra is the ecstatic expression of universal energy, reached through sexual activity. Or so they say. You've heard of the *Kama Sutra*. Well, that's the sort of thing I'm on about. It's about adopting yogic positions, breathing prana, aligning yourself with the universe, getting the kundalini surging up your spine. It can be done with a single lover or a whole group of them. You've seen those carvings of Hindu gods, haven't you? The ones where you can't tell whose hand is up whose sari, and where probing toes are as experimental as fingers? Well, Tantra is what they're up to. Since it's all to do with breath and energy and sacred positions, you can also do it by yourself. As a celibate, instead of having a partner sniffing away at your perfumed garden, you can breathe in the exotic odours alone.

Now don't get the wrong idea. I'm not against sex with a partner. On the contrary, I love the whole rolling, sweating shebang bang bang of it. I've always been ready to go the full nine yards. (Or should that be the full nine inches? Well, we can dream, can't we?) When sex with Vinnie was good – that is, when we still did it properly – it was very good. Trouble was, for the last couple of years we'd only been going through the motions. And for the last few months, we hadn't even bothered to do that. The final split hardly came as a big surprise. I was grateful for it, to be honest. But I'm not saying it wasn't painful. You can get attached to some guys – even if they are mean and miserable and moan on at you all the time. You get used to them being around, don't you? When they finally go, you can't help but wipe a tear from your eye, even if you're sighing out the biggest expression of relief since Mafeking at the same time. That's how it was with me anyway. Call me sentimental but I get attached to the fuckers. And to the fuckees – but, like I said, that's another story.

What I'm telling you here is no tale of woe, though. You won't hear me complaining about nights alone in a bed too big, or not having anybody to take the rubbish out – like Vinnie ever did! No, this is a celebration of celibacy. I sing of the delights of self-pleasuring. Self-pleasuring that has an extra jewel hidden inside, like an exotic black pearl in an insignificant-looking oyster.

Tantric celibacy.

Want to know more? Well, I'm about tell you, aren't I?

I was sitting one afternoon in my tiny conservatory looking out at the wintry garden. A scattering of snow dusted the brown earth of my dug-but-unplanted vegetable patch, like icing sugar on a chocolate cake. The sky was green. You know those winter days – crisp, cold, ethereal. I had the heating up high as I've got a grapevine in the conservatory – well, I call it a conservatory but it's more of a lean-to greenhouse with an old armchair in it – and I was only wearing a T-shirt and a pair of jeans, despite the breath-clouding temperature outside. I was reading a book I'd bought in the Body & Soul bookshop down the road. I'd been getting into the meditation thing a bit more since Vinnie left, doing stuff with crystals and healing, past-life therapy, that sort of thing. OK, I know, for a time I looked like a sad bastard clutching at the straw of spirituality to fill my empty life, but that's not how it was. I'm not one to bother God just because I've got time on my hands. I'm interested in all this stuff. And you will be too when I tell you.

I was reading about Brahmacharya – that's Tantric sublimation to you and me. Apparently, you have to prepare your body for periods of sexual abstinence with yoga and breathing exercises. Well, since abstinence was what I'd decided on, I thought I might as well try it out. Breathing would be easier to do than yoga, I guessed, as I was sitting in an old stuffed armchair in a somewhat cramped space. I read on. You take in the divine prana, that is, breath, and imagine it entering through your root chakra. Now, a chakra is a whirling vortex of energy at the point where mind and body meet, as I expect you well know, and the root chakra's the one located between your anus and your vulva, or scrotum if you happen to be a man. In the prissier books they say it's at the base of the spine. Well, wherever.

I drew in the breath – sorry, prana – and visualised it coming up through my perineum, travelling up my spine and passing through all the other chakras – sacral, solar plexus, heart and throat – until it reached my third eye. They warn you not to go for exiting through the crown chakra, the one on the top of your head, until you're more experienced. It seems you can detach yourself from your body if you don't know what you're doing. And we wouldn't want that, now, would we? The body is a very useful piece of kit. You won't catch me hovering about in the etheric realms without a home to go to.

Well, I tried this rhythmic breathing for a while and soon I started to feel blissed out. Honest. I was relaxed and energised. I was also aware of a warm sensation developing in my crotch area that had nothing to do with thoughts of shiny patent leather thigh boots or being tied face down on a bed, which is what it usually takes to get me going when I'm on my lonesome. No. Just a quiet steady breathing in and breathing out was all it needed. What could be easier?

I'll be frank with you here. I sometimes get bored with the same old heave-ho, tie me up, tie me down, whips and garters stuff. It's good to have a change now and again, variety being the garam marsala of life and all. Well, that's what I reckon anyway.

So, after a few minutes of this breathing, I picked up the book and read on until I got to the bit where you have to start chanting. *Lam, vam, ram, yam, ham, om, aum* – one sound for each chakra, to encourage that curled snake of kundalini to get on up your spine. Lam-Vam, thank you ma'am. I found it difficult to be serious about this. I felt a bit of an idiot, making these sounds, I can tell you. Besides, the bloke next door was out inspecting his cabbages and my lean-to is only plastic. He must've heard me chanting away cos he gave one of those looks that says 'Witch Woman next door casting her spells again.' And it wasn't even Hallowe'en.

Anyway, to get back to the Tantra. By now, my pussy was starting to judder like a two-stroke engine. I had my eyes closed and was seeing a deep-red light behind my eyelids. That's the colour of the root chakra, the one that grounds you, keeps you in contact with the earth. The next one up, the sex chakra, sitting halfway between your pubes and your navel, is orange. And I'm here to tell you that the deep red was turning to orange fast. Vam, vam, vam, vam, vam, I chanted. That's the sex chakra's sound, you see. Vam, vam, vam, vam, vam. Well, that kundalini was starting to flow now all right. It uncoiled itself, slithered between my thighs, up my stomach, round over my hips and buttocks and up my back. It was about this time that I shifted out of the half-lotus position I'd adopted in the armchair and stretched my legs out straight. My jeans were starting to feel strangely tight in certain areas. And I don't just mean at the knees.

I reached my hand down and made a few adjustments. The thick crotch seam was practically embedded in my cunt. And boy, was it wet! I undid the metal button that was embossing my belly with its logo and eased down the zip. Phew. That was better. The red weal of the waistband stood out like a laparotomy scar. I wriggled my behind to loosen the hold the denim had on me. I must've been sweating cos the jeans were sticking to my arse like clingfilm. My knickers were soaked. Must turn the thermostat down in here, I thought. Place was like downtown Delhi the day before the monsoon hits. I struggled my jeans down and managed to get them as far as my knees, lifting my bum up off the chair to slide them under me. I understand why those Tibetan monks wear loose robes now, believe me.

I sat for a while, getting my breathing settled down again, regaining my composure. Centring myself, you know. Cabbage Man was deadheading his roses by now and wasn't looking. Should have had that done well before now, I couldn't help thinking. You'll have gathered I'm a bit of a garden centre buff. Once did it with Vinnie on a pile of growbags at B&Q, but I'll tell you about that some other time.

When I'd got myself settled, I started with the kundalini trick again. Two spirals of energy, called Ida and Pingala, are supposed to coil around the central channel that runs up the spinal cord, called Sushumna. When that happens – congratulations – you've achieved kundalini. Well, I did some more breathing and it didn't take long to get that energy firing up. It seemed reluctant to travel upwards this time though. Instead, it spread in all directions, anywhere except towards my higher, more spiritual realms. It zinged around my nether regions, no bother, though. And now my clit was starting to draw attention to itself, throbbing away like a hammer-struck thumb. My cervix contracted and dilated in time with it, squeezing and clenching like a fist around a tube of toothpaste. I had this urge to lie down on the floor, so, not being one to deny my urges readily, I gave in to it. I hoicked my T-shirt over my head round about then too, and chucked it away. It landed on a low offshoot of the grapevine.

Picture the scene. Me, lying on the coir mat on the floor of a lean-to greenhouse that deludes itself it's a conservatory. Plant pots and trowels roll against my head and a scattering of potting compost softens the corners. And I've only got my bra and knickers on, and a pair of jeans tangled around my knees. Cabbage Man didn't know what he was missing.

First of all, I lay on my back. But that was no good. I'm

a face-down woman when it comes to do-it-yourself. I hauled myself over, the coir mat scratching at my bare skin. I would have taken my jeans off altogether but they were glued to my calves and shins. It would be a waste of precious energy to struggle with them any longer. Next time I'm getting comfort-fit, I can tell you. My face was pressed against the rough matting. I would have a pattern imprinted on one cheek before long but I didn't care. By now my hands were tucked down between my thighs. I lay still for a minute to get myself centred again. Right. What comes next?

Concentrate on the two lower chakras, the book had said. Focus all your attention on them. Visualise these chakras whirling, swirling, vortexing with energy like Catherine wheels. See the colours. Dark red. Orange. Smell the associated smells. Perfume. Incense. Sweat. Sweet genital odours. Taste the associated tastes. Salty skin. Saliva. The secretions of an excited cunt. Hear the sounds. Heartbeat. Breath. Gurglings in the gut. The suck, suck, suck of the contracting vagina.

And don't forget touch.

I slid my hand down to my clit, lingering over my belly, slipping under my damp knickers, sliding over the soft hair of my pubes, dipping down into that warm, wet, secret place. The bud of my clit swelled under my middle finger. *Oh yes. That's right. Just there.* I ran my fingertip gently over it, soothing it, relaxing it first, then rubbing it more vigorously, circling faster and faster, feeling the energy build and build. I spread my forefinger and middle finger apart and slid them down each side of my cunt lips, stroking the roots of my clit. This is an area men can forget about, if you don't remind them. Electrical impulses shot from those roots right up to my cervix. The neck of my womb tightened, loosened, tightened. The contractions were coming so fast that I had to stop myself bursting into orgasm there and then, because that's not the Tantric way. The Tantric way is to build and build and build. To concentrate on the means rather than the end. To hold back as long as possible, so that the final surge, when it comes, is ecstatic. It's all about the contrast between having and not having. Denial is good for the soul.

I put both hands between my moist thighs and slowly caressed myself. I was a good lover. I knew exactly where to stroke, how to stroke, what pressure to use. I wouldn't disappoint myself. I was going all the way. And I was taking myself with me. I was giver and receiver. Doer and done to. I slid three fingers up into my cunt. It was so soft up there! Warm and moist and yielding. No wonder men go mad for it. Juices lubricated my fingers, I could feel them hot and wet, dripping out like melted butter from a crumpet. Well, I couldn't resist, could I? I brought my hand up to my face and breathed in the sweet smell of myself. I wiped my fingers over my mouth and sucked them. Mmm. I could get a taste for this. If only I were more flexible. Imagine what sucking yourself off would be like!

I rolled on to my back. My bra was digging into me. The straps sliced through my shoulders and the underwiring cut into my ribs. Time to get rid of it. I reached back and plucked the hooks and eyes apart and tossed it away. The grapevine nodded its thanks as it caught the bra on a trailing tendril. My breasts bounced forward, full and rounded, the nipples as big as loganberries, ripe and red. I would have loved to take them in my mouth but, damn it, I couldn't reach. Instead I rolled them between my thumb and forefinger. Easy, easy, gently at first, not twiddling away like Vinnie did sometimes, as if he was trying to pick up Radio Luxembourg. Softly, roll them, tweak them, work them up slowly until they're begging to be pinched hard, begging to be squeezed. Then slacken off again, caress them, smooth out the wrinkles of the aureole, cup the breasts. I did all this. And more. I surprised myself with my inventiveness. I played with both nipples at the same time. I squeezed my breasts together and tried to make the nipples kiss. I rolled them under my palms, circling them, squashing my breasts flat. I held my heavy boobs gently then suddenly caught my nipples between the spread fingers of my cupped hands, shocking myself.

To play with yourself. To be playful.

Meanwhile, that Tantric energy hadn't gone away. The kundalini snake was coiling around my lower body, crushing me in its burning embrace. I brought my attention down to my root chakra again, focused on it, breathed the prana into it, felt it begin to spin. I took the breath in steadily, in and out, in and out, bringing the divine energy right into the seat of my being, seeing that blood-red light start to swirl. When it was spinning happily, I brought my attention up to the sex chakra, and got it going as well. The orange disc moved like a fan on low setting, gradually picking up speed until the fluttering energy was hot and growing hotter. When both muladhara and swadhisthana were whirling fans of light, I moved on to the next chakra, the solar plexus, whose colour is yellow.

Soon all my lower chakras were flowering like magnolia trees, the petals opening as in time-lapse photography. They spun, they burst, they blossomed. If you open the lower chakras, the book said, the upper ones will open themselves when you climax. I shoved my hands back down into my groin. It was sticky with sweat and juices. I lay on my back and stroked myself, my eyes closed.

For a long time I lay there, caressing and stroking myself. My fingers roamed through my pubic hair and fondled the lips of my pussy. My abdomen was swollen with pleasure, tumescent with desire. My body was a stiff, throbbing shaft. I didn't want to hurry. I had all the time in the world.

I rolled over, face down again, and worked a bit harder, rubbing, pinching, tweaking. Images of being forced over a barrel and fucked by nameless hordes flickered through my mind. I banished these images. No, this wasn't one of those ordinary wanks. This one was special. I didn't need mindporn to make myself come. My problem was stopping myself coming too soon. My lips were dry and my throat ached. My legs were stiff and my fingers hard as I rubbed and rubbed at my clit. I kept on breathing the breath, focusing on the chakras, keeping them all spinning like plates on sticks. That old serpent, kundalini, was licking at my cunt, flick, flick, flickering its forked tongue, ready to shoot up inside me, splurge up my spine and burst out of my head in a shower of golden rain. The true genitals are internal. My skull was my yoni, receptive, a cup; my spine was my lingum, erect, thrusting. Spinal fluid was my ejaculate. Astral fire my orgasm.

The serpent licked. I rubbed. Between us we brought me to readiness. Warmth spread throughout my groin and stomach. Warmth that held a pulse of orgasmic electric current. AC/DC. Alternating and direct. I was waist high in a Sitz bath of pleasure; a Jacuzzi of juices. I flicked at the switch of my clit, notching the temperature higher. Heat surged across my tits and spread up to my throat and neck. My entire body was tumescent. My face began to burn. My skin ran with sweat as the greenhouse ran with condensation. My windows were well steamed up. I reached that state of total tension that precedes the total relaxation we all long for. Building, building, building. I was almost frantic with anticipation. Anticipation that could not be disappointed.

But I held back. I built and built and built some more. My breathing was rapid now. I was hyperventilating. I was nearly passing out and I wanted so much to let go, to burst into orgasm. I drew my breath all the way up my spine and into my head. My mind was spinning now, as well as my chakras. I kept on rubbing at my clit. My legs were pressed tightly together as I squirmed and wriggled. I was just about dancing horizontally. Man, I was nearly levitating. My cunt was demanding satisfaction, banging against my hands like it had a mind of its own. Hold on, I told it. Remember to build, build, build. Well, we built so high, my pussy and me, it felt like I had a tower block erected inside me. I didn't need a cock to fill me up. My own energy was shafting away like a piston engine. It was no use. I had to let go of the reins that were holding me back. I couldn't help it. I flipped and started to go off.

I was coming. Coming! Couldn't hold it back any longer. Didn't want to hold it back. I had reached saturation point. I couldn't take any more. This was it. It was time.

The first wave of orgasm crashed over me like a breaker at Surfer's Paradise. I let myself crest with it. I let myself drown in its sucking undertow. Wave after wave rolled and crashed and sucked. I bobbed and sank, gasping for air. I kept my hands pressed firmly against my clit as convulsions racked my body. I bucked and tossed. It was like I was giving birth to child after child, and they were all orgasmic. I gave birth to the sun and the moon. My body lurched and rocked. A bushfire raged across my plains and valleys, consuming everything in its path. Lights burst in my head. My spirit soared. I reached climax. I came.

The orgasm was total. It wasn't confined to my cunt but spread through all my tingling limbs, my torso, my head, my mind. My face was scalding. My chakras danced in orgasmic delight as a freight train charged up my spine. I rolled in ecstasy as if I wanted to escape from so much pleasure. I jerked and juddered. It felt like all the openings in my body, even the pores, were being fucked at once. I was making love to the universe and the universe was making love to me. I loved everybody in the world and was loved by them in return. Bliss flooded me, warm, soothing, surging waves of it. Ida and Pingala curled around Sushumna, just as they were supposed to. Kundalini shot up my spine with such force it sent bells ringing in my head. The spiritual semen jetted through me and ejaculated from the top of my cranium in a starburst of golden drops.

And at the moment of orgasm, I left my body. My spirit shot out through the top of my head in a rush of energy, burst through the Plexiglas roof and soared into the fresh crisp air. Hovering above the frosty garden, I looked down on myself. I could see the steamy greenhouse, the tendrils of the grapevine, the old armchair. And I could see myself, prone, an orange-gold aura glowing around me. I hadn't intended to go off like that. I had meant to open up the ajna chakra, the third eye, which grants clarity, but I had gone for the big one, sahasrara, the lotus flower, the crown.

I fell in love with myself that day. I fell in love with myself and with the entire cosmos. I was married to the stars and the planets in an alchemical marriage that never had to pay bills or fight over what to watch on television. My lower self had made love to my higher self. I had courted her, that higher being, wooed her, seduced her, aroused her, and brought her to ecstatic release. Or was it she who courted me?

It seemed like hours later that I rolled over and opened my eyes. I was back. I was limp, but, boy, was I blissful.

Playing With Fire

Kimberly Dean

Playing With Fire

The fifth letter showed up at work.

Erin's hands shook as she slit open the envelope. By now she recognised the typewriter face. There was no return address, but she didn't need one to know what the vile contents of the letter would be. Somehow, she couldn't stop herself from unfolding the paper and reading.

> You're so beautiful. I can't wait to fuck you. I watch you every night on the ten o'clock news. You act so serious, but I don't hear the words you're saying. All I see is that luscious mouth. If I concentrate real hard, I can feel it on my cock.

Her hands shook so badly that the letter slipped from her grip. It fluttered to her desk, but landed face up. Like a magnet, her gaze was drawn back to the filthy words.

> And your hands. I look at those long fingers wrapped around your microphone, and I imagine them on my balls. Your hands kneading my balls and your mouth

sucking the life out of my cock – that's what I want, Erin. That's what I'm going to get.

Blindly, she reached for the phone and dialled her boyfriend's number. 'Mark?'

He heard the tremor in her voice. 'You got another one?'

'Yes.'

'Son of a bitch!' There was a slam in the background and then a long silence. When his voice finally returned, it was under control. 'Is it the same as the others? Is the "f" lifted?'

Her gaze skimmed the words and landed on 'fuck'. She squirmed in her chair but tried to be analytical. 'Yes,' she said. 'It's raised slightly higher than the rest of the lower-case letters.'

'Get over here. Now!'

The drive across town was nerve-racking. With every turn, Erin checked her mirror to make sure she wasn't being followed. By the time she parked and rushed up the front sidewalk to Mark's house, she was a mess. The door was pulled open for her and she fell forward into her boyfriend's arms.

'Are you OK?' he demanded.

She nodded against his chest. Now that she was with him, she felt better.

'Did you bring the letter?'

She shuddered. 'It's in my purse.'

'Let me see it.'

After pulling out of his grip, she rummaged around and found the envelope. Mark carefully took it by the corners and stuffed it into his jacket pocket. It was only then that Erin realised he was dressed to go to the office. Panicking, she grabbed him by the lapels. 'You're not going down to the station now, are you?'

'I have to, baby.' His hands settled on her shoulders and he massaged them gently. 'I need to get this to the lab as soon as possible. I'm sick of this asshole running around terrifying you.'

'But Mark!'

His touch ran down her arms and he gripped her hands tightly. 'Don't worry, baby. Chris is here.'

Chris.

Erin looked sharply over Mark's shoulder. As always, his room-mate was hovering in the background.

'Did you get another naughty letter, love?'

The cool drawl of his voice sent a shiver of energy down her spine. His blue eyes were watching her so carefully. Her throat tightened and she nodded.

'Can you watch over her tonight, Chris?' Mark asked. 'I want to go down to the station and see if I can get any leads as to who's doing this.'

'I'll take care of her.'

Mark softly kissed her forehead. 'You'll be fine here. I'll get this pervert, baby. I swear I will.'

She tightened her grip on him until he lowered his head. His lips covered hers possessively and he gave her a long kiss. She clung to him, not wanting him to go. He gave her a tight squeeze before pulling away.

'Try to relax,' he whispered.

Erin watched him turn and leave. Feeling abandoned, she wrapped her arms about her waist and stared at the door. Chris finally walked over and flipped the deadbolt. She flinched when he turned to face her. His blue look was so intent, so piercing.

'He's right,' he said in that quiet voice. 'You need to relax. You're about ready to jump out of your skin.'

She rubbed her arms, suddenly feeling cold. She couldn't relax. There was simply no way! 'I hate what this guy is doing to me.'

Chris settled back against the door. His pose was casual, but his eyes were alert. 'Are the letters really that bad?'

'They're horrible!' A shiver ran down Erin's spine.

Nervously, she ran a hand through her hair. 'Some of the things he's suggesting are just outrageous. I can't imagine letting anyone touch me that way.'

'Outrageous.'

There was a wealth of meaning behind his one word, but she didn't quite understand his point. 'Yes, they're outrageous.'

'Not "sick". Not "repulsive".'

She opened her mouth to respond, but she found that she didn't have an answer. 'What are you trying to say?' she asked slowly.

'Nothing,' he said as he pushed himself away from the door. 'It was just an observation.'

Stunned, Erin just let the man walk from the room. When she realised what he'd implied, her jaw dropped. Fuming, she stomped into the kitchen after him. 'I don't know who you think you are! I'm being stalked. Don't even try to say that I'm enjoying it. The guy is sick. He's got some very strange ideas, and they scare me.'

Chris filled a cup with coffee and turned round to face her. 'That's what surprises me so much.'

Erin realised that she'd got closer to him than she'd thought. Awareness made the little hairs on the back of her neck stand on end, but she refused to back away. Chris had always affected her that way. He was the strong, silent type. She could never tell what he was thinking, and that unsettled her. 'Explain,' she demanded.

He shrugged. 'I don't know, I always thought you were braver than this. You never seem to take much caution when you're pursuing a story. When you were investigating that prostitution racket last month, you went at it head first.'

She cocked her head and tried to understand. 'This is different. I'm not pursuing a story. A freak is pursuing me.'

'Right – and you're reacting by cowering in the corner.'

'What else am I supposed to do?'

'Fight back.'

'I can't. I don't know who he is. Mark's a detective and even he hasn't been able to track this guy down.'

'So you can't do anything about your little stalker; do something about your fears.'

Erin finally took that step backwards. She didn't know where the conversation was going, but it made her nervous. 'How?'

Chris took another sip of his coffee, but his eyes never left hers. 'How do you conquer any fear? If you're afraid of flying, you get your ass on an airplane. If you're afraid of heights, you go to the top of the nearest skyscraper.'

Erin's cheeks turned pink, but he didn't stop.

'If you're afraid of sex . . .'

Her blush went right up to the roots of her hair. She was mortified to be having this discussion with Chris of all people. Most of their previous conversations had centreed on the weather. She couldn't believe she was standing here, much less considering his idea.

Sexual therapy. Was that the way to ease her mind? The ideas in those letters had been haunting her for weeks. They filled her thoughts night and day. If she could somehow manage to associate pleasure with the kinky threats, would her terror go away? She chewed her lower lip as she thought about it. Finally, she shook her head. 'I can't. Mark wouldn't go for it.'

He took another drink of his coffee, but his gaze pierced her to the core. 'Who said anything about Mark?'

Erin's heart stutter-stepped, but then exploded at a frantic pace. She took another step back, but butted up against the breakfast bar. 'You?'

He set the coffee cup on the counter. 'Why not?'

'Because Mark is my boyfriend.'

Chris pushed himself away from the counter and trapped her. 'This would have nothing to do with that.'

'I . . . I can't.'

'You can. I know you've thought about it.'

The blood rushed out of her face. 'You self-centreed bastard.'

'I've seen you looking at me.'

She couldn't deny it. He wasn't the type of man she was normally drawn to, but there was something about him. Mark was more the dark, handsome type. Chris? Chris had closely cropped strawberry-blond hair, and blue eyes that made her nipples harden every time he glanced her way. And his body. He was built like a brick house. As a fireman, he worked out regularly. The results were enough to make her mouth water. Any time he took his shirt off, she couldn't stop looking at him.

'You know I want to fuck you.'

Her toes curled in her shoes. 'I won't let you.'

'Fine. Walk around like a scared little girl. See if I care.'

Instead of moving back, though, he leaned forward and braced his hands on the bar on either side of her. Erin felt overwhelmed by his presence. He was much taller than she was and probably twice as wide. She felt dominated, and the twinge between her legs shocked her.

'Mark would be crushed,' she whispered.

'It would be our dirty little secret.'

'Do you really think it would work?'

'Take off that suit and we'll find out.'

The order stunned her. Tilting her head back, she looked at him. He was dead serious. He was waiting, though, for her consent. Her breaths shortened as she considered what would happen if she said yes. She couldn't think, though. Her pulse was pounding too frantically. She stared at him with fascination and saw the pulse thudding in his neck too.

His suggestion was too bizarre. She shouldn't even be considering it.

'I don't know . . .'

'Take off the damn suit.'

Erin's insides clenched. She didn't know why she did it, but she reached for the top button. Chris didn't move, but his gaze focused on her actions. His rapt attention made her hands begin to shake. She was taking off her clothes for a man she hardly knew. By the time she got her jacket off, her pulse was pounding at twice its normal speed.

His gaze took in her lacy black bra. 'Now the skirt.'

Her arousal pulsed between her legs. She couldn't understand why, but she reached for the back zip. His gaze nearly singed her breasts. The position had thrust them forward until they nearly brushed against his chest. He was looking straight down into her cleavage.

The rasp of the zipper was uncommonly loud. Erin felt like a wanton as she swirled her hips and let the skirt slide to the floor. She still wore her bra, her panties and her practical journalist shoes, but she'd never felt so naked.

'Now, tell me,' he ordered in a voice that had dropped even lower, 'what does your stalker want to do to you that scares you so much?'

Her stomach clenched. 'I can't . . .'

'Tell me.'

Her breath hissed out of her lungs. The tell-tale sign of stickiness appeared between her legs, and she closed her eyes. God, what was wrong with her? 'He wants to tie me up.'

'And?'

Her face flushed. She knew he would stand there all night staring at her semi-nude form until she told him. Her voice dropped very low – so low she could hardly hear it herself. 'He's got a thing for fire. He wants to drip hot candle wax on my body as he . . . as he screws me.'

The silence in the room was deafening.

'All right,' Chris said, just as softly. 'Then it's on to the table with you.'

Erin's knees nearly buckled. Her sex began to ache when he took her hand and turned her towards the kitchen table. It loomed in the centre of the room. With a tug on her hand, he walked her to it. His hands settled on her waist as he made her look at it. The touch burned against her skin.

'Don't move,' he ordered.

She couldn't. Her breaths shortened as she stared at the table. He was going to do exactly what the pervert had threatened. She got excited just thinking about it. Her panties were wet and her nipples were hard peaks under the cups of her bra. What kind of a woman was she to want this to happen?

Chris wasn't gone long. When he returned, he had a pile of supplies in his hands, including a long length of rope. She shivered uncontrollably when he set them on the table.

'Turn around and sit.'

Her heart jumped up into her throat, but she did as she was told. The table felt cold against the back of her thighs. With embarrassment, Erin realised she was smudging the table's surface with her juices.

Chris gave her a hard look. As he held her gaze, he reached for the front clasp of her bra. It was almost a relief when the confining garment loosened. Still looking at her, he reached for her breasts and caught one soft globe in each hand.

It had been so long since anyone besides Mark had touched her that Erin gasped. The action pressed her breasts harder against his palms, and he squeezed gently. Her breaths went ragged and her eyelids drifted shut.

'Look at me.'

Her eyes popped open. When he saw he had her attention, he began working her breasts in his palms. His touch was so different – almost rough. His occupation was physical, and his hands reflected it. He had a grip that could hurt her if he wanted, and the knowledge excited her. She loved the calluses on his fingers. They scraped against the delicate skin, causing jolts of sexual energy to rush to her core.

'Have you ever been tied up, love?'

Love. The affectionate term made something bloom inside Erin's chest. He'd started calling her that not long after she'd started dating Mark. She'd always thought it odd, but right now, she liked it. It made her feel sexy. 'No,' she said softly.

He pinched her nipples hard and she inhaled sharply.

'Good,' he said. 'I'll make sure you like it.'

He let go of her breasts and swept the bra off her shoulders. His hand ran down her body until it rested on her stomach. 'Lie back.'

Hesitantly, she relaxed on to the hard tabletop. She was a little uncertain. Once he had her tied up, he could do absolutely anything he wanted to her. Her stomach tightened, but she couldn't tell if it was from fear or anticipation.

'Lift your arms overhead.'

She slid her arms upwards. Chris measured out a length of rope. He pulled a handkerchief out of his back pocket and wrapped it around her skin to protect it from burns. Soon, she felt him twist the rope around her delicate wrist. Panic flared inside her, but with it was an overwhelming sense of arousal.

She'd never played these types of games before. Still, she couldn't help but notice that the little smudge of dampness under her buttocks had turned into a pool. She felt like an ancient sacrifice with her arms spread wide and her breasts thrust into the air.

'Oh, that's a pretty sight,' he whispered.

She shut her eyes as his hand settled on her breast again. This time when he pinched her, she was halfway expecting it. Knowing it was coming didn't lessen its effects, though. If anything, her reaction was magnified by the fact that she was bound to the table and couldn't get away. When she finally cried out, he turned her loose.

'That's a good girl,' he said as he moved away.

'Now we're set,' he said as he came to stand at the base of the table.

Uncertainty gripped her one last time. 'Chris, I'm not sure . . .'

'Let's get those panties off of you,' he said in a low voice. His hands settled at her hips. 'Lift.'

Erin's stomach clenched, but she obeyed. The silk was pulled off her hips, down her legs and over her shoes. Chris's strong hands settled on her thighs, and he pushed them open. She could feel the blue heat of his gaze on her most secret place. His fingers bit into her inner thighs, and her pussy spasmed uncontrollably. He bit out a curse when he saw her muscles working.

'Look at you.' His voice was almost a groan.

He swallowed hard, and Erin could almost see the determination cross his face. He pulled back from her suddenly and reached for the back of his T-shirt. He whipped it over his head. Before it even hit the ground, he was reaching for the zipper of his jeans. He stripped in about half the time it had taken her.

He turned from her for a second and doused the lights in the room. Soon, there was the rasp of a match and the hiss of a flame. Erin's fingers bit into her bindings as one of the candles was lit. The fire danced on its perch. Her supine body was bathed in soft light. Shadows emphasised the valleys, while the peaks basked in the glow.

Chris slowly moved the candle down her body. The light danced across her torso until the flame was right over the triangle of her pubic hair. Erin squirmed as he lovingly petted the light brown curls with his free hand.

'Aren't you a pretty pussy?' he said softly as his fingers delved deeper.

She closed her eyes, unable to watch. She felt his fingers part her lower lips. The sensation of heat had her eyelids popping right back open. Her head came off the table as she frantically looked downwards.

The candle was still inches away from her, but he'd

moved the flame closer so he could examine her more intimately. His fingers spread her wide. Her reaction seemed to fascinate him, so he tried it again. He got the same response.

'Careful!' she cried. The candle's flame danced too close for comfort. Sweat broke out on her brow and she locked the muscles of her spine and buttocks. She couldn't afford any more harsh movements.

He pushed her resolve, though, when his fingers moved upwards. With a practised flick, he pushed back the hood of her clit. Erin shrieked and tried to shimmy away. There was nowhere to go. The heat from the candle pulsed around the sensitive bundle of nerve endings. Chris applied direct pressure with his thumb, and her back arched off the table.

'Is the pussy hungry, love?'

'Yes,' she moaned. She wanted him inside her so badly, she could cry.

'All right. Patience.' He reached for another candle and held it up in the flickering light. 'Let's see if it likes this.'

Erin's pulse exploded. 'No!'

Her protest was too late. She felt him placing the hard wax taper at her sensitive opening.

'Yes,' he crooned to her.

He rubbed the candle against her, making her accustomed to its feel. She couldn't relax. She couldn't fight. When he finally gave up teasing and began easing the candle into her, she groaned in delight. She felt so dirty. The taper was long – oh so long – and smooth. He'd put the base in first and the thickened knob pushed deep into her.

'Oh, my God!' she shrieked. 'God!'

Her body went taut and her neck arched as sensations pummelled her. He pumped the candle in and out, watching her hips lift to receive it. When he sensed she was coming close to peaking, though, he pushed the taper in deep and left it there.

'Not yet. I want to be inside you when you come.'

Erin squirmed on the table, so aroused she was almost in pain. 'Oh, please. Chris, please!'

Then she saw it. He'd moved the lit candle over her stomach. Ever so carefully, he tipped it sideways. A droplet of wax poured over the edge. It seemed to fall in slow motion. Her eyes widened, but there was absolutely nothing she could do.

She'd been thinking about this for weeks. Ever since her stalker had painted the scenario in her mind, she'd been able to think of nothing else. The drop fell down, down, down. When it hit her skin, the heat was explosive.

Erin screamed.

The wax wasn't hot enough to burn, but it stung. Another drop hit her skin, lower on the abdomen. Her tummy clenched and, in turn, her pussy clamped down on the candle that was still buried deep in her passageway. She twisted her body, trying to roll away, but Chris firmly pressed her hips flat on to the table.

'God, you're a little firecracker!' Reaching between her legs, he gave the candle a twist.

She responded like a flashpoint. Her entire body became suffused in heat and her hips began thrusting uncontrollably.

Suddenly, hot wax was being dropped everywhere. The splashes hit her so quickly that she couldn't prepare for them. Every one of them edged a little closer to the juncture of her legs. Finally, one plopped on to the edge of her pubic hair.

Everything in the room suddenly went still.

Erin's heart pounded so hard in her chest that she was sure Chris could hear it. He wasn't interested in it, though. All his attention was on the puddle of wax oozing about the fine hairs low on her pubic bone.

He reached a curious hand out to touch the cooling wax. Helplessly, she looked up at him. His gaze was so intense, she forgot to breathe.

Without warning, he gave a yank.

Her pubic hair was pulled out at its root. The hot sting shot straight to Erin's core. Her scream lodged in her throat, but her body went wild. She began tugging at the ropes. Her legs wrapped around Chris's waist and her hips twisted in agony. Her breasts shuddered as she took deep, gasping breaths of air.

'Fuck!' Chris exclaimed. Her volcanic reaction sent him into overdrive. He tugged on the candle. It popped out of her with a slurp and he tossed it on to the floor.

Erin cried at the loss. 'Put it back in!'

'I've got something better,' he said with a ragged breath. He quickly doused the other candle and the room plunged back into darkness.

'Oh, please!' she begged. 'I need something inside me!'

He hooked his arms under her legs and settled his hands under her buttocks. The position stretched her obscenely, but she greedily lifted her hips. His cock poked at her, searching for her opening. He found it in the darkness and, with a hard thrust, plunged into her as far as he could go.

'Chris!' she screamed.

He was much thicker than the candle and she had to stretch to accommodate him. With her hands tied and her legs pulled open wide, there was nothing she could do but accept his thrusts. He pulled out, leaving her almost empty before pushing in deep again.

'Yes!' she whimpered.

With a growl, he dragged her right to the edge of the table and began pounding into her. Erin felt the strain in her arms as the ropes pulled tight. He was fucking her mercilessly, and her blood pounded harder in her veins as it rushed to her core. He thrust one more time, and colours exploded inside her head. Her muscles clamped down hard and squeezed his cock, trying to capture it deep inside her.

'Erin,' he groaned as his own climax overtook him. His

fingers bit into her buttocks and he ground her on his spurting cock. He came for a long, long time before that big cock went limp.

When it was done, his knees buckled slightly. With another groan, he leaned forward and let his weight settle on top of hers. He buried his face in her breasts and closed his eyes.

'Are you all right?' he asked.

Erin's heart pounded in her chest. She didn't know. She'd never been so thoroughly screwed in her life.

He lifted his head and his gaze settled on her like a laser beam.

'I'm fine,' she breathed.

He gave her a strange look. Then, he did something totally unexpected.

He kissed her.

His lips settled across hers and her fingers bit into the rough rope. This wasn't a soft, questioning, first kiss. This was the kiss of a man who wasn't finished fucking his woman.

His hard lips moulded against hers. His tongue sought entrance and Erin opened her mouth. His tongue darted inside and swirled across hers in an intimate mating dance. As just a kiss, it was powerful and overwhelming. She made a soft sound at the back of her throat and he pulled back to read the reaction in her eyes.

'Love,' he sighed. He gently laid a kiss on her forehead. 'Let's get you out of these ropes.'

With infinite care, he untied her. He looked over her wrists carefully, searching for any marks. Convinced he hadn't hurt her, he set about removing the wax from her skin. It had cooled and set. It cracked under his fingers as he applied gentle pressure. He dusted her off before his hand settled against her pubic hair.

'Did it hurt too badly?' he asked. His fingers rubbed the reddened bare spot.

Erin bit her lower lip with embarrassment. 'It was the best bikini wax I've ever had.'

That made him smile. She'd never seen him smile and her heart tripped in response. When his arms swept around her, she went into them willingly. He sat down on one of the kitchen tables and pulled her into his lap.

Erin felt some of her arousal return. God, he was just so hard. She pressed her finger against his pectoral muscle, but his skin had hardly no give to it at all. Giving in to the temptation, she explored the tattoo on his biceps. It had intrigued her forever. As she looked at it more closely, she realised it was a ring of fire circling his arm. She kissed his hard muscle and felt his hand come up to cup the back of her head.

'Scared any more?'

For a moment, she didn't understand the question. Then, with a rush, it all came back. They'd had sex for a very specific purpose – to rid her of her fears about her stalker.

Oh God, how could she have forgotten? Her spine stiffened and she pulled away from him. This wasn't her lover. This was her lover's room-mate!

'I think . . .' She cleared her throat and searched for the detachment she relied upon so heavily as a reporter. 'I think it helped.'

The look in Chris's eyes chilled. For some reason, her response seemed to anger him. Suddenly, the hand at the back of her head tightened. His head swooped down and he held her still for another kiss. The pressure of his lips was hard and Erin felt a thrill pulse in her veins. He filled her senses until she could hardly breathe. Only when he had her limp and writhing on his lap did he let her go.

'Good,' he said in a gruff voice. 'What's next?'

Hours later, Erin found herself bent over a hot gas grill with her ass sticking up in the air. Her heart was pounding, but she was afraid to move. Chris had made it safe for her by covering the lid with towels, but she knew she was playing with fire.

'Lean over a little further, love, so you can grab the legs.'

She followed his instructions, but the move pressed her breasts against the towel. She'd been afraid to let her skin touch the grill at all, but there was no way to avoid it. Heat radiated up through the thick cotton terrycloth and her body was suffused with a dangerous warmth. Her stomach clenched, but the heat on her breasts felt good.

'How's that?' he asked. He parted the curtain of her light brown hair so he could see her face.

'Good,' she sighed.

'How's this?' he asked, pointing his dick at her mouth.

'Better,' she groaned. She opened her mouth and found it soon filled with his cock. She twirled her tongue the way she'd learned he liked. He grunted and thrust. She nearly gagged, but relaxed the muscles in her throat to take him.

His hand ran up and down her spine as she sucked on him. Erin shivered at the picture they must be making. Just as she found her rhythm, though, he pulled his dick out of her mouth. Her lips were left wet and wanting.

He circled around behind her, and her hips wiggled. God, she felt like a woman who'd been stripped naked and put into the stockade. He hadn't bound her, but he'd ordered her to stay in position. He might as well have used the ropes.

'Chris, please,' she begged. She'd lost all her pride hours ago. He'd reduced her to a quivering mass of need with that big cock and those strong hands.

'All right. I'll give you the fucking you need.'

He leaned down to turn up the heat and Erin shifted with some discomfort. She was protected from the hot metal, but her internal temperature was rising quickly. Sweat beaded on her skin and her nipples felt raw from the heat. She gripped the legs of the grill hard and waited for the relief of his penetration.

It didn't come. Instead, she heard him moving around on the deck. 'Chris?'

The slap of water was so unexpected that she went right up on to her toes. Turning her head quickly, she saw that he'd picked up the garden hose and was aiming it straight at her backside. 'That wasn't in the letter,' she gasped.

'I'm improvising,' he said with a grin.

Another zing of water streaked against her and she groaned. The icy stream lashed repeatedly across her sensitive flesh. It felt almost as if he were whipping her with water! As a fireman, he knew exactly how to control the spray.

He walked closer, and the impact of the water increased. Erin screeched when he stopped its random motion and centred it on her pussy. Tormented by the cold spray, she shifted her hips wildly. His hand touched her lower back and she settled into place.

It was too soon, but she felt her orgasm approaching. The heat against her breasts was making her sweat, but the water between her legs was giving her chills. The contrast was overwhelming. 'Oh God! It's too much!'

'No,' he said in that low voice that still made her melt inside. 'This would be too much.'

Her spine went stiff when she felt that icy stream of water become harder and more concentrated on her core. This time, she really did try to get away, but he wrapped his arm about her waist and held her in place. With his other hand, he guided the hose to her numbed opening.

'It will be good,' he promised.

'No,' Erin groaned.

It was too late to deny the pleasure. He pushed the cold metal end of the hose into her. The water gushed deep inside her, chilling her from the inside out. Her hips bucked and swayed as she cried out in pleasure.

She thought she saw a neighbour's light turn on, but she didn't give a damn. All she cared about was the icy douche. Excess water was spilling out of her, but the internal pressure was enormous. She might as well be fucking the Abominable Snowman, as cold and hard as the icy water was inside her.

Then Chris did it; he sent her over the edge. He pushed her hips forward against the towel. The heat from the grill seeped through the material and caught her directly on her clit. It was the only stimulation she needed.

She yelled as her body convulsed in pleasure. She hardly noticed when Chris pulled the hose out of her and plunged his thick cock into her. She sagged over the hot grill as he hammered into her from behind. When he came, he spurted into her almost as hard as the garden hose had.

Erin welcomed the feeling. When he pulled out of her and turned her around into his arms, she was nearly weeping.

'That's enough for tonight,' he said. He pushed her hair back from her face and dried the tears from her eyes.

'Chris,' she said in a tiny voice. There was so much she wanted to say to him, but she just couldn't get out the words. Instead, she buried her face against his chest and wrapped her arms tightly around his waist. 'Promise me there's going to be more than just tonight.'

Chris's body went stock-still. After a moment, he threaded his fingers through her hair and pulled back so he could see her face. He liked whatever he saw there, because he smiled. It was the second smile she'd got out of him tonight and Erin felt blessed. She felt even more special when he leaned down to give her a soft kiss.

'I promise,' he said against her lips. 'Let's go to bed.'

Quickly, he turned off the grill and used the towels to dry the water from her body. With a laugh, he tossed her over his shoulder in a fireman's carry. Erin howled and demanded he put her down. He ignored her as he carried her through the house to his room, stopping only to close the door to Mark's bedroom.

The blood rushed to Erin's head as she hung upside down, but the position gave her a great vantage point of his ass. Tempted into an action she never would have tried with him before tonight, she reached down and gave the tight little globes a squeeze.

'Hey!' he said.

With a whoosh, her world spun again. When her head cleared, she found herself lying in his bed. Smiling, she opened her arms. He lowered his body heavily on top of hers.

'Did our therapy work?' he asked. He brushed a rough kiss across her lips. 'Any more fears I need to address?'

'Stalker? What stalker?' Her hands whisked down his back and settled again on his butt.

He kissed her, and their playful mood turned serious as their ardour heated. It had been that way the entire night.

'Chris, what about Mark?' Erin finally asked. She pulled away from his seeking lips and gave him a serious look. 'I don't want to hurt him.'

'I know,' Chris said. His hand came up to her breast and he squeezed it possessively. 'I'll talk to him.'

'What will you say?' She arched when his thumbnail flicked across her nipple. Panting hard, she tried to concentrate. 'I still love him, but I want to be with you too.'

He soothed the turgid peak with a long lick. 'Maybe we could work out a three-way deal.'

Three-way? Erin knew she should be appalled, but a thrill sizzled down her spine. 'But Mark's so conservative.'

'I think he'll surprise you.'

She couldn't imagine her straight-laced boyfriend sharing her with anybody. Still, Chris had an assured look on his face. 'You really think he'd go for it?'

Chris lifted his head from Erin's breast and looked

down at the beautiful woman in his arms. If anybody had been holding back on this deal, it had been her. His thoughts were immediately drawn back to Mark's bedroom and the old typewriter that his room-mate had forgotten to hide. Laughing, he said, 'Oh yeah, love. He'll go for it like his ass was on fire.'

Keeping Company With Chameleons

Saskia Walker

Keeping Company With Chameleons

Luba was a chameleon, moving from surface to surface, implicitly. Then Luba went deep and still wanted to know how far it was possible to go, pushing back the surface of things with a scarlet-lacquered talon and a wicked smile. Luba was a diva, a totally deviant diva, and Luba invited me to accompany her into her arena of sexual exploration.

But let me start at the beginning, because it was my involvement with Adam that began the rather surreal chain of events that led me to Luba, and beyond.

I had recently moved to a converted apartment block on the north-west side of the City. I fell in love with its elegant Edwardian manor-house façade and was thrilled to find that one conversion still remained on the market. Adam lived opposite me and we first caught sight of each other by the row of numbered post boxes in the ornate hallway. He was dark and lean with an angular face and hawklike eyes. He wore well-cut suits in dark colours, covered over with a charcoal raincoat that swung out behind him as he ran nimbly down the stairs in the mornings. There was an elegant nonchalance about him that attracted me immensely.

He caught me looking at his reflection in the huge mirror over the post boxes, and smiled. I was embarrassed to be caught observing him so intently, but I managed to smile back. I wanted to know more, and it was in my nature to be quietly determined about such things.

We began exchanging pleasantries. Within another week I had discovered that he was a broker in the City and he had learned that I was a press officer for a fashion house in the West End. He seemed interested, and so was I. I started looking out for him, targeting times when I knew he was around, anticipation racing in on me when he responded in kind. The night I saw Luba emerging from his apartment my anticipation tripped up and paused.

She was glamorous and outrageous. Dressed in sleek black from head to toe, slim and elegant, rich auburn hair brushed her shoulders in a chic bob. She was so striking; smoky eyes and ruby lips emphasised her diva looks and her confrontational attitude. I couldn't help staring; she was pure elegance, laced with sinuous sex appeal. She looked me up and down and smiled to herself.

'Hello there,' she drawled, as she passed me by. I managed to utter an appropriate acknowledgement in return, mesmerised by her glamour and the trail of Chanel that held me in her wake. My eyes followed her glossy thigh-high boots criss-crossing the wide landing to the stairway. She pulled her glove a little higher on the arm, before resting her fingertips lightly on the banister. She began her slow descent of the stairs with a seductively smooth sway of her hips. As she turned the corner of the stairway she glanced back at me and smiled to herself again, when she saw that I was still watching her.

Perhaps Adam had told her about the woman across the hallway who had the hots for him. I felt my skin burning up. I should have known he would have a gorgeous woman stashed away somewhere. I fumbled with my keys and slunk inside my sanctuary, poured myself a glass of wine and told myself to forget him. Within a week, we were lovers.

That Friday night, Adam invited me in for a drink. The chit-chat lasted through two glasses – during which time I decided he was a bit off-kilter but very attractive – and then he cut to the chase.

'Is it natural?' he asked, nodding at my hair, in an instant levelling the conversation off on a personal level. I realised my fingers were twined in my hair, which fell loose and unruly about my shoulders.

'Yes, although my parents are both blonde, and they claim they have no idea where I came from.' I smiled.

'Red hair is very special,' he said, suddenly very serious. 'The genes have to be present on both sides, but they are sensitive and very easily overpowered by others.' He arched one eyebrow at me, suggestively. I looked down at my glass, remembering the auburn-haired woman on the stairs. I didn't want to think about her and yet I was strangely curious about her, remembering the way she had looked at me. He was probably obsessed with redheads; he was involved with one of the most stunning redheads I had ever seen. At least, I assumed he was.

He got up from his chair and moved to stand behind the chaise longue where I sat. His eyes had that glimmer that betrayed his intent. I felt a tightness in my breathing in response to the knowledge that this was going to go exactly where I wanted it to. He leaned over my shoulder.

'May I?' he whispered, his hands already resting against my hair. I nodded. His fingers moved over its surface. 'You are a very beautiful woman,' he whispered, as his hands outlined smooth strokes from my shoulders down to my breasts, and then lower. 'I have never seen eyes quite so much like cats' eyes; they are truly tawny.'

His fingers moved assuredly, stroking me. I stretched back in the chair; he bent down as I leaned back into him. The rich smell of sandalwood and his musk raced through my veins. My body was awash with pulsing waves of need. My breasts felt full and hot; I was smouldering. He moved round to pull me closer to him and kissed me. Within minutes we were in his bedroom.

'You're looking for a little danger, aren't you?' he said, as we walked into the sparse, elegant room. I heard my own sharp intake of breath at his blatantness. I had not quite thought of it like that, but given that I was there with a man I barely knew, I could hardly argue the point, could I? The glint in his eye was thoroughly wicked. I remembered the woman's smirk as she had walked by the other night. What was I letting myself in for? I felt the urge to run.

'And you?' I asked, playing for time.

'Judy . . . I simply want you to prove to me that you are a natural redhead . . .' His tone was reminiscent of a lawyer in court, then he gave a dark chuckle, flashing his teeth at me. I was about to comment on his sense of humour when he reached over and slipped his hands beneath the edge of my velvet crop top and pulled it swiftly over my head. As it trailed from my fingertips to the floor, my comment came out as a gasp. He grinned, traced the edge of my lace bra with one finger and then stepped behind me. He lifted my skirt with one hand and slipped the other between my thighs. My heart was pounding against the wall of my chest. His outrageous and direct actions provoked something blatant inside me: the need to be under him. My body was pounding, leaving me weak with need.

'My, my, you are warm and damp. Judy, you should have said!' His chuckle was positively sinister. Bypassing the scrap of silk that betrayed my arousal, he inserted one finger along the lips of my sex and ran it from front to back. He began to explore me; slow, direct, inquisitive strokes, drawing low pants from me as each nerve ending leaped in response to his touches. My body was in turmoil. At that point the roller-coaster ride had only just begun; I wanted him inside me, but Adam kept me waiting a long while for that particular pleasure.

He had me bound over an upturned chair, my ankles spread wide apart, my wrists tethered at my back, my sex thrust back on display to him. He had probed and examined me and tortured my clit into blinding submission three times already, leaving me a panting wreck. I was in ecstasy, blind to anything but this; I was desperate for penetration. But he kept me there, waiting. The room fell silent. I drifted on semi-consciousness.

The sharp cut of stiletto approaching drew me back. A slick digit probed into my aching cunt. I moaned. I felt the nub of his cock against me. One violent thrust filled me to the hilt; I writhed in ecstasy, arching back on to his erection. At last!

It was worth the wait; he was as efficient as he was confident about his sexual prowess and I groaned as he probed as deep as he possibly could, and deeper, pushing vigorously up against the tenderest spots within me. I was in ecstasy, my body about to burst its banks of pent-up desire. As I gripped on to the upturned legs of the chair, almost there, her PVC-clad hands suddenly lay over my arms, grasping at me in turn. My sharp intake of breath latched me on the edge of my climax. The realisation: she was fucking me; that gorgeous diva had played with me all night and was now fucking me to distraction.

'Let it go, you bitch,' he seethed, his vivid synthetic red hair clinging around my cheek, and I did, in total release to him, just as he did.

When I awoke the auburn hair lay on the bedside table, and the sound of whistling in the shower indicated that Luba had left. Adam emerged from the bathroom with a towel around his waist, his short dark hair slicked back and wet. He stood at the end of the bed. I smiled at him;

Adam had turned out to be even more of a dark horse than I had imagined. He looked down at me moving in the bed, then he dropped the towel. As it fell to the floor I saw that his cock was hard and ready for me again. He gave a dark chuckle when my body quickly responded, shifting to face him. He pulled the sheets off me. It was Saturday. I did not leave his apartment until Monday morning.

I watched the swirl of his raincoat descending the stairs, remembering her slow easy steps. When I was with one facet of Adam I was always haunted by the other. Yet both of them somehow remained strangers to me, which I kind of enjoyed. I had always wanted to try sex with a stranger.

'Why?' I asked, much later on, when we were sitting facing each other among the tousled sheets on Adam's bed. I could not stop staring at her; Luba was such an enigma. She was wrapped in a silk kimono, while I sat naked in the tangled sheets.

'Oh, the usual, childhood spent in Mother's wardrobe, watching her string of attentive lovers and so on. Anyway, don't you think I make an attractive woman?' Her laugh was sardonic and decadent. He knew it. I nodded, smiling. He did make an attractive woman and, ironically, I found Luba was a bit less unpredictable to be around than Adam was.

'More than that, I want to get close to you, to women.' Luba looked a little more serious. Her voice was low and gentle, but still recognisably Adam's voice. 'It's more than the arousal associated with the masquerade; I want to know what it feels like to be you, to have men desperate for you. I want to share that with you.' Luba's eyes locked with mine. 'Will you share it with me, Judy?' The question seemed very weighted. She leaned over me and began to kiss my breasts. Her teeth tugged gently on my nipples, tugging at the need deep inside me. I hummed my approval.

'Tell me,' Luba whispered. 'Tell me what you are feeling, I want to know.'

Her hair brushed over my breasts, her hands moving swiftly between my thighs, where a cloying heat awaited those inquisitive fingers. I groaned, my hips pushing up towards her.

'Judy, tell me,' she insisted, when I began to moan and writhe, her fingers flexing and then opening me wide, sending me quickly towards the edge.

'Your fingers are so firm and direct . . . inside me . . . it sends out sensations all over my body.' My words came slowly, drawn out with each movement of her fingers. 'I want more, always more . . .'

'Tell me more, and you'll get more.' It was said through gritted teeth. She stirred her fingers faster, closing her palm hard over my clit, demanding the response.

'Building, it's building up . . .' The effort to speak with the climax so close took immense concentration. I was ready to beg for release.

'You are driving me crazy, Luba! It's like I am on fire there, with the need . . . oh, please . . .'

Luba dropped down and teased my anxious sex with her tongue. She sucked vigorously, taking the juice from my inner sex and bathing it over my ripe clit with her cupped lips, then circling the kernel of flesh rapidly with the tip of her tongue. I felt frantic yet weightless; disjointed words and whimpers flew up from my mouth as the sensations flew up from hers. I was strung out by the dynamism and intensity of Luba's mouth on my clit and it left me barely able to breathe, let alone verbalise. As my moans soared up around us, Luba was wanking furiously.

By the middle of the next month, our explorations of each other's sexuality had become increasingly deviant.

'Tell me your fantasies,' Adam instructed.

I knew him well enough by then to know that he was daring me to challenge him.

'Luba knows,' I whispered, as reckless and extravagant as he was when I was with him. I knew that Luba and Adam would come up with something wilder than I could possibly imagine, and I was their willing accomplice. He unravelled the chains that had held me down and sat back, smiling self-indulgently.

'You are right, Luba does know,' he said, standing up quickly, pacing up and down the room with barely contained energies. What was in his mind this time? I wondered.

'She's getting ready to take you out. She thinks you two should meet a stranger.' I sat up and took his outstretched hand. He looked manic; a shiver of anticipation ran over my bones. I felt almost relieved to see Luba emerge from the bathroom later.

She took me first to what she called TV Strip – the City streets where the transvestites walked. I wore Luba's clothes; she had dressed me. A long slim dress in heavy black satin, cut into a mandarin collar with a keyhole over my cleavage. It was a little tight on my hips and thighs because Luba was leaner than I, and it reached nearly to the ground, whereas on her it was calf-length. She had scraped my hair into a tight skullcap and she gave me her glossed-black wig and full-length gloves to wear.

I looked in the mirror. I looked stunning; I felt fantastic. Luba walked alongside me, tall and elegant in PVC and auburn, proudly watching over her protégée. I felt the thrill surge inside me, excited and proud too, beneath her deviant wing.

As we walked across the street she sang 'Take a walk on the wild side, baby' under her breath, causing me to chuckle. The cars crawled by, blurred faces watching as we clung together on the street corner, kissing and laughing at them as they looked us over, thinking that we were both lady-boys.

I found myself imagining that it was Adam watching us, wanting us. It was, in a way. I kissed Luba; that mouth was firm and passionate, reassuring. I opened my mouth to her and for a moment the world sped away from us. When a car suddenly braked and pulled up close against us, Luba gripped my arm and whispered against my ear as she walked us on. 'Enough of this, this is not what I want for you.'

We moved on to a classy bar that was busy with the spillover from the day's business meetings. I glanced at her, wondering if Adam came there too. Luba's familiarity with the place suggested that was the case. We sat in a leather snug, where we could observe the whole scene without being too obvious ourselves.

'You need a name,' Luba commented.

'Do I?' I twiddled the straw in my Slow Comfortable Screw; I couldn't help smiling. Luba had selected it for me, along with a Bloody Mary for herself.

'I think it should be something to go with your new look . . . how about Camille?'

'OK.' I was enjoying every second of this.

'Right, Camille,' she said, with purpose. 'I think you should choose a man now.' She gestured out towards the rest of the bar. After a moment I realised that she was quite serious. Then I acknowledged the fact that Luba would probably be quite capable of procuring whomsoever I might choose.

'Why him? Just out of interest,' she asked, looking over at the man I had indicated after nearly an hour of contemplation. Her expression was intense; she was fascinated by this game.

I looked back at him. He had come in just minutes before. He was not as tall or lean as Adam, but his body looked firmly muscled and attractive. He was a Latin-type, his skin gently sun-kissed, his features softly classical. He was wearing black jeans with a loose linen jacket over a tight black T-shirt. And he was alone.

'Two things in particular,' I said. 'His smile. Look, watch him when the barman gives him his change.' Luba observed. The man's mouth was exquisite and when he smiled it betrayed his sensuality.

Luba nodded. 'The other?'

'He's watching the people, just like we are.' Luba observed him for a couple of minutes, then smiled.

'Very true, Camille.' She approved my choice and she soon had him ensconced in the snug with us. Apparently a blatant invitation to join us had gone down rather well.

Luba chatted and quizzed him, while he sipped his Southern Comfort, glancing from one to the other of us with curious, watchful eyes. I was even more pleased with my choice when he was closer. He was quite gorgeous and very sexy indeed. His eyes were startling green and heavily fringed. A dark lock of hair fell forward over his brow as he turned to answer her questions. His name was Richard; he was a fitness instructor at a local gym; he was having a drink on his way home and, no, he would not mind at all if we adjourned to Luba's apartment for a bit more privacy.

He rested his hand across the back of my shoulders as I slipped out from the snug. My body was already warm but it was now becoming anxious and pliant.

'You want to see us together, don't you, Richard?' Luba asked, as she settled him on to the chaise longue with a fresh glass of Southern Comfort from Adam's bar. His eyebrows lifted as if surprised, but his eyes revealed that it was not an entirely unpleasant thought to him. Luba laughed. 'That wouldn't be a problem, would it, Camille?' I joined in with her smiles, enjoying the game. Luba stood behind me and began to run her hands over my breasts. I leaned back against her, the pair of us watching the man's responses.

'Are you two dykes?' he asked quite casually, sipping

his drink. I couldn't help laughing, but Luba answered him quite calmly. 'No, not at all, Richard. I do hope that's not a disappointment to you.' Luba squeezed me tight and planted a kiss on my shoulder. I knew Adam would be thrilled that Richard had not realised Luba's true nature.

'No . . . I meant that I hoped that was not the case,' he replied cautiously. He seemed quite collected, if a little wary. I felt a moment of pity for him though – Luba was taunting him. I remembered my first encounter with Adam, trying to keep my cool despite my urge to run.

'May I watch?' Luba whispered against my ear, for my hearing only. I nodded; the idea of it turned me on immensely. Besides, I wanted him; I wanted Richard. I had chosen him, and I was going to have him. My need was becoming insistent and it made me take action. I stepped away from Luba.

'I don't want you to watch us,' I said, closing on Richard. His eyes narrowed – there was caution in him. 'I want you, Richard.'

He gave a controlled and appreciative smile. I could see he was more than ready to take me on, or both of us for that matter; the desire in his expression was naked. I reached out my hand to him and he took it and stood up.

'Is that OK with you?' I asked, quite calmly, as my arms laced themselves round his neck.

'Perfectly so,' he murmured. He looked into my eyes for a moment, then kissed me on both cheeks, slowly; his hands locked lightly around my upper arms. The brush of that full passionate mouth across my face, and the musky scent of his skin, brought a momentary pause to my breathing. Anticipation forced it on again, more rapidly. His lips met mine. My body was burning; I sought the wetness of his mouth to calm the flames, inviting his tongue deeper into my mouth. Meanwhile, Luba moved behind me, undoing the zipper on my dress, taking it off me; she was silent, but I felt her intensity touching me.

Richard looked appreciatively at my unsheathed body, naked but for stockings and boots. He took off his jacket, dropping it to the floor, his eyes dark with lust as he watched me moving towards the chaise longue. He stripped off the T-shirt. His torso was as finely chiselled as one would expect of a fitness instructor. I began to purr.

'You dye your hair black?' he asked, glancing over my body with a quizzical expression. It took me a moment to realise what he meant. It was Luba's turn to chuckle; I had just proven I was a natural redhead, again.

'Um, yes,' I managed to reply, and reached for him to distract him from that particular train of thought.

He rested his hands on my shoulders. As they sank to curve around my breasts, I knew they would be leading the eyes that watched. I was heady with arousal. The touch of his fingers was pure static, a thread of electricity that leaped from the skin of his palm into the tightening skin of my nipples. I was fastened to his eyes, filled now with a blatant, demon sexuality, heat flooding from their intense darkness. He stirred the palms of his hands, his body closing on mine. Passion traversed the breadth of space between our bodies, then the space shrank and was gone. Skin against skin began the swell of lust that burned my skin up in its wake. Then I was raw against him, gripping on to him with flickering hands. Richard responded to my sudden clawing desperation by pushing me down on to the chaise longue.

'Wait,' he whispered, reaching for his belt. There was humour in his expression. I bit my lip and sat into the corner of the chaise longue, my arms draping over the back. I tried to control the throbbing inside me. It was sending deep waves of heat through my body. I shook back my head and closed my eyes for a second, to stop myself snatching at the man. My body wanted more, the hardness of his erection naked in front of me now. He ran his hand over its length, looking down at me with heavy-lidded eyes. He sank to his knees, pushing my thighs open to lean between them, his mouth buried against the skin of my throat. His hands were sweeping the length of my thighs. I felt the slide of my own moistness seeping out, just before his fingers met it in the folds of skin that were swollen with lust for him.

My hands closed around Richard's head, as his mouth opened over my nipple, sucking deep. Warm balm slipped down from his lips to slide over my flesh. His fingers were inside me, slicking the moistness. The head of his cock moved between his fingers, displacing them in its quest for the grip of my sex.

He rose up and grappled with my hips, drawing me forward and pressing my thighs open. As he lunged into me, the pull of my fingers in his hair jerked his head back to align his eyes with those watching from the corner of the room. He smiled and drew back, his arms rigid against the chaise longue, then he thrust so hard into me that I let free a cry of anguish. God he felt good!

For a few moments I wasn't aware of myself or my actions. I was locked into it; my own body moving in time to meet his. Each reach of him was rapidly pushing my pounding cunt to the point of release. I felt only the sensations offered to my body, and the eyes that watched, the hot eyes. I saw the lampshade and the ceiling fade and then my eyes shut.

Moments later I heard a sound and became aware that Luba moved. I glanced over and saw she was behind Richard, lurking in the shadows so he could not see her, but where I could see her over his shoulder. One gloved hand delicately held her PVC skirt up and the other rode Adam's erection with total vigour, while he watched Richard fucking me.

Richard was moving more rapidly, but I gripped his shoulder and arrested his movements. I wanted him angled deeper inside me. It was hard, but I pressed him back from me, forcing him to withdraw.

'I want to kneel for you,' I managed to explain, between gasping for breath. Air rasped into his lungs as he kneeled back on his haunches, the arc of his shining cock resting in one hand.

'Go for it,' he said, with a grin. I returned his grin. I liked his way.

I turned to kneel on the chaise longue. My breasts touched back and forth across the velvet headrest as I pressed my hips back towards him. Richard cursed blissfully and climbed over me; he was ready, so very ready for this. He pulled my hips towards him, aligned himself with the swell of my invitation, and thrust deep inside me again.

He nudged right up to the spot that cracked thunder through my groin. I whimpered. His hands grasped at my shoulders as my body arched back on to him. My fingernails sank into the velvet as each thrust threw out a violent pang of pleasure. I felt the grip of Richard's fingernails in the soft flesh of my hips and the close, firm manipulations of his cock as he came to fruition. The rhythmic jerks moved inside me, echoed in the imminent release of weight from my very core.

'Now ...' I cried out, for Luba, my eyes closing. 'It's coming now ...' My hips rode and flexed without reason. I ground back on to him, desperate, whimpering and panting. The low thunder finally rose up and crashed violently through my body, anchoring itself inside me for several exquisite moments before rolling on and away from me.

Richard held on to me while I rode it out.

My senses groped for direction; I was drenched.

The filter coffeepot burbled at me as I slid it back into its niche. It was two weeks later and I was at a team briefing in the company boardroom. I turned back to the table just as Richard walked through the door. I had to grab my cup to stop it rattling against the saucer.

Laurel, the Managing Director, was shaking his hand. What was going on? I turned back to the coffee table and put the cup back down. *Keep cool,* I urged myself. Last time he saw me I was a raven-haired vamp in tight black satin. Today I was dressed in fluid aquamarine and my hair was clipped up in a pale russet knot atop my head.

'Judy?' Damn. I turned round. Laurel was walking towards me with Richard in tow.

'May I introduce you to Ricardo Vincenzo.' I could barely breathe. Alarm bells were going off everywhere. Vincenzo was the name of the journalist I had to work with on a forthcoming feature, later that afternoon. He was sitting in on the meeting to get a flavour of how the company worked for a Sunday supplement spread.

When I dared myself to look at him, Richard was simply looking back at me with a friendly smile, his hand outstretched in greeting. I took his hand, sensing there was no imminent danger. I smiled; it seemed none of us had been straight with each other that night. Fitness instructor, was it? And how did he manage that alongside his life as a well-known industry and commerce journalist? Adam probably knew his work. It was ironic; perhaps his preoccupation with his own disguise had hidden ours from his eyes.

His handshake was firm and my interior nerve ends suddenly raced alive in memory of his touch elsewhere on my body. I must have held on to his hand overly-long because he began to look at me more closely, smiling back intimately, a glint of curiosity in his eyes. I was suddenly struck by his self-assurity and the intimacy that perfectly augmented his sensual nature. He was quite a man. I gathered my senses, broke the contact and turned away.

I observed him during the meeting, perching my reading glasses on the end of my nose to give me cover to take surreptitious sidelong glances at his profile. The stray lock of hair was slicked back, giving him a sharper professional look that went with his immaculately tailored suit. I started to relish my secret knowledge of him, observing him in the different context. The other women present were all showing interest in him; Laurel was positively simpering at him. Not surprisingly – she was recently divorced – he was a very attractive and attentive man. *And a fantastic lover*, my memory interjected. I bit my lip to quell the urge to laugh.

I led him to my office later that afternoon with a secret smile.

'You seem vaguely familiar to me,' he commented, as he entered my space. 'Have we met before?' His eyes traced the outline of my body.

'Déjà vu, perhaps?' I replied, with a shrug and a smile as I closed the door firmly behind us. I had decided that I wanted to get to know Ricardo Vincenzo, the journalist, properly. And as I mentioned earlier, it was in my nature to be quietly determined about such things.

The Last Deduction

Alison Tyler

The Last Deduction

An audit. A tax fucking audit. Nadine couldn't believe it. She'd filed her forms on time, didn't make a shitload of money, kept careful – well, adequate – records of her expenditures. Why was the IRS harassing her?

'They always go after the little guys,' her friend Daphne explained, 'waitresses, like me, or freelancers, like you. They know you're too poor to afford an expensive accountant and that you'll probably be too scared to challenge anything that they say.' Daphne shot Nadine a sympathetic look. 'You'll be fine, hon. You're so honest. I'm sure they won't find anything out of place.'

'But I don't have all my receipts,' Nadine confessed, impatiently brushing her dark hair out of her eyes. 'I mean, I have a whole shoeboxful of scraps of paper –'

'Give *that* to the auditor,' Daphne said righteously. 'Make him work for it.'

'And some of my deductions might be a little . . .' Nadine's voice trailed off.

'A little what?'

To answer the question, Nadine pulled open the doors to the closet where she kept her writing materials. Like a hostess on some X-rated game show, she pointed to a battery-powered vibrator with harness, a bone-handled crop and a pair of high-heeled fuck-me pumps with tiny studded ankle straps that glistened in the light.

'You put *those* on your itemised return?'

Nadine nodded.

'Under what heading?' Daphne snorted. 'Office supplies?'

'Miscellaneous research items,' Nadine said, adding emphatically, 'I used everything here for my latest book. Every single piece.'

'And I'll bet Steven loved each minute of it,' Daphne said as she stood to take a closer peek, her green eyes wide in disbelief.

'Forget Steven,' Nadine said. 'Help me figure out how I'm going to explain what I do to a tax auditor.'

'You're a writer. Tell him that you need a wide variety of experiences in order to get in touch with your characters.' Now Daphne was slipping into a pair of bright-red feather-tipped mules and admiring the way they looked on her delicate feet. 'Did you write these off too?'

'Of course. They were for a story called *The Death of the Marabou Slippers*.'

'I wish I could be there,' Daphne said, looking longingly at the pink and black-rubber coated paddle, the thick silver handcuffs, the ball gag. 'I can just imagine the guy's face when you show him what's behind door number one.' She started to laugh. But Nadine didn't think it was funny.

Was it really necessary to have bought all the different toys? Nadine debated the question because it was one that the auditor would undoubtedly ask her. If she were a mystery novelist writing about a murder, would she go and buy a gun? No, but she most definitely would hit the shooting range and pump round after round of ammo into some defenceless piece of paper. To her way of thinking, that sort of quest for knowledge was the equivalent to slipping a plastic butt-plug up her heart-shaped ass before trying to write about what that experience felt like.

Besides, her ex-boyfriend had loved it. At least, at first. As she prepared for the audit, she thought about the different kinky times they'd shared together. With Steven starring in the role of her personal sex slave, she'd experimented with a whole assortment of erotic toys. Acting the part of a dominant woman wasn't unique for her. She had done that from time to time anyway, taking charge, being on top. But pushing the limits of that fantasy, getting down and dirty without fear of reprisals – well, that's where the real research came into play.

Closing her eyes, she remembered the time she'd fucked Steven with a massive black strap-on cock. Made to look anatomically correct, the tool was ribbed with veins and sported a rounded mushroom head. Just sliding the accompanying leather harness around her slender waist had turned her on. Having Steven on his hands and knees getting the head of the plastic prick all dripping with his mouth had made her knees weak. That was something she'd never have known if they hadn't played the scene out together. She'd been forced to pull herself together, to act the tough, female dom. Telling him to get as much spit on her tool as he could, because she was going to ream his ass when he was finished. It had been difficult for her not to stop mid-scene and write down dialogue for her book, but she'd managed to wait until he'd come.

Extreme.

That's what the experience had been. And it was why the two had ultimately broken up. She couldn't shake the pleasure at being on top. No reason to go back to anything else. She wanted the power – and, oh, did she have it when she put on her slick, expensive boots, when she wielded the toys that Daphne had so tentatively pointed to.

Yet how was she going to explain all of that to a tax auditor?

'Ms Daniels?' the man in the suit asked, arriving right on time on the dedicated day. The meeting was taking place at her beach-front condominium, because Nadine worked at home. 'I'm Connor Monroe,' the man continued. 'Your auditor.'

My auditor, Nadine thought, irritated by the man's clean-cut good looks, the Boy Scout quality of his carefully pressed suit and polished leather shoes. She was especially irritated because she found him appealing. Connor Monroe seemed more like a male model than someone who served the government in its most hated capacity. If *she* were to create a character who worked for the IRS, she'd have made him heavy, balding, old. Not Connor. He had short dark hair, stone-coloured eyes and a sleek, athletic build that was apparent even with his suit on. In other circumstances, Nadine would definitely have flirted with him, batting her long eyelashes over her deep-blue eyes, stroking one hand sensuously along the curve of her hip to give him ideas. She knew all of the ways to behave in order to make a man want her, but this wasn't the time.

Holding open the front door to her apartment, Nadine tried to put a pleasant expression on her face. 'This way,' she said. 'I have my papers in the bedroom.'

Inwardly, she smirked at his obvious hesitation, letting him suffer for a moment in silence before continuing. 'That's where my office is. I'm not rich enough to afford a two-bedroom condo yet.' Why not let him know that she was angry? He couldn't penalise her for a bad attitude, could he?

As the man followed her down the hallway, he spoke, sounding as if he were repeating a memorised line from a script. 'I know an audit is a frightening proposition for some people. But it's just a regular practice at the bureau.

Not any sort of punishment. Think of this as a routine, like an annual visit to the doctor.'

Nadine let herself smile since he couldn't see her face. In her research closet, she had lots of toys for 'doctor' visits. A box of regulation rubber gloves. A naughty nurse's uniform. A real stethoscope. Playing doctor was something she knew a lot about. She thought about one of her last nights with Steven. How she'd examined him, spread his handsome rear cheeks open as if to take his temperature and then tongue-fucked his ass until he'd shot his load on her mattress, creating a little lake of come beneath his flat belly. No need to share that bit of information with Mr Uptight IRS Man.

'Here we are,' she said, opening the door to her room and gesturing inside. In preparation for the meeting, Nadine had made her bed neatly, the black satin comforter hiding the evidence of her silk leopard-print sheets – another write-off. The room looked as utilitarian as it possibly could, with her paperwork spread out on her writing desk. What receipts she did have were well ordered, and the shoe box was there as well, lid on firmly to hide the mess contained inside. Wasn't that an echo of every part of Nadine's life? The surface looked one way – but take off the lid and see the inner turmoil within.

Regardless of her attempts to make the place look more official, it was obviously the bedroom of someone who liked sex. A dusky, romantic room, with flocked wallpaper and feminine touches in the prints on the walls and the rose-coloured rug on the hardwood floor. The auditor, *her* auditor, looked around, taking in the intricate brass frame on her bed, the two candelabras that stood on small round tables nearby, perfect for wax play when she was in that sort of a mood. How she liked to tilt the candlestick, to let the hot liquid wax drip in pretty patterns along a naked chest . . .

She shook her head, trying to clear the image of doing such a dirty thing with the taxman. He was here to discuss her payments . . . not her panties. Still, she wondered whether he was feeling a pull between them as well. Or did she just have sex on the brain because she'd been looking in her research closet prior to the audit?

'I'm not out to ruin your day, Ms Daniels. We really had only a few questions,' the auditor said, sitting at Nadine's antique desk and waiting while she perched on the edge of her bed. He opened his leather briefcase and pulled out a copy of her tax return, pointing to several lines that were highlighted in bright yellow ink. 'And, honestly, the problem wasn't that we didn't agree with the deductions, it was that we didn't understand them.'

He smiled again and Nadine thought she saw something shimmer in his eyes. A look that didn't match the Boy Scout image at all. His expression made her feel flushed and she looked away.

'Vagueness is something the IRS can't handle,' he continued self-deprecatingly. 'We expect things to fit into neat categories. Phone. Entertainment. Rent. Travel. So, this $6,500 deducted for miscellaneous research supplies. That raised a red flag.'

Nadine sighed, her worst fears realised so quickly in the afternoon. She was going to have to open her toy chest and reveal the different items she'd used as the foundation for her latest novel. Might as well get it over with quickly. Without a word, she stood, walked to the closet and pulled open both of the mirrored doors.

'I'm an author,' she explained, lifting the different implements and placing them on her comforter, one after another, as casually as if they were pens and paper, any other equipment of a serious writer. 'I throw myself into my work, learning every aspect of my characters' lives. My most recent novel took place in an SM environment.' Carefully, she set out the high-end vinyl dress, the handcuffs she'd bought for the equivalent of a month's rent, the shoes with heels so high they couldn't possibly be walked in. But that was OK, since they weren't created for walking. She noticed that the auditor's eyes had opened wider, but he didn't speak.

'If I were writing about pet care, I'd buy grooming materials. If I needed to learn about the art world, I'd have purchased books about Monet and Picasso. I hope you're not going to judge me based on the content of my work.'

The auditor had stood and was now observing the growing pile of items on Nadine's bed at closer range. She noticed that he had the same look on his face that Daphne had had when she'd picked through the toys. Intrigue rather than disgust. She also thought she saw a bulge in his trousers that hadn't been there before.

'Do you understand now, Mr Monroe?' Nadine asked, her husky voice low. 'I had to file everything under miscellaneous, because the IRS doesn't provide neat categories for whips and chains. For bondage gear. For handcuffs –' As she said the word, he hefted the pair, interrupting her.

'Connor,' he said softly.

'Excuse me?'

'My name's Connor. You don't have to call me Mr Monroe.'

Connor. She liked that. And she also liked the way he was playing with her toys, rifling through them as if with a private purpose, stroking the shiny material of the vinyl dress – perfect for water sports – holding up her corset and then looking at her, as if picturing her in it. 'This is all for a book?'

She nodded. '*Paradise Lounge*. It will be out next month.'

'And your character is –'

'A dominatrix,' she said, and again she noticed that flicker in his eyes. Was he getting turned on? She found that *she* was, and she shifted in her faded jeans, feeling suddenly too constrained. As she watched, Connor slid one of the cuffs around his wrist and closed it. Then he looked at her.

'I think I understand now,' he said, 'but maybe you could explain what you do a little more in depth for me. So I get the full picture. I'm a bit anal that way. I like to possess all of the facts before I write up my reports.'

Nadine didn't need any more encouragement. She felt the heat between them and she recognised fully the looks he was giving her. 'Strip,' she said sternly, without hesitation. 'You don't want me to mess with your nice, expensive suit.' Connor did as he was told, like a good boy, and the metal of the handcuff chain made music as he took off his jacket, shirt and tie, then kicked off his slacks, socks and shoes.

'Boxers too,' she said, admiring him for a moment. My, but he had a fine body, even better than she'd expected. Tightly muscled legs, flat stomach and, most importantly for Nadine's particular fixation, a round firm ass. 'You can't really appreciate the image I'm going to create for you unless you give yourself over to it totally. That's how it is for me anyway. I lose myself in my characters. Plunge hard and deep until the rest of the world disappears.'

With his eyes locked on hers, Connor slid off his boxers and then stood, waiting. Oh, he was erect. So hard that Nadine felt a moment of weakness. What she would have liked to do was go on her knees in front of it. Meeting a new cock for the first time was always an exciting prospect. Nadine adored that initial taste, learning how the man's bulbous head would fit into her mouth, stroking the underside with the tip of her tongue, gripping into his ass to pull him forward, harder, at her pace. But not yet, she reminded herself. Take your time. Play it out.

Steeling her inner yearnings, she took hold of the other handcuff, pulled the man forcefully on to her bed, threaded the chain through the headboard and captured his free wrist. He allowed himself to be manipulated without a word, letting Nadine know that he understood she was in charge.

'Now,' she said, 'you want a demonstration of my research equipment.'

'No.' He shook his head, then motioned to the rock-hard monument between his legs. 'A demonstration of your mouth.'

That made Nadine smile, her cherry-red lips curving upwards at the corners. The man had attitude, which she appreciated. But she wasn't about to reward him from the start. Where was the fun in that? No, she wanted to make him pay for the fear she'd had from the moment the IRS had contacted her. That starkly written letter sending panic through her. Nadine hated to feel panic.

'We don't play that way,' she said. 'Not by your rules, but by mine.'

'And they are?'

'That's the fun part.' Nadine grinned, stripping out of her own clothes and sliding into the short vinyl dress and her favourite pair of leather boots, feeling the power start to build within her. She sensed that Connor was memorising the look of her body nearly naked, but she didn't give him a long time to observe her. 'You get to figure out the rules as we go along.'

Connor tilted his head at her, as if he didn't know what she meant.

'You ought to comprehend that concept,' she said snidely. 'Isn't it how the IRS works? Secret rules that you auditors get while the rest of us poor people are forced to guess what on earth will make you happy.'

But what would make Nadine happy?

She considered the question as she glanced over her implements of pleasure and pain. Her auditor continued to watch as she hefted the different devices. The strap-on cock. Yes, she'd had fun with that in the past. Steven liked to be taken, bent over the bed and thrust into, his ass cheeks spread wide, the only lube a bit of spit that Nadine worked up and down the rubber dildo with the palm of her hand, jerking the cock the way a man would.

'Was that one of the items on your tax return?' Connor asked meekly.

Nadine nodded. 'Used it for research for Chapter Twelve.'

Next, there was the wooden paddle, perfect for heating the ass of a naughty boy. This particular paddle had a satisfying weight in her hand and she considered it with an almost loving expression, remembering the scene she had written with the paddle virtually the star of the chapter. She thought of the night she'd tested it on Steven, actually bringing him to tears before letting him come.

'And that was in the miscellaneous items as well?' Connor asked. Nadine heard the note of fear in his voice, but gave him extra points for staying in control of himself. He didn't ask whether she would use the paddle on him, didn't beg her not to. She nodded in answer before moving on to an oily-looking black leather belt, slipping it between her fingers and then leaning forward to use the very lip of it to tickle Connor's balls. He arched his back at the move and a bit of pre-come made the tip of his cock seem to shine.

It wouldn't take much to push him over the edge, Nadine knew. She could do just about anything and he would cream for her. Yet she wanted to have some fun, to make the experience worthwhile. Finally, she decided on one of her five-star toys: a vibrating wand shaped like a cock. Combined with a little of the lube she always kept in her bedside table, she would enjoy introducing this pin-striped man into the world of submission.

'Roll over,' she said.

He tilted his head at her and rattled the chains, indicating that he couldn't.

'Don't mess with me, Connor. There's enough slack,' she said knowingly. 'It might hurt a little bit, the chain rubbing into your wrists, but you can do it.'

Obediently, Connor followed the order, twisting his body on to his stomach, shifting as if to make room on the mattress for his erection. Then shifting again because it was obvious he liked the friction.

'None of that,' Nadine said fiercely, her open hand connecting with his ass in a stinging slap. 'You get off when I tell you. *If* I tell you. Not before. Understand?'

Connor sighed but said nothing.

'Do you understand?' Nadine repeated slowly. 'That's rule number one. I'll give that one to you for free. You answer when spoken to.'

'Yes, Ms Daniels,' Connor said, voice slightly muffled. Mmm. He was learning already. Not calling her by her first name. Choosing Ms instead of Miss. Nadine lifted the leather harness that went with this particular sex toy and fit the large synthetic cock into its resting place. Then she fastened the harness around her slim hips. She did the work behind Connor, so he couldn't see her, could only hear the metal of the buckle connecting. Having a cock on always made Nadine feel different inside. Gave her a little bit of a swagger. But there was still plenty of woman in her, and she wouldn't start with poor Connor without giving him the foreplay he might need before she fucked him.

On hands and knees behind her auditor, she held open his firm bum cheeks and licked once up and down between them, then made a tight, hungry circle right around the velvety rim. Connor sighed and ground his hips again into the mattress, but this time Nadine didn't tell him to stop. Instead, making her tongue hard and long, she pointed it and drove it home.

'Oh, Christ,' Connor groaned, thrusting hard against the bed.

She didn't have to ask whether he liked it. The way he moved made it obvious that he wanted her to fuck his ass and he wanted her to do it now. Sure, sometimes she had played longer with Steven, making him deep throat her massive hard-on before screwing him. But this afternoon Nadine couldn't wait. She wanted the feeling of gripping into his shoulders and sliding the length of her cock deep inside him. First, she reached over Connor's body, opening the drawer on her bedside table and snagging the bottle of lube. Kindly, she spread it along the length of her pinkish cock, her fingers working it and getting extra grease on the tips. To prepare him, she slid two fingers into his ass, opening him up. Teasing him a bit with the intrusion.

'Please –' he said, and she knew somehow that he meant to say 'please stop'. This was all far too new for young Mr Monroe. The fact that he didn't continue with the request let her know that he didn't want her to stop. Not really. And he didn't have the balls yet to say, 'Please fuck me.' So he left it just at that one word. Nadine didn't mind. With both hands, she spread him even wider apart, then placed the huge, knobby head of her joystick at the entrance of his ass.

An evil grin on her lovely face, she found herself repeating the same speech, altered only slightly, that he had given her upon his arrival. 'I know an ass-fucking is a frightening proposition for some people. But it's just a regular practice in my boudoir. Not any sort of punishment. Think of this as a routine, like a visit to the doctor.' Then she reached for the remote control device that went with the toy, holding it tightly in one hand. Now, she was ready.

As she slid the cock in, the power flooded through her. Jesus, but she loved taking a man. In the oval-shaped mirror over her bed, she saw the way she looked as she fucked him. Her glossy dark hair framed her pale face, and her eyes turned a smouldering blue of the ocean in turbulent weather. With one hand on his waist to keep herself steady, she made the ride last. Giving him a taste, then pulling back. Slamming in deeper and holding it. Connor let her know the rhythm that he liked based on the sounds of his moans and the way he echoed her thrusts with his body against her comforter. He was going to come all over it, make a sticky white pool on the black satin, but she didn't care. Because once he got off, she had other plans. Methods to make this afternoon last.

It had been way too long since her last fuck.

Taking Connor hard, she used her free hand to reach around her until she found the mess of toys still spread out on the bed. Her fingers brushed against the handle of the wooden paddle and she hefted it, such a nice weight, and then let the weapon connect with Connor's right cheek, leaving a purplish blush there. Pretty colour. She gave the left cheek a matching blow to even out the hue and, as Connor started to moan, she kept up the spanking. That sound was such a turn-on. The clapping noise, like applause, of a sturdy paddle meeting a naked bottom. She continued to both fuck and punish him until he said, 'I'm going to come, Nadine –' a perfect time to switch to her first name, it made it seem that much more personal '– now.'

With those words, Nadine hit the button on the remote and the cock inside Connor's asshole began to move, startling him as those sexy vibrations worked through his body. 'Oh fucking God,' he groaned. He arched and then shuddered, his whole body releasing, and Nadine threw herself against him, still inside deep, so that he felt the length of her body pressed into his skin. In this position, the base of the vibrator buzzed against her clit, sending her wet pussy into spasms that lasted as long as she kept her cunt pushed forward. Oh, yes, that was perfect, the pleasure that had kept her on edge as she was fucking him now spread throughout her body, making her skin tingle in waves that radiated outwards from the hot zone between her legs.

Sealed deep into Connor's ass, her hair spread out over his shoulders, her vinyl-clad breasts pressed into his back, she held him. This was the way she liked to be held when she came during anal sex. It was comforting, soothing, to be wrapped in another's arms. But after a moment, she pulled out, tore off the harness and stripped.

Out of breath, Connor rolled over on the bed, chains clinking, and watched her. Even lost in the post-climax bliss, it was obvious that he was admiring the curves of her body, her flushed, perfect skin. Nadine felt his eyes on her, but didn't pose for him. She was busy planning round number two. Naked, she stood in front of her closet, and then she found what she was looking for.

'What's that?' Connor asked, pointing as Nadine lifted the bone-handled crop with the braided leather tip.

'This?' Nadine repeated softly as she approached him. 'This is my last deduction.'

Sci-fi Cliché #10

Astrid Fox

Sci-fi Cliché #10

At first, all he could see was blue.

The palace rose up like a hunk of sky in the grey horizon: ostentatious. It was the first thing he noticed. Its windows were smog-coloured, as closed to the world outside as dead computer monitors. But the frosty blue marble of the palace framed these windows like the sky framed clouds. It was impossible to ignore magnificence of this order; impossible to ignore the odd beauty of extremity. Splendour: the silver trim of the bulwarks that ran up the sides of the palace like silver icicles. Splendour: the 7,000 lights embedded in the walls. There, these lamps glittered like neon stars. They crackled with sharp energy. They snapped into 7,000 electric-blue flares. They clicked off again.

The heavens above the castle were upstaged, but received high marks for effort. They moved silver, grey, icy white; two suns winking out their cool rays. For a human, it was impossible not to be moved by the castle, but these inhuman globes gleamed like twinned robin's eggs, pale and perfect and nonchalant in the slate-coloured sky. Suns do not have the responsibility to explain their world to foreigners who walk upon its surface. Click, went the palace lights. Click, click. Sascha felt the wind begin to blow as he walked forward, air forcing its way into his mouth as he inhaled. Cold. Menthol. It was already winter on the alien world.

He kept walking slowly towards the castle. The craft, the metal-lined trap and saviour of a ship that had borne him here, was behind him, crushed in a snowless landscape coloured mist-grey; coloured like those ancient marks Sascha's ancestors made on paper: grey and then grey again, pencil-lead scratchings of grey language on white fibrous sheets, grey graphite, grey as the smoke that rose from cold lakes in the morning, grey and then grey again.

He would walk all the way up to the castle. All the way up to the doorstep he could now see looming in front of him. He would march up to the castle and seek out its tenants, and then he would either be killed or, with their help, begin to look for Severn.

There was a soundtrack that accompanied his steps towards the great blue architecture whose seven-grand lamps twinkled like a circuitboard: he felt like he were about to walk inside an ancient computer. The building seemed devoid of organic life; it buzzed and crackled with the energy of a machine. And this music that surrounded him, this eerie, rather high-pitched music, was not sourced from the palace. It came from the air, from the shadowy ground. Perhaps speakers were implanted in the earth and the melody that rose up was caught invisible in the air, caught in an oxygen net. For surely enough it was oxygen that he breathed here on the alien world, sweet familiar oxygen that had filled his lungs after his ship fell from the sky and the helmet had been torn from his head on impact.

The lights flickered. Click, they said.

The marble rose up in blue sheets a mile above his head when he looked up. He had reached the doorstep.

Click.

He walked through this open hole in the wall, and then he was in a long hallway. The music ceased immediately; he was right, it had come from the outdoors. The lights that had illuminated the castle from the outside were not as apparent now; they had also stopped their clicking. The lamps and their circles of dull blue light were only smudges as he walked nervously down the hallway, which wound deeper and more tightly into what had to be the heart of the castle. Yet there were no other options to his path; this was no maze with choices right or wrong; this was only a single path that coiled towards the building's interior, leading him to a destiny that would itself be ill or good. This disturbed him; he was a strong believer in options.

Now Sascha noticed that the marbled rock from which the structure was carved seemed moist, pliant, nearly vegetable. No circuitboard castle now, after all; no neutered automatons lived here. Of course, because the castle could not have grown itself; it was a construction, wasn't it? Sascha shivered and his skin prickled with fear. Aliens always seemed freakish to him. He never knew what they were thinking. After all, machines and robots do not have the malice or favours of flesh: they might kill, but it is not personal.

There was light ahead, not twinkling lamps but the proverbial light at the end of his tunnel, and Sascha wondered whether he ought to call out, maybe follow local etiquette and sing a soft high melody himself, so as not to sneak up unawares. Then he turned the last corner of the tunnel, and his mouth went dry, and he could not sing.

The whole thing was hollowed out, all the way up to the turrets. It was a gigantic shell of a room once you reached this interior. And maybe the castle was higher than he had even realised, maybe it even pierced past the cloud layer, because the top of the room, when he strained his neck from tilting it back to see how far up the walls went – well, the top was open. Because sunlight shot down from this oversized skylight, straight down to the grey grass that made up the floor of this room. Sascha questioned why he persisted in thinking of it as a castle, but knew he did it instinctively, because of its fantastic appearance. It was like an odd kind of zoo, with its zoned-in version of nature; the sunlight and grass were striking, extremely unusual in an enclosed space. These details were not the most remarkable part of the room.

Oh, and the huge river that ran across the great floor, of course. Sascha stared, open-mouthed. It was a quite natural-looking river – it probably *was* a natural river – and one that flowed from one end of the great room to the other, diagonally, away to his right. The sunlight glittered and glistered on the pull of the water, turning it aqua and even the translucent light blue of Perspex plastic. It was stunning. This was also not the most remarkable part of the castle interior.

The most remarkable part of the castle interior was the gathering of two-legged, bald blue creatures of roughly his own height, of roughly his own features and – aside from the three small but fully developed breasts – of roughly his composition. They were bathing in the river or sunning in the clear white sunlight on the grey grass or just standing around – in alarmingly relaxed bipedal stances – chatting. Or at least he guessed it was chatting. Goddamn.

He couldn't believe what he was seeing, and drew closer. All of the triple-breasted females stood or squatted near the river, exposing their greyish-blue hides to the rays of the suns that beamed across the water. The whole scenario evoked a pastoral scene from his own home of Earth, one where animals drank and cooled themselves in rivers. But these blue-skinned aliens were not animals, or at least they were different kinds of animals. He drew even closer. The light reflected off their greyish-blue skin, their dolphin-like skin.

The suns on their hides made them flicker briefly into several other shades of blue. Yes, the sheen of their flesh glittered neon-blue, glacial-blue, except for what Sascha saw now, as one creature squatted in front of him: he saw the pornographic, close-up genitals of the alien – pink, bubble-gum pink. A sex sticky with thick juice, with white creamy come. He felt himself stiffen as he gazed at the alien as she squatted, her back to him, her thighs revealing a flash of pink colour among all that blue. A pink that was both lurid and obscene.

It wasn't just their trio of small, tapered blue breasts. Judging by their nether regions, they were all, without exception, female.

Now that he was close enough, he realised that his first impression had been wrong. They didn't seem to be chatting or even talking. They made no sounds at all from those wide blue lips, not even a hum. Nor was there any music here, as there had been outside. The only sound was the roll and babble of the river. He found the quiet, natural warble strangely comforting.

He didn't know why he did the next thing. It wasn't like he was attracted to aliens or anything. Maybe it was the sight of the cool blue river, because, let's face it, he could use a bath. Though he was man enough to admit that the sight of the cool blue aliens with their perversely compelling nether regions made him want to strip off. Maybe it was just because he wanted to be equal with them, naked just like them, only without the supernumerary nipple.

Yeah, that had to be it.

Yet when one of them walked towards him, he flinched. She didn't slow her pace, but continued until she stood only several centimetres away and stared him in the face. He was acutely aware of his nakedness, of the heap of his clothes behind him on the grass, clothes that offered no protection now at all. It had been a mistake to take them off.

She was staring at him. He shifted his arm, but didn't yet move it. Her skin looked as smooth as a dolphin's. He wasn't sure if he wanted to touch the blue-grey flesh, even just to brush the tips of his fingers against her skin to feel its texture. What if it was clammy? What if she didn't want his strokings? Sascha risked it. He reached out and put a finger on her arm. It was cool, not clammy; organic but shelled, like the epidermis of an aubergine or an unripe pear. Or even a pupa: the steely grey sheen to the blue was that of a cocoon. He suppressed an impulse to tap on her arm, beckoning out the insect. He kept his finger where it was. But there was the sensation of warmth below, where her blood ran. Maybe it was blue blood too. Still, she was no royal: she had the immediacy of the uncrowned common herd. She was blue, but she was alive and she was breathing in her frosty breath as much as he was breathing out the same air in icy puffs himself. Cool blue. Ice blue. Grey eyes.

They drew him in, those grey eyes. Her hands cradled his head. He sunk lower, lower, down to one of her three breasts. What was he doing? He found he didn't care.

He really didn't care.

He began to suck at one nipple, and sucked and sucked and sucked. It stiffened in his mouth, and the creature began to writhe sensually, and he realised that he was pleasing her. He sucked harder, and her whole body tensed, and then she sprayed into his mouth. The liquid that squirted out into his mouth tasted not of milk but of sex-juice, as if he were rolling his tongue over the well of her pussy instead, as if he were sucking away at her clit and the flow had dripped down to his lips. This genital juice tasted of something like, but not, burned sugar. Burned peppermint, everything tasted menthol, mint, like peppermint candy tablets that dissolve on the tongue, like wintergreen, spearmint . . .

He sucked the juices from each nipple in turn, one-two-three, drinking down this fluid that tasted of pussy. He wanted to drive his cock into her, soak it in her juices.

He continued to suckle but, even as he did so, shock hit his brain at last. Goddamn. It was too much of a cliché, myth that had been related for millennia by misogynists and feminists. He even remembered it from his undergraduate studies of ante-millennial literature (his dissertation had been entitled 'The 1860s: The Industrial Evolution of Literature', and even now he winced at the memory). And there was that mnemonic device he'd used for his exams: *World of Women, World of Men: Sci-fi Cliché #10.* 'World of Women' said more about twentieth-century society than its corrollary. The misogynist take went like this: the females were neutered by their one-genderedness and male potency would set them free; would show them what they had always unknowingly craved – the supremacy of prick. And the feminist version had been utopian; the females had no need of men; they enclosed their own circles and their own needs, carnal or otherwise. In regard to the former, Sascha could even recall an ancient text of a film with the immortal Zsa Zsa: *The Queen of the Venusians*, or something similar. Even that had never rolled his socks up. He had stuck mainly with the eighteenth and nineteenth centuries. Aliens had always kind of creeped him out . . . previously.

This world felt like neither version anyway. It was sufficient unto itself, and yet open to him as voyeur, open to him as partial, and perhaps even full, participant.

The alien was pressing his head down on her nipple again, quite forcefully, and he found he did not want to participate. He wanted to observe nature in its original, untampered state. So he drew away from her insinuating embraces, his cock still thickened and stiff.

Two different females had approached and were observing him attentively. These two were a little taller than the others and Sascha figured that they were more mature. There was something else different about them other than their height, which he realised when they drew closer. On these two, their throats were covered with a layer of well-trimmed fur. One alien's fur choker was greyish, and that of the other female was bluer, bluer even than her otherwise bare skin. For some reason, this adornment aroused him even more; the fur seemed so sexual, so . . . provocative. Like private hair exposed, such as on humans: underneath the arms, between the legs. The creature whose tits he had sucked had seemed as giddy as a twenty-year-old, whereas these two seemed more reflective. Wiser. He grew a little nervous. All the females here were patently adults, but these two had a gravitas that made him think they might be the leaders. He tried to think of something responsible and logical to say in this case, but all he could find himself thinking about was their throat-fur and what it would feel like to come all over it in a fountain of spunk. Oh, damn it. Had he no survival instinct at all? What about Severn? But all he could do now was remember the taste of that juice and stare at the fur round their vulnerable necks, as thin as human necks, as thin as his own. He thought of silver mink, silver furs, ice-queen furs. If he licked his own come out of that silky, smooth fur, it would taste like blue vanilla ice cream. Or maybe blueberry ice cream. Let me taste you, ice queens. Let me lick you. Let me come all over you.

The blue-furred female reached for the grey-furred one – hurriedly, nearly violently – and Sascha took yet another step back, this time completely out of the way. His mouth still tingled from the taste of alien tit-juice. But instead he watched as Blue spread Grey's thighs apart again, exposing all that luscious pink to his eyes. Grey was taller and presumably stronger, but still she submitted totally to Blue's caresses. Sascha swallowed hard, as his throat had suddenly gone dry. Damn it. It seemed like Blue was willing him to look at Grey's pussy. But instead he looked Blue in the eye, before lowering his gaze slowly to the fur ringing her throat. That soft, soft fur ... He jerked his head up again. Yes, they were both staring at him, waiting for him to look down at that pink crotch. He did, and her pussy was wet and gleaming and slick. Then Grey put a hand down on herself and started to rub, started to grind her fingers hard against her stiff clit.

Oh, God. His cock was growing stiff, thickening again, but where else was he supposed to look? This was very perverse too, watching this ... beast pleasure herself with such abandon. Just look at that fur on her. Just look at that satiny, cool blue skin. Just look at that pink wet hole. He broke out in a cold sweat. He made himself look away, but wherever he looked, the blue creatures had started fucking, as if Grey's self-fingering had been a huge big signal for everyone to go at it as well, to go at it like fucking bonobo chimps, actually. There was abandon everywhere: grunting and groaning and the slurping sound of licking and fucking and fisting and deep-tongued kissing.

Sascha tore his eyes away at last. There was an erotic pull inside his gut, one that dragged way down to the pit of his stomach. His cock was tight, too thick. He no longer wanted to come on their throats; now he wanted to shove into one of their pink cunts: take them from behind and plunge his cock into the hot, wet warmth, slick and oozing and wet for him; run his hand over their smooth blue asses and just push and push and push until he came. There was all this female flesh. But he didn't feel right, somehow, touching it. It didn't feel right. Not at the moment. Maybe some other time. If they let him. But he could touch himself, and now his arousal had sweetened, and now it was tightening into something more painful, more desperate.

They were all fucking, all around him. All the blue aliens were screwing in that hot white sun, even screwing knee-deep in the river. He grabbed his cock, and his hand felt so good on himself, felt like a cool quick favour as he stroked himself more and more quickly, the sunlight hot on his neck, and he watched Blue thrust one hand deep into the wide, candy-pink cunt, her blue fingers disappearing into that wet delicious hole, her thumb pressing down hard on the erect blue bead of the other female's clit. Then Grey's tits spurted out a glittering spray of blue liquid, three jets spurting out like miniature geysers, and then he winced with the sugary pain of the rush he felt all the way down the length of his cock.

He wanked and wanked and kept staring straight at the confectionery of Grey's splayed, open pussy, Blue's fingers fucking and Blue's thumb still just a-rubbing and a-rubbing, and he was still watching that same pink, that pink that had now turned nearly cherry with arousal and friction, when he groaned and tightened his fist and shot out his own liquid into the air. His knees bucked and he fell back, on to his ass, back on his hands. His whole body was shaking. His lips were dry. His throat was parched. His heart was beating like a fucking ancient metronome from before the 1860s Industrial Evolution, Revolution, whatever.

He hoped that water was safe, because he was going to go and take a drink from the river. And maybe take a bath as well.

Her pod had crash-landed fifteen minutes ago.

Because impact had been violent, because impact had rent a huge great hole in the ship that let the air roar in, Severn had learned quickly that she could breathe the foreign atmosphere. Then she had stumbled out. Sascha's pod was nowhere in sight, and she thought she remembered that they had ejected at one and the same time, that she had caught a glimpse in the window of another fireball hurtling towards this world.

It was quite possible that he had found himself on the other side of the planet, where it might be evening instead of early morning as it was here, or might not. She hadn't yet had a chance to work out the rotation pattern of the planet in regard to the dual suns, not in fifteen minutes anyway. She wondered how he was coping. She wondered if there was life on this planet and how he was coping with that, because Sascha could actually be a little alienphobic, if there was such a thing as a 'little alienphobic'.

It looked a lot like Earth, except for the two suns. The grass was bright green, the sky was blue and the bright daylight a warm, comforting yellow. She was standing on some form of a steppe, she reckoned, some sort of plateau. Except it had to be a very big plateau, maybe even a prairie, because it stretched out as far as the eye could see, the green grass rippling in the light wind. It was actually kind of pleasant, in a boring sort of way. There were no visible mountains or caverns or rivers to break up the view though. She had once read that the naked human eye could see for seven miles, but she reckoned it was a lot further than that when it came to big things like mountains. Severn always had her eye glued to a lens or a scope anyway, so she had never thought about it much.

Hell. The sunlight really was scorching. She was a little worried about sunburn or, worse, sunstroke, so she constructed a bandanna out of one of the torn parachutes. She had no food or sustenance; she supposed she could eat the grass if it didn't poison her, but she was going to have to find some source of proper water soon. There were no rocks around that she could see, not even pebbles, so she broke off a long shard of her ship door and used it as a kind of marker, gouging a trail into the grass from time to time as she walked further away from the ship. Hansel and Gretel, eat your heart out.

As she walked along in the sticky but necessary lightweight spacesuit, it wasn't long before she began to be aware of two things. The first was that the endless lawn had a line drawn across it, though the line was becoming thicker and expanding as she progressed. The second thing she noticed was that there was a sound coming from up ahead as well, a sound that, as she continued to walk forward, intensified into what was undeniably music. It was spooky and high pitched, uncanny, but it was still music. There was more rhythm to it than the chaotic tune of wind, for example. It sounded a bit like vocal classical music. This meant either that there was organic life, or that organic life had once been here and had created a machine. Severn had been a spacer long enough to know that there was a difference between the two, and long enough to know that there were plenty of deserted, previously inhabited worlds sulking about in this quadrant.

So when the line finally revealed itself to be a huge but narrow chasm separating two stretches of the lawn, and when it became apparent that the music was emanating precisely from that huge, jagged hole, Severn began for the first time to get a little nervous. The thing was, she was also getting a little thirsty. So instead of slowing down, she speeded up.

Then she was standing at the lip of the cavern. Then she was staring down, down into this big crack of a canyon that wiggled its way endlessly to her left and endlessly to her right, made of chalk-like grey rock and dust. And then she was staring, open-mouthed in shock that her years as a spacer really shouldn't have permitted her to feel, at the valley below, a valley of grey rock and green grass and many, many green aliens walking around – too many to count, really. They were the ones who were singing, but this did not at first concern her. The first thing she actually thought was: water! There must be water somewhere. Life means water. Then she thought: perhaps they will kill me.

Of course, if she didn't approach them and approach them peacefully, she would die in a matter of days from lack of water. She vaguely wondered how Sascha was faring (he had always had a problem with aliens). She really did need a drink.

And besides, they had already seen her.

She began to crawl down into the cavern. She got the chance to look more closely at them, as they stared at her, still singing. She could now see that, though their flesh was a pale, almost ghostly green, their lips and mouths were fringed with red, like bright exotic fish.

She was nearly upon them. Their raspberry-red mouths stirred something inside Severn; it was the blood-redness inside their mouths in contrast to their stable, cool melon-green. It was like all the carnality of their flesh was concentrated just inside the lips, indicating God knows what perverse pleasures, and the rest of their pale-green bodies were controlled, even dispassionate. Yet that sharp, animal red – like raw meat, like a wound daubed with lipstick. She found herself watching their lips even when they stopped singing and stood staring at her: chill, dry-skinned, vaguely reptilian. She grew aware that she was looking for that glimpse of red again. She closed her eyes in shame. The image of the red stayed with her, a bright cloud of rouge in her mind. She started to tremble. She found herself wanting to prise their mouths open, to force her fingers in so that she could press them up against all the wet, shiny red.

It was the heat that made her think things like that. She needed a drink.

They were all male.

'Do you have any water?' she asked.

They started to sing again. She pointed to her mouth, miming for water.

One of the green men – fucking green men! she thought, like an old space movie – walked towards her. He was completely humanoid and the odd glint in his eye reminded her of Naomi, her tomboy pilot colleague who had been as cocky as hell until her fighter had been blown out of the sky five years ago. Severn had no idea why she suddenly thought of Naomi. Maybe she was getting sunstroke after all. Those suns were hot. Severn pointed to her lips again. 'Water,' she repeated.

The alien that had walked up to her so boldly – she decided to call him Naomi – stood so close that she hoped he wasn't going to bite her. What was this, a medical examination? A new version of the old 'alien abduction' story? Jesus, how red was that mouth? The flesh was nearly scarlet; it looked almost sexual. Naomi's tongue, lips and mouth were such a darkened, ruby red that the shade was venous, like expensive claret wine. She needed a drink. But of water, not wine.

Though wine would be OK too.

In resignation, she pointed one final time to her mouth, and then pointed straight at Naomi. She didn't even say the word 'water' this time, but she certainly thought it.

Naomi was looking back at her. His alien face was strangely impassive. But surely they were mammals or reptilian or even amphibians of some sort. They needed water, just like she did.

Another alien was joining them. He was more slender than Naomi. It was inappropriate, but she found herself admiring his gait, the swing of his full, plump testicles – like two ripe, ripe pears, juicy and delicious and smooth in the throat. Jesus. Severn thought she might die of heat soon. She had to find some shade, if nothing else. But if she walked away, she might insult them, and then where would she be? Dead, or maybe captured.

The new alien had dropped to his knees in front of Naomi. He was a skinny, pretty young thing. He had opened his mouth.

Jesus. Was he actually going to do what she thought he was going to do?

Yes. And Naomi's cock was already as hard as the grey rock she stood on, only with a smooth sheen to it, like a greased fruit. His attention had shifted from her; he was now groaning instead of singing, and thrusting his prick deep down Slim's throat.

Severn thought she might need to sit down. But she couldn't tear her eyes away from Naomi's melon-green prick, pushing back and forth in the slender alien's crimson mouth; it made her think that the mouths had evolved that way, sexual signifiers, like baboon asses, but then she was a rocket scientist, wasn't she, not a fucking evolutionary primatologist . . .

It was making her hot. She was *already* hot from the sun, and the last thing she needed was an onslaught of horniness. But that slick tight prick sliding into that red hole, with Slim starting to jerk off as well, his hand moving furiously over his own cock, and Naomi grunting with pleasure, screwing his eyes tight like any human guy getting sucked off – well, jeez, it was hot. It really was. She sank down on the slope of the cavern and watched the show.

By the time Naomi was shoving his cock repeatedly faster in a familiar rhythm, Severn had undone the zipper of her suit. By the time Slim had withdrawn his delicious mouth slowly from Naomi's thickened cock, Severn had two fingers up her cunt and was panting. And by the time Slim's strawberry-red tongue was licking its magic over Naomi's asshole and Naomi had his cock in his own hand, Severn had started wanking in earnest. Oh Jesus, it was a hell of a show. Naomi's sea-green body, tight and lean, was visibly trembling as Slim licked his asshole – slowly, so slowly. Severn's fingers were sticky in her cunt and on her clit. Even her own hand felt obscene. Good. God, her fingers felt good. She was really juiced up. She loved watching men have sex together, particularly alien men. She was heading straight for a fucking wicked climax. Hold on, folks. Those red lips, rouged up and plumped, kissing and stroking the tight green hole. She was so fucking wet. Her whole body was shaking. Her crotch was soaking. Her hand was drenched. Faster and faster. It felt so good. The taut red tongue, wiggling and wiggling. Oh, she couldn't look away now.

Naomi would probably come before she did, his body was already cramping, but just the sight of him made something in her coil tight, and she started stroking her clit with her middle finger until it all twisted into sweet and sour pleasure. And it was right then – smack in the middle of her orgasm – that Naomi's jism hit her in the face, right on the lips: his semen was silvery and clear, but it tasted like something much darker, like chocolate or violet or rich coffee. She kept her finger on her clit and licked her mouth, so sweet, so sweet and heavy and delicious. She swallowed and it was like she was drinking a shot of fine brandy: warmth, all the way down.

The sun was still hot. She lay back and lazily watched as Naomi took his turn at pleasuring Slim with a blow job that would roll the socks off any of the guys *she* knew. Green, red, green, red – the colours blurred before her eyes as lips drew back and then advanced over cock. Green. Red. Green.

Jesus, it felt good here in the sun. Basking with her spacesuit rolled down to her hips. She became aware of the greenies singing again and this time she found the melody relaxing, not eerie.

You know, it was just possible that her thirst had been quenched.

Several weeks later Severn hitched a ride with Slim over to the other side of the planet, the grey side, where the girls lived. That was when she hooked up with Sascha again. She was pleased to see that he was . . . thriving.

They compared notes for a good half-hour or so over a glass of exotic peppermint wine Sascha pressed upon her, giggling and blushing together until Sascha heaved himself up to his feet and rubbed his hands together gleefully.

'You know, Severn, I think I've been cured of my little alienphobia problem.'

'That's good.'

'It certainly is. It makes me want to taste new fruits. You certainly gave a stirring description of your little green friends and I'd like to think I did the same with my new friends. Whaddya say we trade sides for a while?'

It sounded good to Severn. She was about to head towards the huge blue castle when she realised that she wanted to say something to Sascha. For a second she hesitated, unsure how to express it, and then remembered that he had studied ante-millennial literature and film. Who was the writer? Well, she couldn't remember the writer, but she could remember the character.

She smiled at Sascha and squeezed his hand goodbye. 'See you in a while,' she said. 'To paraphrase Candide, this is truly the best of both possible worlds.'

Yep.

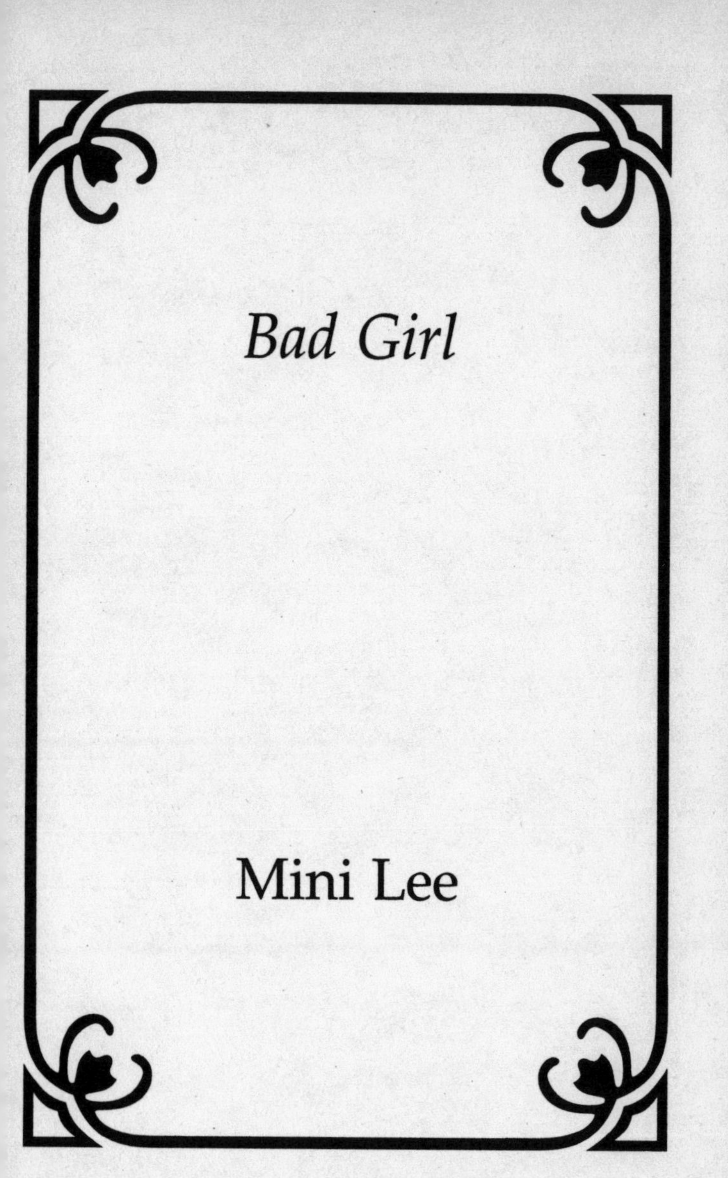

Bad Girl

Mini Lee

Bad Girl

He was middle-aged and had a crew-cut. I noticed him as he was passing through the neighbour's yard. Suspicious. He could be undercover. I watched him and saw him looking for a reason to be there and finally he walked towards the front street. He gazed intently at me, saying hello as he passed. He got into a white car. Had I seen him before?

In the empty lot behind the house was a police cruiser car. I noticed this when I went to my back yard. It gave me sudden shakes. I wouldn't be in touch with John today. Was it because of John, who regularly bought huge quantities of my home-made wine? The heat was on.

Before I reached the back door, I heard a car start up and drive off. I didn't dare look over. After a moment, when I did, the cruiser car wasn't there any more.

I had two reasons for being nervous. I sold wine, which was against the law. Another concern was my penchant for masturbating in my private yard. Paranoid now, I went into my house and felt the place a testimony to my vices. I roamed nervously through the rooms, which seemed liked cages as my anxiety grew. Two rooms in particular possessed the all-too-hot fire of guilt, inhabited by liquor shelves and the sheer curtains where I've stood before, nude, at night. Touching myself.

Was it the fuzzola? Who was that man? My neighbour's boyfriend? I was unsettled all around. In my pit, I was already naked facing authority.

Who was that man today? He was ugly, in a way. Real crew-cut cop. White-haired, with a middle-aged paunch. He wasn't shy about his presence in the yard. The way he looked at me made me feel like he had something on me. I felt he knew everything about me. That I was a bad girl. That he would be back. Was he there right now, outside the house?

Poor naughty girl, had I no purer thoughts to contemplate? What was I to do? I had to do the deal with John, for bloody sakes. I was heavy in wine stock, I wanted to get it out of the house and I was waiting for him to pick it up and lighten his pocketbook.

Yes, I was a bad girl, and I knew it.

Nervous and titillated, I started to fantasise about showing my bare pussy to this man I'd seen, who'd so unsettled me and already possessed me; my cunt was his, the crew-cut man may have it. Just as my doctor did – he who knew all about my bad ways and habits.

Oh, I was a bad girl. Oh, what I've let my doctor do to me, what I'd like to let this bad man do to me. He could walk through the neighbour's yard and right into my garage, where he'd pinch my tits and finger me underneath my wet underwear. And it would hurt; it would feel marvellous. It would not be seen by anyone, but it would happen again and again, wetter and wetter, for I would feel him doing it to me when he wasn't even there. I wanted him to expose my bare breasts, squeeze my nipples, touch the bad girl.

My doctor touched my bare breasts every month. I liked a regular examination. He wanted to bring in a specialist sometime. I would co-operate. Just as I always did for him when we were alone. I remember my last appointment.

The doctor told me to undress and left the room. I put on the gown. I tried to tie the back, but it remained open like the curtains of the proscenium of my bare cheeks. Poor soft ass. I didn't want to think about my own nakedness right here, I couldn't let the doctor think I liked it, but . . . What if I was wet for the examination? Oh God. I didn't want him to look at me. Because I fantasised about him, I felt dirty even though I washed and sprayed perfume earlier and everything.

He entered the room. He didn't look at me but told me to sit on the edge of the examination table. He wanted my feet up and tapped the heel rests on his examination table with his finger. As I got into position he pulled up my gown and reached under to guide my bare ass into place at the edge of the table. All the while, he stared relentlessly at my open pussy, not in the way a doctor properly should. He pushed my legs slowly apart and I felt my moist pussy lips part, open, naked and waiting.

'Spread your legs apart as far as you can.'

I spread my thighs timidly and felt myself getting a little wet as I showed him more. He next lifted my gown all the way up my abdomen past my tits. I was fully naked up to my neck. He looked back down at my well-trimmed mound, my clit protruding. Then he eyed my breasts. He felt around the nipples. 'Any cysts?'

'No,' I said.

'How do you know?' he asked sternly.

'I don't, I guess.' There were butterflies in my stomach as he pinched my nipples.

'They can occur anywhere,' he said, squeezing hard. My nipples were erect and hard. 'Let's check under your arms.' He proceeded to do so, cupping both my breasts in his hands and fingering my armpits. He pressed down with his palms and moved his doctor's hands knowingly in a circle. He looked briefly for my reaction. I looked away and over again only to see his eyes stroll down my torso to my opened legs.

'How's the wine-making?'

My pussy lips betrayed me as they twitched guiltily, and he moved away from my breasts, now intent on my lower nakedness. His eyes were fixed on my clit and I tried not to look at him. 'Spread more.' I could hardly part my legs any wider, but I tried, and my juices visibly gushed out of me. I caught a brief smile on his face.

'Are you drinking much of it?' he asked accusingly.

'Umm . . .' He slowly forced my legs further apart, so far that it hurt and I groaned unwillingly.

'How much are you drinking?'

'Well, more than I should,' I answered, knowing his game, trying not to sound disturbed by what he was doing.

'You're selling most of it, aren't you?' His fingers rudely circled the wet lips of my pussy. I felt dirty and aroused. Suddenly he thrust a finger deep inside my hole. It hurt, his jabbing, but I deserved it and I loved it. I closed my legs on his hand and moaned in spite of myself.

'It's against the law, you know.'

I gasped and spread my legs again; he knew how to make me uneasy. I had once confided in him that I made a little extra money from home-made brew. Since, this irrationally made me feel sexually aroused, this confession. Though I wished I'd never told him, he used it mercilessly against me. He pulled his finger out of my wet pussy.

'It's all right.' He patted my clit. 'Did that hurt? I need you to relax now. Just tell the doctor everything.'

I remained silent and aroused as he slowly patted my sticky clit. The patting became a little more rapid. He looked at me, but I couldn't look back. He smiled and began to spank my pussy. Hard. It stung hot red. I tried to close my legs. He allowed me to and then pushed my knees to one side, exposing my bare ass, which he proceeded to spank several times, harder and harder. I turned to get away and was flat on my stomach.

'You are a dirty, bad girl. I could report you to the police.'

'I've stopped.'

'I don't believe you! You're going to make yourself sick with worry about getting caught. I'll take your temperature. Put your knees under you and raise your bum up for me, you bad, bad girl.'

I obeyed, shivering, my eyes wide with fear. He used my undammed pussy juices to moisten his thick thermometer. It was cold and smooth inside me.

'You're all wet.'

'I'm sorry.'

'No, you're not. Look at this.' He pulled on my cunt lips, separating them, elongating them. He fingered the wetness between the folds, moving the juices up to my asshole. Slowly, in and out, he worked the thermometer into my hole. I pulled away in shock, falling on to my belly whereupon I received many more sharp slaps to my naked ass. Following that he made me tell him about how I was a bad girl, and what I did around my house. All the while he did many more shameful things to me, and he made me do things to him.

Perhaps my doctor had told the police all about me and they were watching my house now. Hence the crew-topped man. Was he a friend of the doctor's? All I knew was I'd best call off the deal with John tonight.

What kind of life was I leading? I was married, respectable ... I needed to lie down. I was feeling shaky. I got into bed and lay still, feeling warmer, safer. Peter would be home shortly. I could rest for a moment and not think about anything.

But I did think. I fantasised about the man I saw in the neighbour's yard. I thought about him confronting me because he knew of my underground business affairs. Or perhaps he'd seen me touching myself in my yard. In my bed, I felt my heart beat fast and my clit fill so that it was fat with arousal.

I envisioned the scene from under my covers. I moved my hand down and inside my panties. I was already slick wet thinking of him coming through the back gate of my yard, looking for me wearing my short skirt on a hot summer's day. In my private yard, I have never minded that, when I leaned over, anyone could see I had no panties on. Perhaps the crew-cut man had already seen my pussy. I pushed off my bedcovers and felt my clit, erect as a small penis.

What if this man came back to punish the bad girl? What if he found me in my yard, when I had a short skirt on with no panties? I started to tell myself a bedtime story.

I could see myself bending over, exposing my naked pussy to the sun. But I heard the gate open and close around the corner. I nervously straightened up. I cast my eyes in the direction of the gate, but no one appeared. I continued my garden work, bending over again. My naked bush was in full view, out in the sunshine; I had an open, warm, wet pussy. With my ass, I reached up to the sun, moaning more loudly than a bad girl should have. Like an echo, I heard the moan again. But it wasn't me and I looked around.

The man with the crew-cut was standing a few feet away. He had seen what I was now attempting to hide, my naked pussy. I rose, embarrassed. He was looking at me without expression.

He said, 'Excuse me, miss.' He approached, looking me over.

'Can I help you?' I asked tersely.

'I have a search warrant,' he announced as he drew nearer.

'For what?'

'For bootlegging and for what I just saw you do, dirty,

bad girl. Shall we go inside?' He roughly took my wrist and drew me close to him. 'Get in the house.' He held me with his hungry eyes. He looked at my breasts inside my flimsy shirt. My nipples were erect and I had no bra on to conceal them. He started to caress my ass under my skirt, gently, feeling its shape. The doctor must have sent him. The policeman knew I might be in for trouble, in trouble with him, with the law.

'I have nothing to hide,' I said with a nervous voice.

'Where are your panties then?' He lifted my skirt slightly and poked my bare pussy with his finger. The bad girl was all wet. I pulled away, but he still held me by the wrist. 'Let's go inside and see.'

As he led me towards the house I was shaking like a leaf. What if he found my stash? The wind lifted my skirt to expose my naked ass cheeks, or was it him?

A long bursting orgasm moved me in my bed. Just then the door sounded below and Peter arrived home. I dried my soaking wet pussy with a tissue. After I washed my hands, I'd make dinner, I thought. I'd got him out of my system and I hoped I would never see or think about the white-haired, crew-cut man again.

Later that night, needing more release yet from my day, I had little sleep. I wondered if the crew-cut man was going to spank me sometime. My husband snored beside me.

I was tired the next morning. All when I had so much to do. I had put off tending the garden this spring and seedlings wanted to be planted. The sun was going to be hot on the south side of the house; I would wear shorts, or a short, wide skirt, perhaps with no underwear. I could feel the breeze already. It would be great. The prospect roused my energy for the chore when I was so weary. I dressed and I chose a shorter skirt than planned and went out into the garden. I lit a cigarette and let the feeling of my daring and vulnerability creep over me. My energy rose quickly. The bedding plants were over on the garden table and ready. Without hesitation, I set to the task. I was aroused by the way the breeze played with my skirt; it excited me. I remember how I had told the doctor what I sometimes did; it made me feel like I was a bad girl. I was faced with a feeling of concern for what I'd told the doctor and a yearning for redemption for being a bad girl. Like the things he'd done to me on the examination table. I was feeling wet. I was feeling the breeze up my skirt. How much could be seen of my naked pussy?

Bending over in the garden was easy, my wide skirt provided ample movement. I wondered if I should go in and put on some underwear but when I felt the warm sun touch my pussy lips, I enjoyed it too much to stop. It felt so good, healing, intense, deeply penetrating. I could have picked the gauze skirt, which was somewhat safer, it went lower, but still provided ample exposure and it was practically like ether. But since my yard was relatively private, I felt I could freely enjoy this pleasant sensation of my fully naked pussy exposed to the sun. I briefly wondered what the doctor would say if I had a tanned cunny. I felt myself getting wet at the thought of his discovering it – the spankings I would get; I liked being a bad girl. I heard the gate open and I straightened up. Then there was no noise at all. I rose and listened carefully for a while. Finally, I went around the corner to look and see. There was nothing and the gate was closed. My heart was beating hard. I thought of the crew-cut man and neared the fence to look over and see if there was a police cruiser car parked there again. Nothing. I hid by the fence momentarily, feeling completely culpable with bootleg wine in my house and the wind playing games with my skirt. Enough paranoia. I was simply leading my life. I had nothing to regret, I was smart, resourceful. I crept back over to where I was working, wanting to get back to the job. I leaned over; there were so many trees, no one could see, I thought, and the sun was so warm and so sensual. I spread my full cunt out to the sun. Mmm.

I sighed.

Then I heard a sigh. I straightened up immediately. Someone was close by. I felt my pussy release fluids, wetting me mercilessly. I looked around. The man with the crew-cut was standing over by the elm tree. He looked at me without expression. I knew he'd seen me with my skirt up, seen my naked pussy. I was a bad girl caught. As he started towards me, he smiled and said, 'Good day, miss. I have a search warrant for these premises. Do you own this property?'

'For what do you search?' I asked innocently.

'For bootleg products,' he replied as he pulled out his official documents from his chest pocket. I reached for them and with one hand he took me by the wrist. 'Take a look.' He held them out for me with the other hand. As I tried to look, I felt his eyes looking at the hem of my skirt, which was blowing up a little in the wind. He slid the papers down into my shirt, pulling it downwards, exposing my hard, dark nipples and he said, 'It looks like you're in trouble, little girl.' He cooed, 'You can't go around dressed like that.' I felt his dry hand brush under my skirt, touching the skin of my sun-warmed ass. I tried to pull away but he held my wrist tighter.

'I have nothing to hide.'

'Where are your panties then?' He guided me to the back door of the house. The wind picked up, lifting my skirt, exposing my bare ass to the crew-cut man. Perhaps it was he who pulled up my skirt. I heard him groan as I opened the back door.

Once inside, the crew-cut man pushed me up the stairs. I fell forward along the steps, whereupon my skirt went up and I tried to scramble up the steps, my thighs and ass nude and trembling. I felt several sharp slaps on my bare bum. 'Get up. Show me where you stand all naked at night.' I turned to him angrily.

'I wasn't expecting company; let me get dressed.'

'Just get up the stairs.' Then he pinched the inside of my leg, close to my wetness. I sprang up with a frightened gasp. He lost his grip on my arm and so pulled me down by the ankle. Angry now, he pushed my skirt fully up and spanked my bare ass again, harder and several times. I moaned and squirmed, but this only made his spanking harder. Finally I lay still and he stopped slapping me. My ass was hot and red and he felt it with his hand. 'You're all hot and red.' I was wet and, when he slid his hand between my legs, I felt his fingers slippery along my twat. He groaned. So did I, helplessly. 'Get up,' he ordered. I climbed the steps while he kept hold of my arm. I stood in the middle of the kitchen, trembling. 'Is it in front of this window?' He pinched my nipple; it was erect and jutting through my shirt. I tried to back away. 'I've seen you, bad girl.' He pinched my other nipple and I turned away. I was breathing hard and so was he. I knew he would be able to do whatever he wanted, incarcerate me perhaps.

'What I do in my own home is my business,' I pleaded.

'I know everything that you do, I know where everything is,' he said, lifting my skirt, looking at my naked pussy. 'The doctor told me; he told me many things.'

'Are you a friend of Dr Nuds?' I felt my face go red as I pulled away.

'Oh you're in a great deal of trouble, you know. Do you like trouble?' he asked.

'You're my trouble right now, sir.'

'Don't you know it.'

'Please? Please don't report me.'

'The bad girl will tell me the whole indecent story. Would she like to take me down the basement to her wine cellars? Bootlegging bad girl!' His hand brushed over my breasts slowly. Lingering, dragging the tip of his finger across my right nipple.

'There's nothing in the basement.'

'The basement is where I will see everything,' he said menacingly. He reached from behind and turned me, holding me by my tits, directing me back to the stairs. He slid one hand between my legs as we went down the stairs, his finger poking into my pussy and my asshole.

As we reached the bottom of the steps, the boxes of wine were lined up along the wall. 'What's that? How much do you sell?' He pushed me towards them. I regained my footing and turned to face him.

'None,' I said. I slowly lifted my skirt to show him my nakedness, neatly trimmed by the doctor. All my folds were showing and wet.

'Bad girl!'

I parted my lips for him and I pulled up my shirt to show him my erect nipples. I made my nipples wet with my juices.

'You dirty girl.' He unzipped his pants and slowly pulled out his large, pink, throbbing cock. 'Here, suck it with your dirty mouth.' He neared me, massaging his hard cock with his hand. 'Kneel down.' His cock was hot and sweaty as he pressed my face into it. I took him into my mouth. 'You going to break the law?' he asked, moving his prick deep inside my mouth. 'Hmm? You bad girl. I could put you in jail, you know.' He thrust his cock in and out of my mouth a few times. Then he withdrew it quickly. 'Take off your top.'

I looked up at him. 'Will you keep my secrets?'

'I can do whatever I want to, can't I?'

I drew in a quick breath, feeling myself involuntarily releasing juices inside my pussy. I wanted to pee and my clit was burning. I began to pull off my top.

'I have to pee.'

'That's good. Hold it, little tits.'

He was right: I had small firm breasts, but I knew my nipples were beautiful – small, dark and true to the touch. He pinched them. 'Show me the rest of your basement,' he urged, his cock wet against my upper thigh. I felt I was dripping, such a bad girl that I was. I led the way into the nether regions of the basement. The light was crude and bright around the washer and dryer. He pushed me up against my dryer, from behind. 'What do I do with you? You deserve more than a spanking.' I leaned forward against the dryer and my nipples got harder against the cold metal. He spanked me several times. Then he felt my moist pussy from behind, sliding his fingers into me. It made such a noise, my wetness . . . He transferred his attention to my asshole. Then he poked with insistent wet fingers. I moaned, feeling his cock near the hole, pressing to get in. Wet enough, he squeezed his hard cock into my asshole, his fingers reaching to pinch my clit at the same time. He pushed his cock deep into me and then guided it into my pussy. I peed a little into his hand.

'Don't pee. Does the doctor do this to you? He told me all about it; he's my brother, you know.' He pulled out suddenly and flipped me over, lifting me by the pussy on to the dryer, whereupon he had me spread my legs wide. He licked my wet opening and then his tongue circled my clit in slow, wet strokes. 'Do you need to pee? Go pee.' His lips sucked on my clit. I peed in spurts all over his face. 'Mmm,' he said. When I was finished, he looked up at me. 'A urine test, eh? You should see the doctor soon. We'd like to meet with you together, you know. And a bad girl like you, you'd better come to see us. Discuss your illegal and dangerous lifestyle.' He leaned on my naked pussy with his hard cock, his mouth pressed against mine. His cock eased into me and he leaned back again so he could squeeze my nipples while he drove his large hot cock in and out of my wet, wet, orgasming cunt. He watched me rub my exploding, convulsing clit with my finger.

'I'm a bad girl,' I whispered.

Opening the Veins of Jade

Renée M. Charles

Opening the Veins of Jade

For a brief, magical time just after it's been applied, and all the colours have been pushed deeply under the epidermis with a bee-hum of sound and furious motion, a tattoo seems to hover just above the skin, the submerged tones all but cleaving from the newly pierced flesh like moist cloisonné resting on a bed of fine-napped satin. Oh, I know it really isn't magical, just a reaction of injured, dye-infused skin to the surrounding air, but yet, as I finish each new permanent embellishment on a customer's bared flesh, just before slathering the area with antibiotic cream and applying a patch of gauze with pre-ripped bits of tape, I can't help but feel like a shaman-woman who's just created a sacred sand painting in vivid, blood-strong colours, or who's finished the application of ritual body art before a coming-of-age ceremony.

Customers who can crane their necks to see the results of my labours often comment on how *real* raised tattoos look; some wistfully ask if there isn't a way to keep tattoos puffy, so they might stand out better, be more eye-catching . . .

That's when I smile, shake my head and remind them that if they keep out of the sun, or use sunblock as religiously as their diaphragms, a tattoo will remain incredibly vibrant, thanks to today's improved dye spectrums ... but if they want puffy decorations on their bodies, they'd best visit those shops specialising in invasive body modification.

It's funny, although my clientele is roughly an even male/female split, women usually ask if they can keep a tattoo raised; maybe it's the being-used-to-jewellery thing, or an extension of the ages-old emphasis on jutting breasts and a swollen belly and bottom (not to forget the Bushman's – Bushwoman's? – abundant *mons pubis*) ... Anyhow, if a client sees that glistening, jewel-domed tattoo jutting out of her flesh, she'll invariably ask if there isn't something I can do to make it stay that way. One even suggested I try a collagen injection under it – although she already had enough of that in her lips to shoot some down to her upper arm!

But since there's nothing I can do to keep tattoos raised, I usually remind the client that her new piece of bodily adornment is hers and hers alone: like most tattoo artists, I stamp each selected design SOLD once it's been chosen. Which is no more than fair – after enduring hours of stinging, vibrating-to-the-bone pain, plus the loss of some blood, every customer deserves the exclusivity of his or her bodily illustration. After all, there's no easy way to shuck it off if everyone else is 'wearing' the same thing.

When the client comes in with a design he or she has drawn or commissioned themselves, the whole 'sold' issue is a moot one, since I'm not going to tack their design outline up on the studio wall once the person walks out of the salon – for one thing, I wouldn't want some of the designs they bring in *on* my walls (why they'd want them on their bodies is beyond me) and, for another, such designs usually have a meaning unique to that person alone, so for another client, they'd have no appeal.

So, on that late afternoon when the trio of ageless, ebony-haired women walked into my salon, moving with a close, silky smoothness, like pearls straddling a silken thread, past my postered-to-the-ceilings walls, straight to the padded table where I do most of my work, each of them holding a folded sheet of creamy pale parchment with the unmistakable seep-through of black lines on the inner folds of the paper, I knew instinctively that these ladies would be wanting me to ink designs of a most idiosyncratic sort upon their smooth-fleshed bodies. As it was, each of them wore clothing that showed off previous examples of the tattooist's art: delicate, fragile-hued designs that reminded me of ancient Chinese and Japanese bamboo scrolls, with what looked like single-needle outlining, and interior wash of colour so delicately faint it looked more like daubs of watercolour applied to the top of the flesh rather than tinted ink inserted under the skin. Finely etched bracelets of interlocking blossoms and angular faux jade adorned each woman's bare arm, and on the barely cloth-shadowed folds and valleys of their jutting small breasts, I saw gauzy cloud-obscured animal shapes of a most fantastic nature. The trio stood silently, watching politely as I finished cleaning off my electric tattoo gun, their eyes demure under the Asian single-fold of their eyelids, their exquisitely formed small mouths pursed slightly, as if in anticipation of answering my inevitable question:

'How may I help you, ladies?'

The tallest one, with the glistening chin-length hair whose straight fringe hovered a precise inch above her delicately winged brows, said softly, in a voice free of accent or inflection, 'We wish to be tattooed, please. We have brought our own designs.'

With that, each of them extended her paper-holding hand towards me, so that I could see what designs had been painstakingly inked on to the translucent paper. The one who'd spoken to me held a design that resembled a blooming peony, albeit one with a most unusual horse-shoe-like configuration, one with a high and wide top and trailing buds and leaves fanning out to each side. The woman to her left, with the longest hair and the fullest hips, showed me a similarly altered lotus outline, while the third woman, whose shining hair hugged her rounded skull in finely tapered layers of soft jet, held the stylised delineation of some sort of stone gateway, also in that oddly familiar configuration of a wide-arched top and tapering sides.

The designs had been expertly drawn, clearly with an understanding of my needs as a tattoo artist, yet there was something about them, something so specific, yet unexpected to my eye, despite my having done countless similar inked designs on hundreds of other patches of bared flesh. A small inner voice told me – these designs aren't meant to be readily seen – and when I took my eyes from the sheets of pale parchment, I saw the tallest one motioning with a slim, taper-nailed hand towards her abdomen, then gently outline the contours of her mons through the tight-fitting sheath dress she wore, before saying, 'These designs . . . you can do them, here?'

Now, in the ten years I've been a working artist (plus the two other years I'd experimented with the craft on my boyfriend's back and other bodily contours) I've had some strange requests for tattoos in intimate spots, but the seriousness of these women took me aback. Usually, when someone has genitals done, it's at the urging of a lover or spouse, who comes along to witness the embellishing (until the blood comes, that is, and then many find the process quite *un*erotic!). But, judging from the way these ladies related to each other, they didn't seem to be members of a DC *ménages à trois* – there was no overt touching, no nuzzling or sly winks and blushes. And they weren't tarts – too classy, too refined, even for high-rent girls.

And they were clearly of age; while their flawlessly smooth skin and uniformly sable hair spoke of youth, their bearing and presence spoke of an accumulation of years impossible to feign.

Three pairs of depthless dark eyes regarded me with polite coolness as I looked at each of them in turn and replied, 'Yes, I can do a tattoo anywhere . . . but you realise that this will be extremely painful, and there will be a lot of bleeding, more than when you had your arms and . . . everywhere else done. I'm not allowed to give painkillers, so I have to warn you before I –'

'Pain is not a problem for any of us,' the long-haired one cut in, then smiled enough to reveal a top row of small, tightly spaced white teeth, before her crop-haired companion added, 'Pain, if anticipated, can function as a form of pleasure.' Their taller consort nodded briefly in agreement, her eyes briefly lit from within with what might have been pleasure – or at least anticipation.

The obstacle removed, I found another reason to delay their request, this one far more practical, at least from my point of view.

'Well, if you say so on that . . . but I'll have to do this after hours, on account of the privacy matter and all. People come in unannounced, and it can be embarrassing when I'm working on someone's bum, or their breasts . . .'

Three lustrous black heads bobbed in agreement, before the short-haired one said, 'We understand your concern for us. To us it is not a problem, but your own discomfort should be considered.'

I'd never thought of it in that way before, yet once she stopped speaking, I understood. After all, if someone wanted a design on their bum, or on a breast, apparently they did want at least one person to see it – or more than one person. And if it didn't bother them for me to see their exposed privates . . .

Nodding, I said, 'Then would it be all right with you to return at, say, nine o'clock? I close at seven-thirty, so that would give me time to ink these drawings, get everything ready – oh, did you have specific colours picked out, or –'

'We do have colours in mind,' Short-Hair interjected, pointing to the gate-like design on her square of paper. 'This is the Vermilion Gate, so a suitable red will be necessary, as well as darker shading. The Golden Lotus should be a natural aureate tone befitting the original blossom, while the Open Peony Blossom shall be pink, with veins of darker blush and, of course, dusky green leaves. For now, we will leave the Jewel Terrace and Jade Vein unadorned,' she concluded, after glancing at each of her companions in turn, who nodded assent to her instructions.

Apparently *they* understood all this talk of Jade Veins and Jewelled Whatnots (the capitalisation of the words was implicit in her pronunciation), so there seemed no need to translate for my benefit. After resting their drawings on my workbench, they bowed their heads in my direction, then walked en masse towards the door, with a silken swish of fabric rubbing against bare flesh, which reminded me to call after them, 'Ladies, you'll need a shave or wax before I can do the tattoos, OK?'

Without turning to face me, Long-Hair replied, 'That has already been arranged.' Then the trio exited my shop with a light tinkling of the bell attached to my door – which was softly echoed by the flesh-obscured muffled jingle of the ben-wah balls one or all of them had concealed within their bodies.

It was only after they'd left that I noticed the faint, gingery smell of their perfume lingering in the air, a scent that made my own pussy twitch, before I felt an inner trickle of moist warmth against the tight fabric of my jeans. With a groan, I glanced at the clock, whose hands stubbornly rested in the five-o'clock position. Never before had four hours seemed so unbearably long to wait for what promised to be a most . . . unusual job.

Perhaps if my boyfriend hadn't been out of the city that week, acting as a judge at some tattooing convention, I wouldn't have found myself bubbling from within in anticipation of that night. But, as it was, I was already aching for him when those three exotics sauntered into the shop, inked parchment in hand, ben-wah balls secreted within, so, since I did know better than to actively seek out companionship of a temporary sort during his absence, I was looking forward to being able to caress (albeit with latex-filmed hands) those smooth folds and mounds of musky flesh while inking on those intricate, bizarre designs, then again caressing the slightly raised skin while slathering on the creamy white ointment . . . That there were three of them only made the waiting all the more anxious and sweeter, even as it removed the temptation to go *too* far with any of them (sure, I had a boyfriend, but a beautiful body is still a beautiful body).

My heart lurched in my chest as I flipped over the OPEN/CLOSED sign in the door and drew the ring-topped curtains across the shop windows, shutting out the sight of the evening crowds spilling out of the bars and theatres. Behind me, I'd readied the drawings for application – judging by the size of each illustration, the trio had exquisitely small, tight-lipped pussies – and the fresh sets of needles (single and multi-tipped) rested next to unopened bottles of vermilion, golden yellow, sage green, light and dark pink, and black inks. Three pairs of latex gloves rested next to the inks and needles, and I'd placed extra folded sheets near the tattooing table, as well as a box of gauze pads and a roll of white tape. And next to those, a tube of antibiotic ointment, fresh out of the box.

Just looking at the array of equipment and materials made me shivery inside and I ran to the bathroom at the back of the shop for a quick session with my vibrator, the one with the gentle curve to it and the nubby, bump-studded tip. Resting the back of my head and my shoulders against the wall, I arched my pelvis forward to brush my upper lips and clit against the vibrating nubs, allowing the rubbery tip to tease the lightly stubbled flesh (my boyfriend's doing – he'd been after me to allow him to tattoo some flowers and vines down there, but I'd always demurred for one reason or another, despite having many decorations on my limbs and breasts), until my clit twitched on its own and a shuddering rush of rippling, over-lapping waves of pleasure moved through me from the deep centre outward. Clicking off the vibrator, I spritzed some body shampoo on to a flannel, then rubbed it over and around my mons.

As I went to rinse off the flannel, I noticed a thin sliver of red – I hadn't realised my time of the month was due so soon.

With a sigh, I unwrapped and inserted a tampon (it did feel a bit like a non-musical ben-wah ball), then scrubbed up and went back into the shop, where I saw the silhouettes of three slim, yet subtly curving, bodies standing behind one of the shaded windows, their forms outlined intermittently by a flashing bank of lights across the side-street. Hoping they hadn't been waiting too long (even though they were a good half-hour early), I hurried to the door and opened it with a soft 'Come in, come in,' before backing into the shop.

This time, the muted jingle of their ben-wah balls was unmistakable. Instead of the tight sheath dresses they'd worn earlier, they now sported shorter wrap-style coat dresses, belted loosely at the waist with self-fabric belts. They wore high heels whose soles and thin points clicked in sharp descant to the interior tinkle of their hidden pleasure-balls, as they approached my work station. Pressing my thighs so tightly together the tampon felt like a hard stone shoved high into my pussy, I licked my lips briefly before asking, 'Which one of you would like to go first?'

They glanced at each other, not speaking, until Crop-Top hoisted herself up on to the table and began to undo her belt. The others stood politely off to one side, out of my light and out of my way. But I had to walk between them to get to my work table, and it took every bit of effort on my part not to casually brush against one or both of them as I made my way to the waiting needles and inks.

I busied myself with pulling on my gloves (which reminded me of condoms, all slick and shiny without and powdery-soft within) then I put black ink in the needle gun (I'd use the vermilion later, to add natural colour and contouring). I picked up the design and approached my first client of the evening. Her dress was spread open, and her thighs were parted invitingly, to reveal a smooth, waxed mons and a tight pinkish-tan twist of pussy lips, topped off by a taut, rounded nubbin of clit flesh. She was resting with her shoulders and upper back touching the wall behind the bench, while her head was craned forward enough to watch me as I worked.

I heard the subtle jangle of the ben-wahs as I applied the inked paper to her pliant mound, rubbing firmly to transfer the outline of the pattern to her flesh, while her soft breathing made the slight roll of skin over her mons move in time with the rubbing motions of my gloved hand. Her skin was an extraordinary shade of palest, purest pinkish-tan, and before I was finished with the rub-on, I could tell that the tattoo would be startling against such delicate flesh.

Once the design was in place, I reluctantly asked her to lie down, so I'd have a more stable surface upon which to work; she did so only after asking her companions, 'You will inform me about the progress of the Gate?'

As each nodded in reply, I found myself asking, 'I know it isn't any of my business, but is this a special sort of tattoo? It sounds like you're capitalising the words – are they significant?'

A beat of mutual silence on their part, then, with a soft sigh that might've been one of consternation or one of relief, the tall one said, 'Where we come from, originally, the names of one's sexual organs were most descriptive, and poetic, in keeping with the titles of the associated sexual positions. For women, the labia and the mons were more specific: the Vermilion Gate, the Open Peony Blossom, the Golden Lotus. And for the clitoris, the Jewel Terrace, surrounded by the Jade Veins, or Golden Cleft. Men possessed a Jade Stem, or Heavenly Dragon Pillars –'

'– or Red Bird, or Coral Stalk,' added Chin-length Bob.

Her companion continued, 'All names that implied a natural reverence for the sexual act – unlike the terms more commonly associated with such bodily parts.'

Wondering if these birds really were call girls of some sort, albeit very classy ones, I let their information sink in, as it were, before saying, as I approached the inked outlines of the Vermilion Gate with my needle, 'I agree they're far more aesthetic terms – beautiful, really. I just hope this is all worth it . . . I know what you said about pain and all, but *this* will hurt.'

In unspoken answer to my first pass with the single needle over her softly curved mons, Short-Hair merely closed her eyes and arched her lower back upwards, while her confidantes described the blossoming inked design in hushed, almost reverent tones:

'The first pillar of the Gate is growing redder, while the top arch is now filled in . . .'

As I worked, inking on the wash of dark red with multiple needles, I had to lean closer to that crimson-toned flesh but, as I wiped away the excess ink and resulting blood with a moistened towelette, I soon noticed that, in addition to the jingling undercurrent produced by the vibrating of the skin surrounding the ben-wahs, there was something else unusual happening – instead of the skin merely rising from the action of the needles piercing the flesh, it now felt *harder*, and ultra-smooth, like organic armour over her pubic bone. And the mingled scent of blood and ink was different too – far spicier, far more musk-like than usual.

Yet, when I glanced at her gently wrinkled inner lips, it was still fairly dry, without that sheen of inner juices that might be associated with personal musk.

My head was swirling from the humming drone of the needles, the tinny clink of the deeply inserted balls, and the rise and fall of the other women's voices above and behind me. I was in a daze as I reached for the tube of ointment, uncapped it, then squirted out a generous clear dollop on to one gloved palm, before gently smoothing it over her Vermilion Gate-embellished mound. But daze or no daze, the feel of polished, deeply carved stone beneath my fingers was unmistakable, and in the stark white light above, I easily made out the indentations of carving *in* the surrounding cinnabar-stone gates – 'carvings' I'd inked *on to* her flesh only minutes earlier. It was only as I reached for a patch of gauze that she spoke again. Gently waving off my hands, she smiled and said, 'No need . . . the air will be much better on it,' before closing her legs and the dress flap and climbing off the table.

Shaken, I shucked off my gloves, then eased on fresh ones while I heard the rustle of another of the women getting up on the bench and undoing her dress. When I turned around, I saw Long-Hair, who'd requested the Golden Lotus, sitting with her dress completely open. There were banks of clouds tattooed on the top of each breast, and fine thin hoops of burnished gold jutted from pierced, raisin-tight nipples. Her nipple rings were joined by a fine cord of golden mesh, twin strands cunningly twisted into a swaying rope between the pale orbs of her breasts.

Thin, deep-blue shadows cast by the suspended chain fell across her slightly convex stomach, and my hands ached to caress the mounds that surmounted that hovering shadow, so much so that, as I took up the paper with her chosen design on it, my hands shook, making the paper flutter like a trapped butterfly caught in my palms.

But, as I bent down to rub the pattern on to her smooth plate, I felt her hands running lightly along my spine, as she whispered into the mass of wavy hair that covered my left ear, 'This will ease your shivers.' Then she ran her hands down my back, along the curve of my jeans-covered arse, then in, towards the thick seam of denim that covered my throbbing sex. Steadying myself against the bench with both hands, I closed my eyes and she – and her companions – continued to lightly massage me through my clothes. The sensation of their hands pressing the fabric tightly against my skin was incredibly sensual, like being massaged by dozens of French tickers.

Once the last undulating ripples of orgasm swept through me, I was able to continue transferring the last of the inks blossom on to her powdery soft skin, before switching on the single-needled gun and filling in the delicate tracery of petals, stamens and curling leaves with deep-pulsing ink. As Short-Hair before her had done, with each piercing stab of the needle, she sunk deeper into a swoon of ecstasy, her eyes closed under blood-suffused lids.

And with each arc of the double needles, as more and more brilliant colour filled in the outlines of the Golden Lotus, her newly tattooed mons took on an unmistakable softness and pliancy, a tactile delicacy matched only by dew-brushed flower petals – a difference in texture I could easily feel through the confines of my latex gloves. More stunning, though, was how each separate petal was raised to a slightly varied height above her pelvis, so that when I smoothed on the glistening cream, I felt the distinct outline of each petal I'd embellished there – as well as the rougher surfaces of the surrounding leaves.

As she sat up, the swaying shadow of her chain-linked

breasts momentarily shifted across the surface of her newly illuminated mound, and I swore that I saw the shadow break into a jagged line as it crossed over the varied surfaces of her genitalia, as if passing over a terraced hillside dotted with small hillocks and shallow valleys.

This time, as I peeled off my second pair of gloves, I was bold enough to gently run my bare fingers over her cream-smeared flowering softness – and was rewarded with the sensation of caressing the most tender flower petals imaginable, petals which nonetheless throbbed with an inner heat, and which even shifted slightly under my delicate probing touch. When she sighed, I caught the scent of some unknown but heady floral fragrance, before she covered the top of my hand with her left one, and guided my fingers deeper into her Golden Lotus, past the fleshy cloisonné of ink and artistry, down to the barely damp tucks and folds of her Golden Cleft, whispering as she did so, 'You've noticed the fruits of your handiwork – do not doubt your senses, or question them. What was once flesh is now so much more.'

As my right hand rubbed and massaged her hidden treasures, my left slowly began caressing her lower belly, then her gently heaving chest, until my fingers found those twin mounds of gold-roped softness; cupping each breast in turn, I tentatively ran my fingertips over the cloud-like formations embellished there, and was rewarded with the slightly moist, singularily amorphous sensation of fondling the clouds themselves. And when I gave the linking chain between her nipples a gentle, playful tug, I was astonished to see the inked clouds shift and gather all the more tightly over each satiny hillock of warm flesh.

Only after she reached a softly panting, eyes-tightly-closed orgasm did Golden Lotus Woman slowly slide off the bench, and as I pulled on my third pair of gloves that evening, prior to readying the ink and fresh needles, I noticed that Short-Hair was now sitting on one of the small chairs in the studio, dress parted to the waist, admiring the now stone-solid contours and shining vermilion surfaces of her finished Gate, before flexing and relaxing her pelvis, so that the ben-wah balls within her tinkled with a silvery metallic whispering, as the studio's bright lights glinted off those seemingly polished cinnabar-carved walls. After reluctantly taking my eyes away from that alluring, exotic sight, I concentrated on preparing that last tattoo – the Open Peony Blossom, easily the most intricate and exuberant design of her three.

Her chin-length bob shone like ebony lacquer in the lamp's clear white light, with scintillations of reddish-blue highlights, while her finely plucked brows formed graceful arcing wings on her smooth, pale brow. As I approached her, she untied her dress and ceremoniously spread open the folds of fabric, to reveal a feathery tracery of muted yet gem-like colour that formed a pair of phoenixes perched on each small, firm breast, whose tail feathers trailed in long, spiralling plumes down her rib-cage and along the gentle convex curve of her belly.

Wishing I'd left off my gloves for just a bit, I traced her phoenix-plumage with a rubbery fingertip and, even though the latex, I felt the distinct ripple of feathers under my fingertip – a sensation which had to have been equally real for her, for she let out a deep, throaty sound that might have been mirth, might have been incredibly intense pleasure, before staying my hand and guiding it back to the piece of inked paper resting on my work table. This time, no mere orgasm would steady my hand; holding the piece of peony-outlined paper aloft, out of her reach, I said, 'I must know what's happening . . . this is so . . . *unreal.* I see it, I feel it, but . . . I can't understand it. Is it me, or you, or what?'

She slumped back against the wall, legs still invitingly parted, red-painted mouth forming a moue, until she finally said, 'As my sister told you, what was once mere flesh *is* so much more – as it has been for us for many, many centuries. Yes, we're ages old, ages wise – but not very wise in your special art, that of tattooing. Many times we have sought one who could adorn us in the most meaningful of fashions, and many times we've had to be satisfied with mere trifling embellishments, small tricks of the inked needle, with no intrinsic value.'

Feeling strangely calm, despite the fantastic revelation she'd just made, I again looked at each of them in turn, at the glorious 'tricks of the inked needle' that adorned their creamy-pale flesh (Miss Vermilion had opened her dress, to reveal upturned breasts embellished with the shiny smooth hardness of lacquerware-like inverted bowl shapes, which turned each breast into a deliciously gibbous orb), and asked simply, 'How did this happen to you?'

'This was not a gift from birth,' Golden Lotus explained, as the clouds on her linked breasts grew slightly grey, as if overcast by memory. 'We were born as any other women, with gifts and pleasures possessed by any other and, when we matured, we became concubines to a most wealthy and powerful man. Our lives were intertwined with the joyous giving of our natural gifts, and sexuality was our art. We were masters of the Winding Dragon, Bamboos by the Altar, and the Cleaving Circada ...' Here her voice trailed off, as her cheeks reddened at the mention of remembered pleasures, but Vermilion Gate continued: 'So highly prized were our gifts, that our master and lord made a gift of us to a travelling man of great power and esteem. A man who was far more than he appeared to be, both in terms of power and in terms of his manhood. His Red Bird was far more than mere flesh – it *was*, literally, a living bird of incredible redness, not the symbolic representation of a rising Red Bird. The sensation, against the Jade Veins and the Jewel Terrace, was a heretofore unknown delight. After him, our dildoes and Burmese Bells – what he called

Rin-no-tama bells – were of little use, so great was the need and longing he stirred in each of us.

'And he in turn was so taken with us, and so moved by our plight born of longing, that before he was to take leave of our host, he bestowed his own special gift upon us, a gift tempered by the stinging passion bites he left on each of our bodies, bites that burned with the magic of his hard kisses, and his enchanted Red Bird, which, he revealed to us before that final parting, was once simple ink pounded into his flesh – ink made feathery by the enchantment of his thriving blood.'

'But, before he left,' added the one who sat, waiting in all her phoenix-adorned glory, 'he had one of his own servants decorate our breasts, as proof of the gift he'd bestowed on each of us. But before his servant could give us the Golden Lotus, Vermilion Gate and Open Blooming Peony we craved, our lord banished him from his estate, after having seen the servant's handiwork. Our master thought it the work of evil spirits and banished us as well – but other men found our special charms all the more enticing.

'It was then that we discovered our benefactor's other gift – while those with whom we performed the Phoenix Sporting in the Cinnabar Cleft and the Unicorn Horn gradually grew old and died, we remained young and supple. Through all the centuries following our expulsion from our first master's home, and through all the time spent in a "green bower" with other givers of flesh and other more homely delights . . .'

'But even as men partook of our unique charms, and our own brand of sexual symbolism not found in the classic alchemy of *Ts'an-t'ung-chi'i*, they eventually feared us, and so we found ourselves cast out again, this time from our own land,' explained Golden Lotus, but then went on, as she drew her dress flaps over her clouded breasts and still-glistening Lotus mons, 'Our main concern, however, was to complete what our original . . .

initiate's servant had begun, so many sunsets ago. In other regards, our lives were most self-sufficient, but lacking in the sexual sense. Occasionally, we passed on our gift to others, men and women alike, although those people chose different paths of self-expression, some with small rings and chains of precious metals, others with embellishments that lived in other ways, in other places. But, sadly, in all our wanderings, we had yet to find an artist who was either willing or suitable in ability to grant us our most deeply desired gift . . .'

While listening to the lilting sing-song of Golden Lotus's words, and her tale of gifts passed on to others, a small voice began whispering in my ear, hissing soft tales of a most different sort.

'Are you ladies . . . vampires?'

'Of a sort,' the woman on the bench replied, while reflexively undulating her hips and pelvis, so that the metallic balls within underscored her words with a silvery descant. 'Although nothing like the vampires of *your* mythos, or that of the imaginative Irishman so lauded by your people. Night time *is* our time of sexual feasting, and sexual giving, but we need not fear the day. Through the magic of our blood, the eyes of flesh can see, and the lips of the skin can taste – but only if those eyes and lips are placed on flesh whose blood runs deep and hot with a burning alchemy born of lust and desire. Although the enchantment of our blood is strong, our abilities with the needle and the ink are weak, very weak . . .'

'Just as mine is strong in that regard?' I found myself asking, while unconsciously adopting their syntax for my own.

All three nodded solemnly, and only then did I take up my inked outline and rub it against her shorn, smooth mons . . . and once each petal was transferred to her skin, I picked up my needle gun and began fulfilling her long-held dream, a dream born long, long before my own time of remembrance. And with each completed petal, each inked-in section of the magnificent, spreading blossom, she sighed and began caressing her jutting breasts, stroking and smoothing down the inked feather and plumed contours of the great mythic birds, whose small eyes followed the motions of my needle in slowly rolling watchfulness.

Once the tattoo was finished, and I rubbed on the antibiotic lotion with tight, circular motions, which displaced the petals of her labia and mons briefly, before they slowly moved back into place, I found myself rubbing my own tightly clipped mons against my jeans inseam, wondering how I might feel with a pelvis adorned by silky petals, or made blissfully slick and smooth with an armour of needle-carved cinnabar . . . and how my boyfriend would regard such a change, not only in my appearance, but in *me*.

Before she had a chance to slide off the bench, I stripped off my gloves and then quickly unzipped my jeans and stepped out of them, asking, 'Instead of paying me with money, would you pay me with your . . . gift?' The women glanced first at one another, then at my naked mons with its light covering of fine dark hair – but then their eyes moved in unison to my existing tattoos: the small winged dragon on my left hip, and the fanged tiger on my right hip and buttocks. Then Golden Lotus said softly, 'Such a payment is most possible – but first, your flesh will have to be freed from the danger that lurks there.'

'Danger?' I echoed dully, before Vermilion Gate reached out to stroke the trapped-ink tiger on my hip, and Blossoming Peony traced the outline of the dragon on my other side.

Golden Lotus continued, 'Once your blood is like ours, the eyes of your flesh will see – and the fangs will bite. A grave threat to you, and your loved one, but one which we can negate – if you still wish for our blood-gift. Remember, it is also one of eternal life, which goes hand in hand with eternal loneliness, unless you choose a suitable partner for such perpetual pleasure, which results from your *own* stinging kiss.'

I thought of my boyfriend and his deep-humming needles caressing my flesh as he'd created the dragon and the tiger, but I also remembered his constant request to give me more 'special, intimate' adornment, one for our mutual benefit, and I asked the sister, 'Do the bites show like scars, or do they go away?'

'Ours were on our breasts, which were decorated, but yours will be on each hip, which likewise will be re-embellished, with more mutually pleasing designs,' Lotus explained, before guiding me over to the stool where I usually sat to do my work. Before I'd had a chance to completely sit down, Vermilion kneeled down beside me and, without hesitation, opened her painted lips wide and sunk her incisors into my flesh. The pain was brief, intense . . . yet highly erotic, like losing one's maidenhead on a smaller scale, followed by the soothing pleasure that comes after that first, yet final, pain. Seconds after she bit me, I felt a small fuzzy warmth on my skin, which just as suddenly departed from my flesh, leaving an odd coolness in its place. When I glanced down, I saw the translucent streaking movement of something small and orange-black-striped darting away, until it became utterly transparent and finally vanished in a haze of small dots of colour that disappeared into the surrounding air. But before the last of the flecks of freed ink, which had once been my tiger, vanished. I felt a second sharp, moist quadruple jabbing in my other hip, and I turned my head in time to see a quartz-bright flurry of flapping wings and an undulating serpentine-fanged head rising up from my bleeding flesh, up past the bent head of Peony and into the warm air of the studio – before it, too, turned into a miasma of blue, emerald-green and bronze-yellow freed ink, which rained down on the tiled floor in tiny, splashing droplets of pooling colour.

Following my earlier example, the sisters lovingly applied daubs of ointment to my hips, then Lotus bent down over my lap, tongue aimed at my mons, before I said, 'Not now – I'm having my monthly.'

This brought a smile of surprise to her face, and she said, 'This is an auspicious sign – you're in a time of great power, of flowing *yin*, which mimics *yang* action. The magic of a woman's blood is most potent, and when added to the alchemy of the lusting blood . . .' Her voice trailed off seductively, as if allowing me to come up with the possibilities inherent in my new-found condition. She then used her hands to massage my mons (being careful not to dislodge the tampon string trailing out) and motioned for her sisters to likewise caress my breasts through my thin T-shirt.

Only after I'd come once more, the musky gushing lubrication pleasantly cooled by the surrounding air, and I shuddered under their expert, soothing petting, did they offer a more tangible payment to me, after properly tying their dresses closed, and smoothing down their ruffled hair. With a sweet, secret smile, Vermilion reached into her coat-dress pocket and extracted a small black and red embroidered satin pouch, while saying, 'Wear these when your own special tattoo is applied – the sensation will be most exquisite while the needle vibrates.' Then she handed the pouch to me.

Opening it, I saw the liquid metallic glint of two beautifully carved ben-wah balls within and, as I started to voice my thanks, Peony added, 'These can also be attached with a silken string to the underside of a man's Jade Shaft or Heavenly Dragon Pillar while *it* is being tattooed. Our original benefactor assured us that the sensations are equally erotic. Perhaps he who will embellish *you* will appreciate them once it is time for you to decorate him – he was the one who applied your tiger and dragon, no?'

Nodding, I merely smiled as they departed my shop, all the while creating suitable designs for my own mons in my head, although I'd allow my boyfriend the pleasure of choosing his own design once I'd bestowed my new-found blood kiss on him – after he'd tattooed me and discovered just *how* real a tattoo could actually feel.

Of course, I'd have to do some boning up on Chinese sexual literature first – after all, once a customer of mine gets a tattoo, it *is* uniquely hers, and her alone.

But I did recall the term 'Jade Veins' for the labia, which I found *most* appealing . . .

Two-Timer

Louise Demartigny

Two-Timer

Melanie liked to make her views on pornography clear as early as possible in her relationships.

Men were usually full of admiration for her no-nonsense approach to the subject, she'd found. They'd agree when she asked how could porn possibly be exploitative when people were being paid so much money to get their kit off? And they'd laugh when she said if it was OK to buy a burger when you were hungry, what was wrong with making a beeline for the top shelf when you fancied a wank? It made her more attractive, she thought. Well, a porn-friendly woman who wasn't going to get insecure about the cover of *Loaded* was bound to be a bit of a goer in bed, wasn't she?

Strangely, although she'd been dating Jamie for over a month now, the subject had never been broached. Since they'd met, literally bumping into each other as they reached for the same vintage denim jacket in Oxfam, there'd always been so many other things to talk about and do – bands she'd never heard of to see, parts of the city she didn't know existed to discover, second-hand record shops to rummage around on a Saturday afternoon. Even the things that sounded really corny like walking in the park and playing I-Spy were oddly enjoyable. As for the sex, it was the best ever. With Jamie, Melanie had never felt the need to show off in bed – or anywhere else, for that matter. Hell, he'd even seen her without make-up once! As most of Melanie's relationships didn't last as long as a month, she had no idea whether this was normal behaviour or not. It had started to worry her. Was she becoming boring because sitting in front of the TV and talking about each other's day at work was suddenly a perfectly acceptable way to spend an evening? Maybe it was time to remind Jamie just how broad-minded and liberated she was, she decided. She didn't want him to lose interest, after all.

'Did I tell you about the time I encouraged my friend Ann-Marie to do a topless shoot for a men's magazine?' she began one evening, stretching herself voluptuously on Jamie's sofa. She'd chosen her moment carefully. Their evening of pizza and *ER* was showing every promise of turning into a full-on snogging session at any moment. 'I saw the advert, persuaded her to do it and went with her to the studio. She said she hated it but she earned loads of cash. I think those sort of mags are great. I'd do it myself if I had bigger tits.'

Jamie shook his head incredulously and wriggled free from Melanie's virtual mouth lock. 'You mean you agree with how those tacky magazines turn women into sex objects?'

'They celebrate women! And do you think we can't get turned on by them as well?' Melanie pressed her breasts against him. She'd been hoping he'd contradict her when she said her breasts weren't large enough.

'They just seem wrong.'

'What's wrong with earning money from the assets nature gives you? You've met Ann-Marie. You know she's like a one-woman episode of *Baywatch*!'

'Nature also gave her a beautiful mind.' Jamie pulled himself away and stared fixedly at the TV. A little girl had just been told she'd never walk again following a hit-and-run incident on the streets of Chicago. Jamie studied George Clooney's grief-stricken expression with a furrowed brow. 'Ann-Marie's a really nice person,' he said finally. 'There are other things you could encourage her to do.'

Melanie was speechless. This wasn't going to plan. Couldn't he see this wasn't the point? She chewed on some cold, hardened pizza crust. Jamie might be gorgeous, funny and clever, but he had a hell of a sense of timing.

She pondered the discussion the following morning. As a freelance interior designer, she could pick and choose her working hours. Jamie had got up early to take the sixth-formers he taught at the local comprehensive on a geography field trip. Although he'd left her with a cup of tea, a slice of toast and a spectacular orgasm, she felt a sharp unease pierce her domestic bliss. What did he mean when he said that Ann-Marie was a 'really nice person' and had a 'beautiful mind'? Had he watched her that closely? OK, so he was a kind and compassionate sort of guy. That's why she liked him in the first place. Hell, even his teabags came from organic plantations run by fairly paid Kenyan workers with full access to trade unions. He was bound to care about the people he met, but still . . .

Melanie tried to pull herself together. What was she playing at? She was almost thirty, a self-made woman, and perfectly at ease with herself? This was real life, not some Valentine world of hearts and roses and promises of everlasting devotion! So what if Ann-Marie was the archetypal sex goddess, all flowing raven locks, pouting smile and gravity-defying curves? Was it really that strange or catastrophic if Jamie did fancy her? Maybe, years ago, Melanie occasionally felt a pang of jealousy when the usual Saturday night stampede of hunks pushed past her to slobber over Ann-Marie. But that was all in the past. That was before Melanie had started her own business and become a success on her own terms. She wasn't going to start feeling threatened by anyone, least of all her own best friend!

In fact, where was that book that Jamie had been reading in bed the other morning? There'd been something in it about everyone being beautiful in his or her own way. Melanie fumbled under the bed and, pulling out a slim volume, settled back on her pillow. A few meditations on her own inner loveliness would soon have her feeling better. But just a minute! What was this? Half a cup of ethically produced tea spilled on the duvet as Melanie came face to face with Jamie's modest collection of porn. Was it some kind of joke? After all, wasn't this the very material that he'd denounced as 'tacky' just hours ago? He was obviously ashamed, Melanie decided. Bless him! It was all quite funny in a way. They'd have a laugh about it later, maybe look at it together. It was cool.

She began to flick through the glossy pages and, noticing a bookmark fall out of the centre pages, settled back with what was left of her tea to see what turned her boyfriend on in his deepest, secret fantasies. When Melanie's eyes met those of the model, however, her smile froze. For there, staring straight at her was Ann-Marie. The topless photo shoot! Melanie gasped at the sight of her friend reclining, under the title 'Secretary Sluts', on an office desk, clip-charts, staplers and graphs on the wall behind her. Was it really Ann-Marie, whose eyes were smouldering behind a pair of sensible glasses, and whose shiny, scarlet lips were pursed together, as if preparing to give someone his tightest blow-job ever? She certainly didn't look as if she was hating it, as she pushed her huge, oiled breasts together and forced them to spill out of her neat, white shirt, her large nipples swollen and ready to be sucked and licked. Her legs, propped on some ring-binder files marked 'Sales', were so wide apart that her open crotch, just visible under a short tartan skirt, offered itself completely to her audience. Under the tight, white knickers – which would have been wholesome, had they not been two sizes too small – the juicy delights beneath could only be imagined from the soft, shaved lines and curves of her half-hidden pussy. 'I usually wear tight blouses, short skirts and no knickers to work,' Melanie read under the picture. 'I cross and uncross my legs in front of my boss. He pretends not to look, but I know he can see right up to my bare pussy. I also splash cold water on my nipples before walking through the Accounts department. I like to raise temperatures and probably a few other things! There are five or six horny men in there and I often fantasise that I'm stuck in the lift with all of them at the same time. I'd really have my hands full and no one would rush to press the emergency button!' Melanie could almost hear the rustle of smart shirts, the unzipping of tailored trousers, as many a stirring cock sought relief.

The magazine slid to the floor. It was one thing approving of porn, she thought, and another when the model was a living, breathing person, ideally positioned to steal your man! Melanie felt betrayed, even though no one had actually done anything. Or had they? Was there really such a big difference between Jamie masturbating about Ann-Marie and having sex with her in person? And did this mean that he thought about Ann-Marie when he was in bed with her? Sick and dizzy with confusion and hurt, Melanie waited for the pounding in her heart to stop. But it didn't. Neither could she stop the barrage of images that had started to flicker, unbidden, across her mind's eye like videotape. There was Jamie, alone at night, his cock swelling at the sight of Ann-Marie's huge tits, the knickers, pulled tight across her cunt, the hungry look that beckoned to him alone. What did he imagine doing to her? With astonishment, Melanie realised that the dampness between her legs wasn't post-orgasm bliss but pre-orgasm craving. She brushed an exploratory finger between her labia and almost dissolved in fierce pleasure. As she started to circle her clit, she pictured Ann-Marie as the new admin assistant at Jamie's school, starting work amidst a blaze of rumours that she'd only been successful because she'd given the headmaster a blow-job under the desk. Or that at her last company, she'd let three of her colleagues fuck her in the toilets, one at a time while the others queued outside. Now here she was, working late one night in the office. 'Is there anything you want, Mr O'Neill?' She'd walk across to Jamie in her tight blouse and short skirt. Then she'd sink to her knees slowly, silently and his face would contort with desire as she undid his flies. Tilting her head backwards, she'd take him in her mouth all in one go and he'd sigh and pant as, trousers around his ankles, he thrust vigorously, the sound of her sucking turning him on more. It wouldn't take him long to come and he'd be so far down her throat, she wouldn't taste a drop. Melanie's fingers juddered against her slippery insides as she hurtled towards the strongest orgasm she'd ever had.

When she got her breath back, she felt no better. How could she let herself masturbate about her boyfriend masturbating about her friend, for heaven's sake? The situation was serious. It didn't need further complications: it needed answers. It was eleven o'clock. With any luck, she'd catch Ann-Marie before she started work. She had a favour to ask.

'You want me to try to seduce Jamie?' Ann-Marie almost dropped the kettle in shock. 'Are you mad?'

'I don't want you to seduce him for real! Just give him, you know, a tiny shred of an idea that you might be up for it. I want to know what his reaction would be.' Melanie couldn't help seeing Ann-Marie in a new light. The plain white T-shirt strained across her breasts and the old jeans hugged her arse so tightly they were like a second skin. 'Before I go any further with the relationship,

I need to know if I can trust him and to see how he copes with temptation.' She explained, as Ann-Marie bit into an éclair. That could be Jamie's cock she was licking, she thought. That wasn't cream that she was wiping from the side of her mouth, it was his spunk.

'What if he can't?'

'He's history and you'll have done me a big favour.'

'So what am I supposed to do exactly?'

'I don't know. I guess I didn't really think that far.'

'And what about Simon? Or did you forget that I have a serious partner?'

Simon was Ann-Marie's live-in lover. Melanie and he enjoyed a straightforward relationship, in that they were both at ease with their plain and simple hatred of each other.

'Well, it's not as if you're actually going to be unfaithful.'

As if on cue, the door swung open and Simon walked in, worse for wear after a busy morning plumbing or building or joining, whatever it was that Melanie could never remember he did. He looked pointedly at the glittery clip in Melanie's hair. She glanced with undisguised loathing at his short, over-gelled hair and the skin-tight vest that she supposed he thought enhanced his unnaturally pneumatic muscles. Simon always provoked a mixture of utter repulsion and abject pity in Melanie. Didn't he realise that he looked like one of those sad men who toured working men's clubs and called themselves something with 'boyz' in the title?

'It's Barbie girl!' he sneered, putting a possessive arm round Ann-Marie's waist. 'Not going already, are you?'

'Much as I enjoy seeing you, Simon,' Melanie replied sweetly, 'I seem to have this reflex action to grab my coat whenever you're around. Odd, isn't it?'

She let herself out, embarrassed. What had possessed her to think of such a stupid idea? Although Simon was a vain, sarcastic dick-head, it was obvious that Ann-Marie only had eyes for him. And if Jamie preferred to be with someone else, he would be, wouldn't he? How many times had she thought about Brad Pitt or Keanu Reeves or the cute one from the programme about vets in a state of undress, after all?

Melanie would have all but forgotten if Ann-Marie hadn't called the next day. 'I'll do it,' she whispered, 'but on one condition: you do the same with Simon.'

Melanie spluttered. 'But why? You and Simon are a proper couple! You've been living with each other for years. You're on first name terms with each other's grandmas. You haven't got anything to worry about.'

'I'm curious.'

'Well, maybe it's not such a good idea really.'

'Come on, Mel! It's an excellent idea! And I've got a really good plan. How about next Saturday we arrange to go for lunch, just you, Jamie and me? Tell him I've been feeling depressed lately and need a shoulder to cry on. He's a caring chap, so he'll be chuffed to be invited. You get called away by a client and . . .'

'And?'

'Leave the rest to me!'

'And what plans do you have for me?' Melanie tried to picture herself, naked except for a hard hat, swinging from scaffolding on one of Simon's building sites, or sitting next to him in a low-cut top, murmuring, 'Ooh, Simon, show us that lead piping again.' The thought of having any sort of charm that would turn Simon on, let alone encourage two words that weren't 'fuck' and 'off', was ludicrous.

'While I'm with Jamie, you'll be at ours, making sketches of the lounge because I've asked you to give us some advice on redecorating it.'

'Have you?'

'I'm about to. When Simon comes back from the gym at around one, there you'll be, alone . . .'

Melanie squirmed. The rules were vastly unbalanced. Ann-Marie knew that Simon was devoted to her. Why would he stray when he knew he had a sex goddess at home? It would be as pointless as eating fish fingers when you could have prime salmon on a silver platter for a lot less effort. Ann-Marie was obviously only pretending that she wanted Melanie to test Simon. It was nice of her to try to create the illusion that Melanie wasn't the only suspicious, neurotic bag of insecurity that she'd obviously come across as yesterday, but Melanie wasn't fooled.

'It's up to you,' Ann-Marie urged.

Then again, now she had the chance, wouldn't it be a shame to waste it? If she didn't take it, wouldn't she always wonder whether she could really trust Jamie? And if there were doubts, she might as well end it now.

'OK, it's a deal.' Melanie had the uncomfortable feeling that she really had no choice.

It wasn't until the following Saturday that Melanie realised what she had to lose. She watched Jamie get up, smelled the familiar morning smell of fruity shower gel and fresh coffee, heard the rattle of crockery, the click of the toaster as if for the last time. Tomorrow, she might be waking in her own bed as a single woman. And Jamie might have turned into just some bastard she used to go out with. Melanie couldn't help feeling that somewhere along the line there'd been the opportunity to deal with her doubts differently. They could have had a sensible discussion about the magazine like the adults they were supposed to be, for instance. But now it was too late. The plan had taken on a life of its own and Melanie was being carried in its unstoppable current, unable to help herself. Besides, it wasn't really up to her, was it? The forbidden fruit would be there for Jamie's taking. It was his call, not hers.

'Damn, I can't make lunch,' she said, as Jamie buttoned his shirt. 'Those clients who want me to design their new restaurant called when you were in the shower and today's the only day I can meet them. Are you OK to meet Ann-Marie yourself?'

'No problem!' Jamie's enthusiasm was discouraging. 'I know how important that deal is. How about I cook later and you tell me all about it?' He kissed Melanie on the cheek. Any seeds of guilt she might have felt dissolved in the fumes of his special occasion after-shave.

Melanie didn't feel any better when she saw Ann-Marie. She was looking even more gorgeous than ever in an ultra-feminine mini-dress, whose frills and flounces gathered at the top, Brigitte Bardot style, to guide all eyes, as if by accident, to a teasing inch of cleavage. The 'sexy, moi?' look was completed to perfection by a high, girlie ponytail that oozed the same accidental horniness as the dress and a careful coating of make-up that made the rosy cheeks and dewy eyes look completely natural. Melanie looked down at her own combat trousers and vest that she'd always thought were sexy in a kind of ass-kicking woman-of-action type of way and suddenly felt as seductive as a sack of potatoes.

'There's been a change of plan.' Ann-Marie fluttered her Bambi eyelashes apologetically. 'I completely forgot. Simon's old school friend Harry's visiting this weekend, so they're both out all day. I'm ever so sorry. Look, shall we cancel? We could do it another day.'

'No,' Melanie said, relieved. Ann-Marie knew as well as she did that Simon had nothing to do with it. It was about Jamie. Generous of her to keep up the pretence, though.

'Well, if you're sure that's OK?'

'Sure. I'll hang around here for a while. I might as well do those sketches for you as I've got my sketchbook. I'm going to Jamie's at seven. Call me beforehand if you can.'

'I'll make sure we've stopped shagging by half six, then.' Ann-Marie started to giggle, but stopped as soon as she caught sight of Melanie's face. 'You know I'm only joking, right?' She planted a smooth, lip-glossed kiss on her cheek. 'He's safe with me.'

The door slammed decisively and the room seemed to echo with finality. Melanie sat on the sofa and tried to concentrate on her drawings. However, there was something about the hushed sound of her pencil gliding across the smooth paper, like fingers brushing naked skin, that made her think about sex. She pictured Jamie, sitting outside the café at one of those discreet tables with the parasols that could be tilted inwards for optimum privacy. He'd glimpse Ann-Marie walking down the street and drink her in, lap up the way her breasts strained and swayed gently under the thin fabric of her dress, the way the flounced hem climbed her bare leg with every footstep. She'd sit down and he'd try not to stare at her deepening cleavage as she kissed him on the cheek. Maybe they'd order a bottle of chilled white wine, talk, laugh, share secrets and slowly meander into that special, intimate place where people go when they share too much personal information and alcohol. Maybe he'd suggest going back to his place to lend her one of those New Age books he was always reading about self-esteem and inner confidence.

Back in his flat, he'd make coffee and they'd talk more. She'd be tearful and grateful for his advice about her problems; he'd be tipsy and flattered. She'd touch his arm, look into his eyes, tell him how understood she felt and, before they could help themselves, they'd be pulling at each other's clothes. Her dress would slide down silently, effortlessly. He'd see that she'd been wearing no knickers and all the blood in his body would make a beeline for his cock, although he'd already be iron-hard after an afternoon staring at the body he wanked about. He'd tug at her lacy bra, feel the huge nipples harden between his fingers, and, cradling a full breast in each hand, push her towards the sink. She'd turn round, spread her legs wide and hold on to the taps for support as he pushed his swollen cock into her from behind.

Melanie realised that she was hot and damp between the legs and started rubbing herself feverishly as she relived the scenario her imagination had created. Well, what harm could it do? Hastily, she removed her trousers and knickers, the thrill of being half naked and masturbating on someone else's sofa adding to the rush of excitement. Would Jamie have reached his climax already? At this very moment was Ann-Marie pushing her arse into Jamie's groin, manoeuvring him, skilfully moulding her own orgasm from her best friend's boyfriend's dick?

Melanie must not have heard the door click open, must not have noticed the footsteps padding down the hall, entering the lounge, and finally stopping abruptly at the sofa. Because when she opened her eyes, who should be staring down at her but Simon? And not only Simon, but a sort of Simon-mark-two, who might have had shoulder length, sun-streaked hair and a different designer's name splattered over his too-tight T-shirt but appeared to be from exactly the same brainless-beefcake-and-proud-of-it mould.

'Um, right.' Melanie squirmed and grabbed her trousers, glad that she'd kept her bra on at least. 'Sorry.'

'Is this some sort of early birthday present, Si? You got a whore in for me!' The stranger took off his wraparound shades and ran his eyes over her approvingly. They were distant, appraising, as if she were a new product he was weighing up at the supermarket. 'Cheers, mate!' He rubbed his hands in greedy anticipation and started to unzip his chinos.

'Who the fuck do you think you are?' Melanie hurriedly fumbled on the floor for her knickers, trying to display as little as possible to the stranger's probing eyes.

'Harry,' he said, and gave a deep, throaty laugh, which, if it was supposed to make him sound attractive to her, was a dismal failure. He held out his hand. She ignored it.

'That's not a whore; it's one of Ann-Marie's mates.' Simon grabbed the TV remote control and sighed as if the whole thing was a minor inconvenience. 'Nothing worth getting excited about, mate.' He looked distinctly uninterested as he sat down on the chair opposite and channel hopped to the football. Melanie felt a pang of rejection. How dare he? Sure, there was no love lost between them, but he could have looked slightly more, well, interested. She was naked and masturbating on his settee, after all! He hadn't even given her a second glance or tried to get a furtive glimpse of her tits.

'I know you're an interior designer, Mel,' he began, concentrating on the match, 'but can't you get off on our new light fittings in your own home? I can lend you an Ikea catalogue if you want.'

'Well, your light fittings are a whole lot sexier than you, I suppose.' Melanie glowered, ignoring Harry's gurgles of laughter. 'And a hell of a lot wittier to.'

'Shame!' Harry sighed, his finger still poised over his zip. 'I could have done with giving her one. I haven't got it up for fucking weeks, man.' He ran his hand over his bulging groin.

'Wonder why?' Melanie couldn't help saying. 'Look, has one of you hidden my knickers? The sooner I find them, the sooner I'm out of here.'

'See what I mean?' Simon said to Harry. 'She thinks she's sexy, but give her a chance of a good fuck and she'll run a mile. The frigid cow could turn yoghurt sour.'

Melanie felt a surge of pure anger, too sudden to be diluted by sense, logic or reason. What gave this wanker the right to judge her? What made him think he knew her? 'What would you know about a good fuck, Simon?' she hissed.

'I'd show you, but I just don't fancy you, darling.' Simon shrugged apologetically. 'Sorry, love.'

The bastard! Right, she'd show him. Before she knew what she was doing, she lay back on the sofa and, giving her best pornographic stare at the gob-smacked Harry, spread her legs wide apart. She started to stroke herself again, not gently this time, but urgently, defiantly, pulling her lips apart with the fingers of both hands. Simon turned up the volume but Harry needed no further encouragement.

'Bloody hell, are you sure you're not paying her?' Harry bent over her and shoved a rough hand up her bra. Melanie was going to protest at his uncouth approach but one look at Simon's sneer stopped her. Besides, wasn't her groin flooding anew as, kneeling above her, with one leg at either side of her body, Harry started to rub both nipples brisky between finger and thumb, pinching and pulling them outwards, teasing them to their full length. 'Nice and pert,' he murmured. Her breasts had never been touched so firmly before. Usually men fondled them gently, assumed she liked a gentle hand, wanted to give her pleasure. This man obviously had no such altruistic reasons. He just wanted to grope some tit and hers happened to be available to him. Accompanied by the fleshy sound of fingers grappling with lace and a televised football roar, Melanie found her bra being deftly whisked from under her.

'Why don't you come and suck some tit, mate?' Harry called across to Simon. 'If you don't like the bird, this'll take your mind of it.' Melanie shivered as, without warning, half a can of lager frothed over her naked breasts. 'Come on, a tit each.'

'You want to watch it, mate,' Simon said flatly, without looking. 'She'll kick you in the balls in a minute.'

'It's all right, isn't it, love?' Harry wiped the liquid around her swollen nipples. 'It's only a bit of fun, isn't it?'

'Course,' Melanie said brightly. She wasn't going to admit that having half a pint of Tennants Extra drip down her belly wasn't high on her list of sexual fantasies. Mind you, Harry had started to suck it nice and vigorously off her tits, so maybe she'd have to re-evaluate that one.

But bloody Simon was still riveted to the football! Melanie had an idea that would teach him not to judge her so easily. Reaching out suddenly for Harry's crotch, she pushed him gently backwards on the settee and, kneeling over him, her arse in the air, unzipped him and started to lick his prick. It wasn't bad, she noticed, as far as cocks go. It was a bit too slender for her tastes, but had a good length and was nice and smooth. Even if he had the worst, ugliest, most misshapen cock in the world, she'd still be giving this plonker a blow-job he'd never forget though, and then they'd see if Simon still found Manchester United so fascinating! She started to flick her tongue around his tip in long, fast strokes and felt a thrill of triumph when he shouted, in a voice hoarse with desire, 'This one's good, Si. You should have a go after me.'

With Harry's cock down her throat, Melanie couldn't see whose hands had started to stroke her upturned arse, or which man was rubbing her buttocks, gently at first and then more vigorously until she felt them being stretched and pulled apart. She gasped at the unexpected but delicious, cool feeling of her anus being exposed to the light of day.

Over a televised American voice enthusing about stone-ground pizzas 'just like they make 'em in Chicago!' Melanie thought she heard a bottle being unscrewed. Not more lager! Then a familiar fruity smell coincided with the sensation of oiliness on her buttocks. Olive oil! They were oiling her up! She felt flushed with victory. Simon had relented. Otherwise, how could one man be holding her buttocks apart and the other delicately circling her anus like that? Around and around went the oiled finger. No one spoke. On TV a cartoon penguin was telling children how good Readybrek was for them when, suddenly, the finger pushed its way into Melanie's greased-up arsehole. She bit her lip. She'd never liked the idea of anal sex, had never understood how it could possibly feel sexy or pleasurable, yet, as the finger pushed higher and deeper than she thought possible, she felt as if a shock wave had just arced to her clit like lightning. What was this feeling? Pain or pleasure? Yes, she'd squirmed, but it was painful; why did she want more? As not one, but two fingers now slipped into her, filling her totally, she felt that the pleasure was somehow too much, that the waves of delight that were flooding across her, cancelling out every other sensation in their path would drown her, suffocate her. Which man was doing this to her? Or was it both of them? They were sniggering, so were they sharing her? And, more importantly, how could she possibly answer the urgent calls of her clit in this position?

She was relieved when Harry's cock started to twitch in her mouth. As the fingers were pulled out of her, Harry suddenly kneeled above her. 'Hold her up, Si!' he called, wanking furiously, and there was just time for a jet of hot, white spunk to land on her face. She wiped it away on the back of her hand, not able to help tasting its bitterness on her lips. She didn't like him that much. In fact, come to think of it, she didn't like either of them, so how was she managing to feel so damned turned on?

'Atta girl!' Harry looked her in the eyes for the first time. There was no tenderness, no intimacy, just a quick wink – the acknowledgement of a favour. 'Fancy a go, Si?'

Melanie looked at Simon. Although he couldn't hide an impressive hard-on that was straining in his jeans, he shrugged nonchalantly and glared at the screen. Melanie was now desperate. She was no stranger to satisfying herself, but with two men there, it was criminal. Still, she wasn't going to demean herself by asking for it, especially from Simon. She squirmed her legs together, wondering how long she'd be able to get away with it before anyone noticed.

'Thinks she's too good to be fucked by me.' Simon downed the rest of the lager. It was true: she was too good to be fucked by him, but that wasn't the point. For the first time Melanie realised that sex wasn't always the same as making love.

'Well, I like to see them come.' Melanie tried not to show that she was grateful when Harry jumped up and kneeled at the end of the sofa. 'Spread your legs, sweet-heart!' Melanie promptly shoved her dripping cunt into his face before he had the chance to change his mind. Harry's tongue was hot and agile. He completely ignored her clit – well, what did she expect? – and plunged his tongue deep into her hole. She moved against it slowly, trying to pace herself. Although waves of lust were trick-ling from her groin like high tide, she wanted him to work for it. She twisted her head around to see if Simon was watching and the sight almost made her come there and then. Not only had he taken his cock out of his trousers, but it was by far the largest and plumpest she'd ever seen. So when he straddled her chest, she put her lips around it triumphantly, even though the juices of his friend still coated her mouth. Maybe he did only have eyes for Ann-Marie but, right now, it was she who was driving him to distraction, she whom he desired and wanted, just like Jamie desired and wanted Ann-Marie when he looked at her picture. Empathy worked in strange ways, she thought.

'A tenner you'll come first, Si,' Harry panted. There was the rustling sound of a condom and suddenly it was Harry, hard again already, pushing his cock at her entrance, nudging it impatiently to make a swift entrance. Then Melanie was full of cock, as she took both of them deep inside her. Harry held her legs over his shoulder to get a deeper thrust and, Melanie realised happily, to make desperate grabs where he thought her clit might be. She wanted the moment to go on and on. Two men made sex twice as good. There was twice the grinding and panting, twice the deeply sexy smell of sweat and naked flesh, twice the exquisite pulse of pure pleasure, and twice the filth when she thought that she really, really shouldn't be doing this. But it was she who broke the moment, coming to a spine-tingling orgasm that streamed from her groin to every millimetre of flesh and beyond. Seconds later, to a husky cry, she felt her mouth fill with so much spunk that it spilled from her lips. Finally, Harry crashed to the floor like a log.

Melanie was the first to speak. 'That's a tenner you owe me,' she said to Harry.

'You've got nothing to worry about.' Melanie's hand shook so much at the sound of Ann-Marie's voice that she almost dropped her mobile. 'It's obvious Jamie would never stray. We had lunch and then went our separate ways after an hour.'

Melanie panicked. Should she tell Ann-Marie? She was already feeling as guilty as hell, as Jamie flitted around her, filling her glass with wine and planting small, tender kisses on her cheeks. She bided her time and changed the subject. 'So, um, what did you do this afternoon then?'

'Nothing much. Watched TV with Simon and Harry.'

'This afternoon? With Simon and Harry?'

'Yes,' Ann-Marie said calmly. 'Why?'

'Oh, nothing.'

'I'm glad our little plan didn't work out.' Ann-Marie laughed. 'Glad we're not single women, crying on each other's shoulders tonight.'

'Yes! Stupid idea!'

'Was that your clients again?' Jamie placed a home-cooked nut-roast on the table with mock flourish.

'No. It was Ann-Marie.'

'Ann-Marie was here this afternoon,' he breezed, lighting a candle. 'She borrowed some books.'

'She didn't go home then?'

'No, she left just before you came. Why?'

For a moment, Melanie thought Jamie looked nervous, but it could have been the candlelight.

'Nothing, nothing at all.' As they clinked glasses, Melanie knew that things were going to be fine. Just fine.

Dorian Gray Never
Did This

Maria Lloyd

Dorian Gray Never Did This

'Do you know that you look as beautiful and boyish as my mental image of Dorian Gray?'

'Well, thank you, I guess.' I shrug.

'It is a true compliment, you know. I must have read Oscar Wilde's book a dozen times and I've a firm visual idea of Dorian. It's amazing. You *are* my Dorian. That's rarer than looking like a celebrity, I can tell you. It's as if you walked straight out of my imagination. And my imagination is anything but straight, darling.'

'Yup, I can believe that. But I ain't no figure from your imagination and flattery won't get you any free drinks. Now what'll you have?'

The young transvestite pouts her coral lips; her false eyelashes flutter as she decides. 'Bottle of schnapps please, chilled.'

I open the chill cabinet, flick the bottle open and swing back in one easy rhythm.

'I really mean it, you know. It's uncanny. Your bone structure's fantastic,' he-she continues to enthuse.

I take the money and smile.

'Well, thank you, darlin', but I'm afraid you're the wrong sex for me, however femme you look.'

He-she pouts once again, flicks back blonde corkscrew curls, hands on hips as cleavage leans closer to me across the bar.

'You don't think I'm woman enough for you?'

I shrug my regrets, smile.

'What's your name, Barkeep?' the trannie persists.

'Del. Short for Delia,' I say.

'I'm Karla. Long for Karl. And you don't know what you're passing up.'

I smile once more. Flattered but bewildered by Karla's intense stare, the provocative tongue waggle. He means it, it's beyond a joke this come-on. Dorian Gray must have figured large in this man-girl's fantasies. I shake my head apologetically as Karla hits on her schnapps, turns away in defeat.

'See you around, cunt-tease,' I can't resist adding.

'You sure will. Ciao.'

Karla is very tipsy but I can't help liking her style, as she swings those hips in her tight skirt and strappy high heels. Sassy.

Karla walks over to a guy in leathers, who is sitting alone at a table in the corner, and no doubt Karla starts some seductive spiel because the guy is soon smiling, making room for her. She turns round to check I'm still watching, winks and mouths 'score'. I wink in congratulations, get back to polishing some wine glasses with a linen tea towel.

I like my job in this mixed gay bar in Holborn. The place has been restored to genuine Victorian splendour. Frosted-glass windows, mahogany booths, half-tiled walls, bare wooden floor. The bar is dark and glossy and curves the whole length of the main room. Brass lamps and framed prints from *Punch* or *The Strand* magazine adorn the walls. There's a proper Music Hall or Gin Palace feel to the place. Dorian Gray himself might have frequented somewhere like this a hundred years ago if he had fancied a bit of rough and had been, like, real.

Nowadays we get a lot of straight-looking gays dining with long-term partners during office lunch hours (we have a Thai chef in Monday to Friday) and a young gay and lesbian crowd early evening before they move on to art cinemas or nightclubs. Followed by the gay students from London University, already tanked up on cheap booze from the union bars, cruising in the hope of capturing a handsome stranger for the night. Occasionally a shocked group of tourists ends up in the middle of this for a drink or two before they beat a retreat. But we never get any trouble from anyone.

Yes, it's a mixed clientele and I'm never bored people-watching from my side of the bar. I've a few old lovers and many good friends among the regulars. On Saturday nights we have a disco in the back, usually with a fun theme, and Sundays is the drag queen cabaret. We try to ring the changes and come up with different ideas. Next Saturday we're holding an eighties revival disco; everyone can dress up as New Romantics for a bit of a laugh and the winner gets a bottle of vintage champagne. I've decided to dress as the thin white duke – always had a soft spot for Bowie.

The young trannie, Karla, is still glancing back at me, even as the leather-clad guy puts a hand on her stockinged knee and they start to neck. I give a half-smile, wonder what the hell her game is. She's been in most evenings these past couple of weeks, with a crowd of art students from the Chelsea. I'm guessing she's an art student too. This is new though, coming here alone on the pick-up, goading me to test how much of a real woman she is. She must have a thing for butch dykes. I wonder if Karla's suddenly discovered drugs, but dismiss the idea. Nope, just a fledgling trannie testing the boundaries of sexuality, just like I did when I first moved to London two years ago.

Karla, however, considers I haven't tested the landscape of my own sexuality far enough. Would love to play the pioneer with me. That much is apparent from his Dorian Gray come-on. Well, I once considered myself a possible bi, but that possibility has receded since most guys I meet seem far too obvious or crass for a good sensual fuck. Maybe Karla's got a point though. Never say never in this libertine world.

As Karla and the guy eventually leave, Karla lingers by the door, turns to blow a kiss, mouths, 'Next time, Dorian' over to me.

How cute.

Next lunchtime Karla comes in the bar dressed as Karl. Black jeans and T-shirt, still traces of last night's make-up on his pretty, mobile face. He orders a Guinness from Jack in muted fashion while I'm taking a food order. I guess the Guinness is his liquid lunch, plus hair of the dog. He sits at the bar, flicks listlessly through a copy of Q magazine. So I've plenty of time to size him up.

It's funny, but he's more attractive to me in this downbeat version. He is really feminine in a young-boy kind of way. His skin is good; his cheeks are high and he sports a neat little nose. His eyes are tawny-hazel, quite almond-shaped and lidded in a 'come to bed' fashion. His natural hair is dark blond and cropped close to his head. His lips are his best feature though, generous and at rest form an angelic bow, a bit like Liv Ullman's. As he hunches over and reads the magazine, his long fingers idly rub the back of his cropped head in a feminine, vulnerable gesture. It makes me want to smooth the back of his neck and nuzzle him affectionately. I guess he must about 20, and I'm 25. Quite mature and street-wise compared to his young trannie persona.

'Anything worth reading?' I ask eventually, bored by the lack of customers to serve. He looks up, blinks and smiles.

'Oh, it's you, Dorian. Didn't notice you were working today. Not really, only an interview with Marilyn Mansun if you're interested. You can keep this copy when I've finished the album reviews.'

'Ta.' I watch him take a sip of his Guinness. A little milky foam clings to his upper lip. 'How did it go last night?' I can't resist asking. He sighs.

'Oh, not so bad. I'm afraid I had brewer's droop from too much beer and schnapps, but he seemed well satisfied with his blow-job.'

'Will you see him again?'

'Naw, don't think so. Not really my type.'

'What is your type?'

'Well, I think it's Dorian Gray. What's yours?'

I laugh. 'I'm not sure. It used to be Louise Brooks but I gave up on that long ago.'

He smiles. 'That combination of unapproachable vulnerability appeals to you?'

I shrug. 'Doesn't it to everyone at some stage?'

'I guess.'

I consider a moment. Why not take a chance? He's so sweet. On impulse I hand him a voucher from the newly printed stack on a shelf behind the bar. He narrows his eyes to read it.

'Invitation to the eighties night this Saturday? Thanks, Dorian. Should be fun. Maybe I'll meet a lucious Bryan Ferry if I can't have my Dorian Gray.'

'Will you dress up? Bottle of Moët for the winner.'

He smiles, perks up. 'Yeah, neat. Will you?'

'I plan to.'

He puts the invitation in his jeans pocket, knocks his Guinness with an elbow in the process, catches the glass just in time to save most of the dark liquid.

'Sorry.'

'That's OK.' I use the towel beside the pumps to mop up the spill. I'm surprised when he reaches out to stroke my forearm with his long fingers.

'Wow, your muscles are impressive. Do you work out?'

'Whenever I can. And I practise Wing Chun.'

'Cool. Explains your enigmatic smile. Do you fancy an arm wrestle?'

I laugh, remove his long fingers with ease, unsettled by their warm dry touch on the down of my forearm.

'Naw, leave it out. You wouldn't stand a chance.'

'Saturday, maybe?'

'Maybe.'

Then I go to serve a couple of biker-dykes that have just walked in and are waiting at the other end of the bar.

I don't see Karl or his alter ego Karla over the next few days, but he starts to prey on my mind. After all, straight sex with a guy is the one deviance I have never experimented with yet. As I explained, it's never really appealed before. But, well, I hate the thought of being a virgin in any respect, especially now I've been propositioned by someone I find quite attractive. And Karl/Karla moves me in some way. Maybe it was the frank chat-up line, the obvious attraction he feels towards me. No sophistication or face-saving indifference. The little trannie must be new to the London scene. And his fragile androgyny interests me. He exudes sexual longing from every pore. He has obviously wanked his way through some teenage-hood in small-town hell and wants to try everything the big bad world has to offer. What fun to help him let rip, help break in a young thoroughbred. The sudden idea made me laugh out loud – as if I would have a clue what to do with a man's prick. And, for all his boasting, would he truly have any finesse with a fanny? The mental picture was ridiculous.

But the very image of us fumbling and experimenting like rampant 1950s teenagers made me unexpectedly horny. Hell.

I did my best to dismiss all this from my mind as quickly as it cropped up. But this Karla-prick thing was starting to obsess me. Me. I had once considered myself the most confirmed lesbian in London. What on earth could I do to preserve my sanity? The memory of Karl's pouting lips, the mystery of the thing between his legs, was tempting me as much as if I'd been randy old Socrates before taking the hemlock. What would Karla's provocative lips look like encircling my nipple? What would his real live prick look like, all engorged and horny and easing into my wet fanny? How different would it feel to the black rubber dildo I keep beside my bed?

This mixture of sexual curiosity and sensual obsession raised a fever in my blood that could not be cooled. Except, perhaps, by surrendering to the temptation Karla offered. Such depravity, to seriously consider trying out straight sex in a gay bar.

Something tells me Dorian Gray never did this.

As Saturday approached I felt as nervous as a teenager. Then I started to worry. What if Karl had forgotten his proposition of me already? He was only testing out his universal attraction factor, bless him. I had no excuse for my own brand of temporary love-madness. In the end I vowed that even if he did turn up, I would do my best to avoid him and any potential embarrassment.

Still, I took great care with my thin white duke disguise. It was fun, putting on make-up to look gaunt and decadent in a Berlin-cabaret kind of way. I sprayed a blond streak into the front of my short hair. I wore dark pleated-front trousers from an old suit I found in a charity shop, winkle-picker shoes, a crisp old-fashioned white shirt, with a stiff collar and cuffs fastened with mother of pearl cuff links. Gold-tipped black Russian cigarettes, bought from a specialist tobacconist's, and an antique gold lighter, slipped into my trouser pockets, completed the image. I have to admit I looked pretty chic in a world-weary kind of way.

OK, so Bowie in this phase was really late seventies, but he influenced the whole UK eighties pop thing with those Berlin albums. And I've always longed to play the jaded decadent.

It was a fun crowd that night, and many had made the effort to dress up. There were a dozen Siouxsie Siouxs and Adam Ants. Some had dressed in frothy cocktail gowns or dark Goth gear. The air smelled of cigarette smoke and the tons of hairspray required to support back-combed hair, along with a sharp tang of cranberry juice from the sea-breeze cocktails on special offer during Happy Hour.

One of the art students, Georgie, was taking Polaroids of everyone, waving his arms about to position groups of friends in pretentious or erotic poses, sticking the snaps along the dance-floor walls for people to examine while they danced. Monica and Tara had been roped in to DJ; they were the right age to have all the eighties stuff, from Yello's 'I Love You' to New Order's 'Blue Monday'. Not to mention 'Stand and Deliver', or 'Tainted Love'. The old Goths were busy showing the silly New Romantic moves to laughing younger regulars, more used to the dance routines of boy bands.

I was carried away by the spirit of the evening, joking with the customers as I did the rounds collecting glasses. Some asked in mock sympathy if I was still feeling 'Low' or hummed 'Heroes' and offered a kiss by the wall. A young Siouxsie clone kowtowed and asked to be my groupie, which was rather sweet. I must confess I drank quite a few of the sea-breeze cocktails, which were offered to me as I squeezed my way between the tables and the dancers, kissed many of the willing mouths, enjoyed my butt being fondled anonymously.

Then I saw her through the tipsy, disco-lit haze. The Louise Brooks of my dreams.

She was dressed in a black flapper dress adorned by jet sequins, a glittering dark sheath that stretched over flat breasts, hourglass hips and reached down to shapely ankles clad in adorable 1920s button boots. A string of pearls wrapped around her slender neck reached down to her navel. Long black-satin gloves dressed up shapely arms. The good-quality wig, in the distinctive bob, was a dark shining perfection. Pale powdered skin, dark kohl eyes and red Cupid-bow lips completed the illusion. Louise perched on a barstool in the corner of the bar, sipping a sea-breeze, holding a long cigarette holder, which she wafted towards me with elegant disdain.

It took moments to look beyond the immaculate vamp and discover the tawny eyes, the seductive smile, of Karla. She beckoned me over by crooking a gloved finger.

I felt kind of shy. Kind of excited. Back in first-date territory.

Slowly, I sauntered up to her, resting a few collected cocktail glasses on the table beside her.

'Hiya.'

'Hi.'

'Got a light? The damn thing keeps on going out in this cigarette holder.'

I took out my antique gold lighter and held the little orange flame to the end of Karla's cigarette. Watched with fascination as Karla's full, rouged lips pouted and sucked at the ivory cigarette holder's mouthpiece. Eventually the amber glow of ash resumed and Karla smiled, exhaled the smoke with satisfaction.

'Thanks.'

I was about to collect the glasses and carry on with my circuit of the bar when Karla's gloved arm snaked over my shirt sleeve.

'Please stay, have a cigarette break with me?'

I thought about that for several moments. Then I exhaled slowly and smiled.

'OK.'

And so the decision is made.

Suddenly I'm in the moment, and enjoying every shiver of anticipation. I take out one of my black Russians and light it swiftly, exhale. I like the gritty dark tobacco taste; it's something to focus on while Karla is stroking my forearm affectionately, looking up into my stern, thin duke face.

'Boy, do you look great. Like Dorian Gray if he had survived into the 1930s and taken his picture with him to an attic in Berlin. The make-up is just a vain attempt to hide his everlasting youth.'

'I'm meant to be David Bowie.' I laugh.

'I guessed.'

'You look pretty good yourself. But Louise Brooks is hardly eighties.'

She smiles; her face glows.

'Ah, but she wrote her memoirs, *Lulu in Hollywood*, during the eighties. You like it? I dressed up specially to seduce you, you know.'

Karla is stroking circles along the inside of my wrist now with a gloved index finger. The warm satin caress is delicious. I can feel myself relaxing closer to her, my pupils dilating as I admire her beauty. Then I sigh, take a drag on my cigarette and shake my head sadly.

'It can't be done. I just don't go for men.'

'And I told you that I'm more woman than you can handle. I'll worship you until you're in heaven, Dorian. You don't have to touch the thing between my legs if you don't want to. It hardly exists as far as I'm concerned.'

I chuckle at his rather odd statement. But his soft honeyed voice, which I strain to hear above the strains of 'This Charming Man', is very persuasive.

'So, you're a girl-boy who really wants to forget his prick? What exactly do you want from me?'

He juts out his tongue and waggles it slowly, strokes the front of my pleated trousers.

'I just want to be your bitch-whore, Dorian,' she says sweetly.

What an offer. Too good to refuse.

I take hold of Karla's rope of pearls and pull her

towards me, finally get a taste of those maddening lips. The lipstick is warm and moist and tastes slightly of citrus. Karla does not even try to pull away. Her lips answer mine; compliant and eager, they part to let my tongue search out and twist against hers. I kiss harder, more urgent, feeling a twitch of kundalini in my groin, because she is so yielding and this feels like forbidden fruit. The lips are rougher than a girl's, even through lipstick, and I nip the lower lip, teasing her into surrendering completely.

My hand supports the back of Karla's neck and I press against her, bend her below my kiss so that she teeters on the bar stool, and my other arm encircles her waist to hold her steady. My biceps flex under her weight. This is much more fun than the promised arm-wrestle.

She is totally at my mercy, and I can feel the curves and planes of her young body stretched beneath the gorgeous dress. I nuzzle against her breasts, smell her intoxicating scent – a mixture of fresh musk and Chanel No. 5. I can see glints of abandoned lust in her hooded tawny eyes as she squirms against me, begging me in whispers to take more liberties with her. I take my time, even though she whimpers softly and plucks at my shoulders, fondling the shaven hollow at the back of my head, her cigarette holder clattering forgotten to the floor. I press my palms against the small flat breasts and feel the nipples protrude. She begs me to pinch them between my fingers. I twist and tease her nipples between my fingers and then between my teeth through the sequinned dress until she cries out with joy.

I part her knees with one of my legs, let my hand sneak underneath her long skirts. I stroke nylon-clad calves, lace stocking tops, my palms circle the bare flesh at the top on her thighs until she's arching further back in abandon. Her mouth moves across my cheekbones and nibbles my earlobes until I'm desperate with sensual overload. I kiss along her exposed throat until I meet the tender flesh where the base of her neck meets her collarbone. I nibble and suck longingly like a vampire, deliver my first hickey for many a year.

A Polaroid flashes behind us.

'Hey, you two,' Georgie yells, 'leave it for the bedroom, you gender-bender perverts!' He laughs and moves on.

With an effort I come up for air.

'You still want to be my bitch?' I murmur as I pull Karla upright on the stool, leave her wavering.

She immediately takes my hand, laps at my palm, suckles on my fingers and thumb, gazing up at me, soft with longing. I feel a white-hot wave of lust, a melting of my pussy, just to look into those dark-amber eyes.

'Dance with me,' she says as she releases my thumb, 'for just one song.'

'Just one.'

I follow her on to the dance floor, pull her close, my hands mould the curve of her buttocks. Our loins are locked as we circle to the music. It takes a while to register that the long bulge I can feel against my pelvis is her erect cock. We glide together and my breasts graze her sequinned dress, my nipples harden as her hands trace my shoulders, stroke my flanks, circle my butt. Soon we're kissing, tonguing once more. It's strange to be so obsessed with these lips, this tongue, this body, oblivious to what is going on around us. I realise that we're dancing to Roxy Music's 'Slave to Love'. How very apt.

We can't pull away from each other at the end of the song. Our pheromones have taken over and we're glued together by sweat and need and narrow-eyed lust.

'Come with me,' I whisper. She grabs her purse before I take her hand and hurry her behind the bar, into the small locker room kept for the staff. Jack notices, winks to me. I know he'll keep watch, but that means I'll have to stay late and lock up tonight. A small price to pay for this arrangement.

The room isn't much. A few lockers, a washbasin and

waste bin, a high-backed chair, a full-length mirror screwed to a brick wall. I dig out a few night lights, which we use in the bar, from a cardboard box in the corner and light them, strew them on top of the lockers and between the washbasin taps. Their soft glow is more romantic than the naked overhead light.

I turn back to Karla and we embrace, continuing our dance. Karla undoes my flies and strokes me through cotton boxers, caresses my buttocks and sweeps gently across my moistened cunt when I least expect it with her satin-sheathed fingers.

When I can stand this heavy petting no longer, I step out of my trousers and sit down on the chair, open my legs wide, and point to my pussy. Imperious in my need. Karla gladly kneels to comply. She nuzzles her face up against my cunt, while one of my heels rests on her shoulder blade.

'My God, you smell wonderful,' she murmurs, 'like roast beef and caramel.'

I love the way she starts to gently lap around my cunt lips, then gets lost with total abandon. Her soft and insistent tongue teases my clit into erection, then my whole pussy blossoms and opens.

'Harder,' I order eventually. 'Faster.' I'm writhing against her flat broad tongue. She pauses to blow on my clit, circle my lips, slide sly little stabs of tongue deep inside me. I glance up at the mirror in front of me, watch Karla's arse waggle as she grows absorbed in pleasuring me. My face has relaxed into sublime horniness under her gentle ministrations. This thin white duke is being shown a thing or two tonight.

I groan as Karla's gloved fingers start to stroke against my hot pussy, and her little finger traces circles over my sensitive clit with such skill that my butt almost rises from the chair and my hips rock, eager for more. She looks up, my juices on her full red lips, lipstick smeared and wig slightly askew.

'Can I fist you, please?' she begs.

I nod, beyond words. I pull off the wig, grab Karla's real short hair and drag her towards me for a kiss as her fingers wriggle their way into my willing cunt.

My God, she's so *good* at it. She knows exactly where to stroke and tease, while the flat of her other hand is pressed against my pelvis, increasing the erotic pressure. Then she's down licking my clit again; her tongue sucks and gives delicate dabs and twists in double time to her insistent hand. I grip her head and ride her like the horny duke I am, until it's like someone has opened a door of pure light in my head and my whole body is undulating to the gentle orgasm flowing deep within my pelvis.

Wow. Some time since I've had such a gentle and glorious come. I'm weak with ecstasy. Slumped in the chair, fondling the back of Karla's bare neck with mute gratitude.

'Where the hell did you learn to do that?' I gasp.

'That would be telling. A girl has to have her secrets,' Karla murmurs. 'Just tell me that I'm good.'

'You're good.'

But Karla does not leave it at that. Oh no. Still she's lapping at the juices and teasing me with the tip of her tongue until I groan in near agony.

I'm beside myself with passion and I want to do something for her.

'Stand up,' I order breathlessly. She obeys, but the little grimace shows she would rather not. She is truly in love with my pussy.

'Pull your skirt up,' I say.

She does, with a slow wiggle of hips.

She's wearing camiknickers of raw silk above her stockings and it's strangely arousing to see the bulge of her hard cock against the filmy softness. Undeniable physical evidence that Karla's turned on.

'Does it hurt, to be that hard and not be brought off?' I ask curiously.

'Only in a masochistic kind of way.'

I nod, beginning to understand. I'd heard somewhere about delayed orgasm, a delicious dry come.

'Can I touch it?'

'If you want to.'

I put out a hand and stroke the length of Karla's shaft. I'm gratified when it twitches and grows even harder under my searching fingers as I stroke the tip.

My other hand reaches round to feel her tensed buttocks through the fine silk. I can hear her ragged breath, interpret her silence as willingness to let me do whatever I please.

I put out my tongue, experiment with licking the length of the shaft, then circle the head. Karla stiffens and swears softly.

'Is that good?'

'Oh yes.'

My lips and tongue explore the high, hard balls through the soft silk camiknickers.

'And that?'

'Exquisite.'

I feel like a novice in new territory here. But I'm surprised at how turned on I am at handling this prick. I am so very horny, sliding my thighs together across my slick and hungry cunt. No dildo handy, why not try the real thing? It looks so ready and willing. What will it feel like inside me?

'Do you carry any condoms, Karla?' I whisper.

'Always.'

'Will you put one on for me?'

She nods, reaches in her black sequinned purse for a packet. I pull down her camiknickers and let her hard prick spring free. Hastily she pulls off her gloves and, with trembling fingers, unfurls the sheath across the swollen cock.

Her cock is good and thick and riding high, jutting from her narrow hips, as she holds her skirts out of the way so I can admire it more closely. The cock glistens softly in its sheath of rubber.

'You have a good-looking cock, Karla. Better than any Greek god's.'

'Thank you.'

I take the tip of it in my mouth experimentally and Karla moans.

'Your lips feel so soft,' she exclaims. 'Stop or I'll come.'

I stop. I stand up, kiss my beautiful girl-with-a-prick.

'Sit down, Karla,' I order. 'I want to sit on your cock and try it out for size. Could you hang on for long enough to give me a ride?'

'I'll try.'

She sits and drapes her skirts behind her over the back of the chair, so that I can straddle her.

It takes a little while until I get the position right. Then my wet cunt lips slide easily over Karla's waiting cock.

Well, my first flesh-and-blood cock fits like a glove. Better than any made-to-measure dildo. We both moan with the bliss of this final embrace. Impending consummation.

I've got to admire my young trannie's self-control. Worthy of any tantric-sex guru. We kiss again as we circle against each other gently, groin to groin once more, this time locked together in genuine lovemaking, which any respectable missionary could almost approve of.

It feels strange to look into my man-girl's kohl-encircled eyes, see the lust I've aroused, and know that it is her flesh-totem that's circling high inside me. I can feel hard balls roll against my soft crack as our delicious tempo increases.

'Please,' she whispers against my lips, 'can I see your breasts?'

The thin white duke rips open his shirt to display high, pert tits.

'Look, don't touch,' I order wickedly.

'They're beautiful. So firm, like hard pears. And those nipples . . . please, can I suck one?'

I consider, then nod, watch those voluptuous lips I've admired surround my hard teat. She suckles hungrily on my right nipple and my abdomen tightens, twitches in response. I can feel her prick press harder into me and it's wonderful to feel my pussy muscles grip and undulate in easy reply to the stroke. We're fucking, and the act is running away from all our desire and control and need to make it last.

'Let's do this, man-bitch,' I hiss at last, letting my hips rock harder against her. 'Come inside me.'

Karla's wide sensual mouth fully encircles my breast and I feel her shudder as she comes. My stomach muscles quiver and I cry out with orgasmic bliss for a second time. This is fast and fierce and wonderful, the full release of what's been building up between us, and I bite into her shoulder as she grazes her teeth across my nipples in happy ecstasy as we fuck ourselves off the chair and on to the floor in the final consummation.

Eventually we giggle and disentangle ourselves.

'I believe you lasted quite well for a young buck,' I say at last. My cunt feels soft and satiated, but strangely empty without her as she slides out of me.

'I wouldn't dare come until you told me to,' Karla says humbly, disposing of the condom in the swingbin below the sink before she washes her prick at the washbasin. I watch with fascination as the softened cock slowly shrinks and lies nestled against her relaxed balls. She catches my eye, gives me a wicked smile.

'So what did you think of your first real prick? Have I converted you? Turned you straight?'

I pretend to consider this as I get dressed. I don't want Karla to know how much she's got a hook in my groin. The sight of my man-bitch semi-naked and soft turns me on more than ever. Maybe attraction is beyond gender, and Karla's pheromone signature, his prick, is truly the one for me.

'I'm not sure. It may take a few more times to know one way or another,' I say doubtfully.

Karla pouts. 'Man-girl, you are hard to please.'

'But, baby, you were more of a woman than I ever thought you could be.' I smile in mock consolation.

'And you're more of a man than I've ever met.' She giggles and rearranges her gorgeous black dress, slips her camiknickers back on. 'Will you fuck me next time?'

'How?'

'With your strap-on of course. No mercy, just jump on me and take me from behind. God, I'm almost hard again already at the thought.'

'Shut up, will you?' I was getting wet myself at the very idea of Karla crouched beneath me, her bare buttocks riding high and lubed, quivering and waiting for my dildo-plunge . . . I shake my head to free myself from the fug of re-awakened desire. 'I've got to get back to work or I'll be in trouble,' I say sternly. Indeed, Jack would be wondering how much longer my quickie was going to last.

Karla comes over to help me with my shirt buttons because I am fumbling so much. She smoothes my shirt front, holds on to my shoulders and gazes into my eyes. I like the soft expression, the earnest need I find there. Those shining tawny eyes are heart melting.

'I can wait for you till the end of the night, right? I can go home with you?' she begs.

The thrum in my ears, the dry spot at the back of my throat, must be me getting all hot and bothered and yearning for Karla all over again. With an effort I pull away.

'Sure.' I try to sound off-hand. 'If you still want to by the end of the night.'

I'm such a tough guy.

* * *

So I get back to the mundane task of collecting empty glasses while Jack looks heavenwards to say 'What took you so long?' Quite a few friends stop me, point to the Polaroid of me and Karla in shameless embrace, stare at me in amazement.

'Is it true, you and the trannie are getting off?'

What can I say? Word gets around. Karla's back on her barstool, drinking cocktails and smoking, hair and make-up immaculate, as though butter wouldn't melt in her mouth. I shrug.

'Try anything once, except folk dancing and incest, right?'

They laugh, run off to spread the rumour.

At the end of the night the winner of the fancy dress competition is announced.

'It's a draw, between Louise Brooks and our very own thin white duke!' Monica announces. Arms propel me forwards to the spotlight. Karla is given a packet of fancy condoms and I get the bottle of champagne. We kiss on the little stage, blow kisses to the audience, which cheers enthusiastically, before we are allowed down from the spotlight again.

'I can't help but think this was fixed,' I growl at Monica, who winks and applauds as we depart.

'Don't knock it, the prize will come in handy tonight,' Karla purrs before she goes back to her seat. I put the vintage Moët in the fridge cabinet to chill.

Now, as the evening finally ends I'm left by Jack to clear and lock up.

But Karla still waits for me at her corner of the bar. She waves the prize packet of condoms at me, a wicked smile on her face, and sings stanzas of 'Slave to Love' as I collect the bottle of champagne.

I've a feeling that Karla and me are going to be an item.

Thank you, Dorian Gray.

The Pillory

Mathilde Madden

The Pillory

Ted gave the horn a tap and, after a couple of moments, Angela then Jim appeared at the door. Friday nights always followed the same routine. Ted would pick me up and then we'd go and collect Jim and Angela. We'd drive to the pub in the next village have a few drinks and stagger home. And Ted would have to go and pick up his car the next morning.

It was for solely financial reasons that I had come back to live with my parents after I graduated, while I looked for work. I hadn't planned to get back together with Ted, my old school boyfriend; it had just kind of happened.

Ted and I had dated when we were fifteen but when I stayed on at sixth form and he got a job as a carpenter, we had drifted apart. I knew I had probably broken his heart back then, but after I moved away to university I hadn't given him a second thought.

It had been his idea that we got back together when I returned and I was grateful for the company. He, Ted and Angela gave me a ready-made crowd to hang out with, as most of my other old school friends weren't around any more.

And the sex was nice, a distraction from boring village life, though not much more. Ted was a good lover, attractive and well built from his years of manual labour, but the sex was essentially pretty mechanical. He wasn't very imaginative.

As Angela bounded down the path with Jim walking stoically behind her I could still feel the tension in the air between Ted and me.

I had been up to London just that day for a job interview, for a marketing job, of exactly the kind I had set my heart on. The interview had gone well and the prospect that I might actually get this job had caused Ted and I to revisit an old row: whether or not he was coming to London with me when I inevitably moved there. He was keen to; I was adamant that he would not.

Angela opened the door and slid across the back seat. She was very pretty, with long dark hair and a slight figure. She had been Ted's next door neighbour when they were younger, literally the girl next door. I knew she didn't think much of me and wasn't surprised to see a slight smile cross her face as she clocked the tension between Ted and me.

Jim followed. Jim and Angela had been married for about three years, which I found odd, as Angela was only my age, but she came from a culture where girls, especially pretty girls like her, married young. Jim was some years older than her and ex-army. It still showed in his crewcut hair, solid build and excellent posture. I had no idea what Jim thought of me, as he hardly spoke most of the time, but I knew I found him desperately attractive. Sometimes, when we were all in the pub, I would notice him looking at me, with a stern, almost angry expression on his face and I would always feel a private thrill at the thought of being taken firmly in hand by him.

As the car pulled away Angela said, 'You two OK?'

'Fine,' said Ted grimly, staring at the road ahead.

I shifted angrily in my seat. Clearly Ted was going to let our stupid quarrel ruin the whole evening.

'You're not fine, Ted,' said Angela soothingly, completely ignoring me, 'what's wrong?'

'Well, if you must know, Angela,' said Ted, 'this bitch has just confirmed to me, again, that I am nothing more than some dumb bit of rough keeping her happy until she swans off to her big London career.'

'Ted, I didn't,' I countered, unhappy at having this aired in front of Angela and Jim.

'You're just using me,' he said angrily. 'You used me before and now you're doing it again.'

'Oh, Ted,' I soothed, hoping to get the subject dropped, 'it's not like that, really it isn't.'

'Isn't it?' he said softly, still sounding angry but also sad. I could already see the lights of the pub ahead of us and decided to give up. It was bound to be a rotten evening.

We pulled into the country pub car park, with tension still hanging. As I opened my car door and climbed out I found Angela was standing in front of me, barring my way.

She looked angrily at me. 'I'm sick of you,' she snarled. 'You lead my Ted on, break his heart and now you come back, just to get his hopes up again. You know how much he loves you and yet you just play with him. You are such a bitch.'

I was shocked. I suppose I couldn't blame Angela for feeling like this, it was basically the truth, but she had never said anything before. I was pissed off too – it was nothing to do with her.

'Mind your own fucking business, Angela,' I snapped back, pushing her out of the way.

As I moved past her, Jim grabbed me by my wrists, stopping me getting any further. 'Don't touch her,' he said, in his usual level tone.

With Jim holding me still, Angela pushed her face close to mine and went on, 'You need to be taught a lesson, you stuck-up bitch. I spent months listening to Ted sobbing his heart out over you and now you waltz back into his life. Well, you won't hurt him again, I'll see to that.'

'You've been watching too many soap operas,' I sneered at Angela, struggling to get free of Jim's grasp. I looked over my shoulder at Ted, on the other side of the car. He looked at me and then glanced at the floor.

Suddenly, while I was distracted by Ted, Angela hit me, a hard slap around the face. I cried out and tried to protect myself but Jim held me fast. Shit, I thought, she was going to beat me up.

I looked over my shoulder at Ted again, assuming he would come to my aid, but he just stood there, looking helpless.

'Bring her.' Angela snapped the order over her shoulder to Jim and set off through the car park into the beer garden. At this time of year it was deserted and in darkness. As Jim marched me firmly through the picnic tables, behind Angela, I suddenly realised where we were going.

At the back of the beer garden was a pillory, a type of wooden medieval stocks, which was designed to hold a prisoner in a standing position with their head and hands locked into wooden holes. It was an original, the pub claimed, that had been used for centuries on that very spot, to imprison and humiliate wrongdoers.

They were going to put me in the pillory, I thought, frantically. In a panic I began to kick out and scream but Jim was too fast for me. He lifted me off my feet and hoisted me right over his shoulder. I swung upside down, beating my fists against the small of his back, but he barely seemed to notice and just walked on after Angela, ignoring my screams of anger.

Ever since I had first seen that pillory, over ten years

ago, on a family outing to this very pub, it had haunted my fantasies. I had squirmed in my bed, before I even understood what I was doing, thinking of the pillory and what it must be like to be locked into it and helpless in front of a jeering crowd. At first I simply imagined how it would feel to be so exposed and defenceless, as the crowd pelted you with rotten fruit, unsure of why I found such a fantasy pleasurable. But as I grew older, and more sexually aware, the action changed subtly and I imagined strangers from the crowd coming up to me, caressing and molesting and eventually fucking me, as I stood there, unable to resist them.

It didn't take much effort for Jim to get my head and hands in position in the device. He closed the top half down over my neck and wrists and Angela snapped the padlock into place. I struggled and twisted but it was useless. It held me as fast as it had those prisoners in years gone by.

Slightly bent over, unable to move my head or hands, I realised with a start that I was totally helpless and vulnerable. Angela stood in front of me, flanked by Jim and Ted. Any bravado I had had left, sparked by my anger, drained away.

Angela reached out and took hold of my chin with her hand, tilting my head to meet her gaze.

'We are going to teach you a lesson you won't forget, you little bitch. You think you're so much better than us.' She smiled a cruel smile. 'Well, who's in charge now?'

'I don't know what you think you're doing,' I began, praying my voice wouldn't give away how turned on I was, 'but it's ridiculous. Ted and I, well, that's our business and –'

Ted cut me off. 'I asked them to help me,' he said slowly, 'and everything Angela's said has been true – you do deserve a lesson. I just asked them to help me to teach it to you.' I stared at Ted. He was both angry and in control and he looked so beautiful.

'We need to keep her quiet,' Angela said, half sneering. 'She'll start to scream the place down when we leave her.' Ted picked up a small holdall from the ground. He handed a small rag to Angela, which she stuffed into my mouth. Then Ted cut a short length of tape from a roll and passed it to Angela. This was stuck over my mouth, holding the rag in place. I tried to say something, to protest, but the gag held fast.

Then I could only watch as the three of them turned and, without a word, walked down the path between the picnic tables to the back door of the pub. I struggled again to make a sound but, through the gag, only a muffled mumbling was possible. I was left alone, silenced and helpless.

After some time – I have no idea how long it was, but it felt like about twenty minutes – I saw a figure come walking back up the path towards me. I stared and as the figure drew closer. I saw it was Jim.

Instinctively I tried to speak, to beg him to let me free, but the gag kept me silent.

'Stop trying to talk, silly bitch,' Jim drawled as he arrived to stand in front of me. 'You're fixed up good. Me and Ted saw to that.' He kicked the wooden upright of the pillory as if to illustrate its strength. Then, seemingly to admire his handiwork further, he walked slowly around it to stand behind me. Held fast, as I was, I couldn't make any attempt to see what he was doing there. I was forced to stand dumbly and wait.

Suddenly I felt his hand stroke my arse. 'I think I see what Ted sees in you,' he murmured softly.

Instantly, like a switch being flicked on, I was flooded with arousal. I got so wet so quickly that I felt sure he must be able to feel it through my jeans. He ran his hand slowly along the seam between my legs, making me feel like I could come right there and then. I sighed into the gag and Jim gave a soft laugh in response. 'It's just a shame you're such a stuck-up little cow,' he went on. 'I'm so glad you are finally going to get what you deserve.' I felt him undo the fly of my jeans in one easy movement, quickly pulling them down to my ankles and taking my knickers with them. I gasped as the night air hit my wet pussy. 'This,' said Jim, his voice sounding much colder, 'is for treating Ted like shit.'

I felt the air move and then a sudden explosion of heat and pain as his large hand hit my exposed arse. I had never been spanked before; although I often fantasised about it, I had never realised it would hurt this much. I felt like all the breath was being knocked out of my body.

The spanks sounded so loud in the still air that I was surprised they couldn't hear it in the pub, but no one came to investigate.

Although my arse was starting to feel like it was on fire, somehow the pain seemed to be becoming more bearable as the sharp blows continued. I was also thrilled to find that each strike pushed my bare pubic mound into the wooden upright of the pillory and, gradually, each spank became a wave of pleasure as I got closer and closer to coming.

Before I could peak he stopped. I quickly stifled an involuntary moan of frustration as I heard him open his own fly behind me. Next I heard his trousers drop and then felt him slide easily inside me, clearly as aroused by the spanking as I had been.

Now it was his thrusting pushing me into the wooden frame. The feeling of being fucked in this demeaning position and the whole thing being in public spurred me on and we both came quickly with me twisting against the pillory and his firm grip.

The next thing I knew Jim had withdrawn and fastened himself up. He walked around to the front of the pillory and I squirmed with humiliation as I realised he was clearly going to leave me stripped from the waist down with our mixed juices running down my legs. He said nothing, just gave me a wink as he turned and sauntered back to the pub. I watched him go. I had no choice.

The cold air around my exposed wet pussy was making me need to pee. I shifted uncomfortably, hoping they would decide to release me before I wet myself. I waited in the silence and eventually I saw someone else coming up the path. This time it was Angela.

She stopped in front of me and carefully released the gag. I gasped with relief as it came off.

Looking up at her, I began to beg, 'Please, Angela, please let me go. I'm sorry, I've learned my lesson, really . . .' Angela pushed her hand over my mouth to silence me.

'Shut up,' she hissed, 'I don't want to hear your begging. I'll decide when you've learned your lesson.' She held a wine glass of water, which she had been carrying, up to my lips. I drank it gratefully, realising how thirsty I was. After I had drained the glass she bent down, placing her face inches from mine. 'I really am sorry it's come to this,' she whispered. 'I gave you every chance to make it up to him but you would keep on acting like an evil little bitch.' Leaning further forward, she kissed me softly on the lips.

'Please, Angela,' I breathed as she pulled away, 'I need to pee. Please let me go.'

Angela didn't reply; she walked around the pillory to stand behind me, and then she stroked my exposed cunt. The pressure from my full bladder was making me feel aroused again and I whimpered with pleasure at her touch. Then I felt something hard and cold between my legs. I realised she was holding the empty glass to catch my urine. I took a deep breath and began to pee.

I sighed with relief as the liquid gushed out of me. I was slightly embarrassed at the thought of Angela standing behind me watching, but I was so desperate I had no choice. When I finished she walked back around to face me, carrying the glass with her. It was about one-third full. She hadn't managed to catch it all.

'Are you sorry?' she asked.

'Yes.' I even felt tears begin to prick my eyes as I realised I truly was.

'Then prove it.' She held the glass to my lips. 'Drink this, as penance, and I'll let you go.'

My stomach seemed to flip over at the thought of it, but at the same time I knew there was no way I was going to drink my own piss for Angela. So I looked her in the eye, relishing the defiance, and softly said, 'No.'

'What did you say?'

'I said no, I won't drink it.'

'Oh, you will.' Roughly she grabbed my nose, pinching it, and forced my head back until it banged into the wood behind it. Involuntarly I opened my mouth to breathe and, as I did so, she poured the entire contents of the glass into my mouth. She laughed as I choked and spluttered and spat it out, dribbling at least half of it down my chin. She slapped me round the face. 'So you want to stay out here, do you? Well you can stay here all night if you want to.' She raised her hand to slap me again but her wrist was caught by a familiar figure standing behind her.

'Thank you for your help, Angela,' said Ted, 'but I'll take it from here.' Angela gave Ted a challenging glance. She seemed as if she was about to say something but she didn't; she just turned on her heel and walked swiftly off down the path.

'So, do you like what I've made for you?' he said, stroking the top of the pillory.

'You made this?' I asked, confused.

'Oh yeah, couldn't use the original, it's an antique and, besides, it would never actually hold you. It's far too old and worn. I knocked this one up in my workshop and did a switch; my design's better anyway.' He smiled. 'Well, I think it's better; as far as you're concerned, it's a lot worse. For example.' He bent down and fiddled with something towards the bottom of the upright. I gasped with confusion, feeling a sudden pressure from above on my neck and wrists. Then I realised the whole of the top section, which held me, was being lowered.

'It's height-adjustable, see? My innovation,' said Ted from below me. 'It's like a mike stand; it works sort of like a telescope.' I was oblivious to this technical information, as my head and shoulders being forced downwards was somewhat distracting. I bent my knees to adjust myself, struggling to keep my balance. With the frame adjusted how he liked it, Ted tightened something at the bottom and stood up again. Now his crotch was level with my face.

'See?' I heard him say above me. 'Clever, eh?'

I struggled with my uncomfortable new position. 'So,' Ted continued, 'what shall I do with you now I've got you like this?' He paused, as if considering the question. 'Oh, I know, undo my trousers, bitch.' His voice was suddenly sharp and cruel.

I looked up at him, confused. 'I can't,' I muttered, wriggling my hands, which were imprisoned some distance from his fly.

'Come on,' he growled, thrusting his crotch into my face.

His fly was right in front of my mouth. I carefully probed the button with my tongue, realising that if I pushed hard enough I could probably get it through the buttonhole.

'Good girl,' he soothed as he saw me start to struggle with it.

It wasn't easy but I got the button undone, then swiftly gripped the zip between my teeth and pulled it down. He jiggled his hips slightly and the trousers fell to the floor.

'Now get it out.' he muttered. His voice was suddenly thick with arousal.

I pulled his underpants down with my teeth, liberating his familiar cock. It seemed bigger and harder than I had ever seen it before. I gasped and, unable to wait for his command, took it eagerly into my mouth.

I felt my cunt thump with arousal as his pheromones surrounded me. As I sucked hard he sighed in response and pushed his fingers into my hair, grasping handfuls and forcing my head further down. I had no choice but to surrender to him, so I relaxed my throat and let him slide himself right into my mouth as far as he wished. My eyes began to water as he thrust harder and harder. I heard his moan as he came suddenly in fast spasms. I eagerly swallowed.

He staggered away from me, doing himself up, and then grinned. 'Good girl,' he said gently, 'I think you deserve the present I have for you.'

He reached into his holdall on the ground and pulled out a long black riding crop. I heard myself gasp as horror and delight flooded through me.

'I made this for you too,' he went on. 'It was quite easy; I found some info on the net.'

Slapping the small piece of black leather on the end of the crop into his palm ominously, he walked around behind the pillory to where my still naked arse was quivering in the cold air.

I felt him pull me backwards until my legs were straight and my arse sticking out, provocatively. The air moved slightly as he took aim. Then the crop crashed into my arse, still sore from Jim's spanking, feeling as if it was leaving a line of fire across it. 'Count,' he ordered.

'One,' I gasped, barely able to get the word out with the shock of the pain. Then I softly added, 'Sir.'

'Good girl,' he said and hit me again.

'Two, sir,' I said. My pussy was now screaming for attention. At the third stroke I felt like I was seeing stars. 'Three, sir,' I said, fighting to keep my voice level.

Gently he slid the crop between my legs, pushing up and drawing it across my aching, swollen clit. It was enough and I felt myself begin to come. He drew the crop across me again and I screamed, feeling a wave of moisture seem to come pouring down my legs. I bucked so hard I felt as if the wooden frame might break.

When I opened my eyes again, Ted was standing in front of me.

'Ted,' I gasped with relief, 'where were you?'

'Just there.' He pointed to a small clump of bushes a couple of yards away. 'Did you see me?'

'No.' I was still shaking with the aftershock of the greatest orgasm of my life and found myself being pretty monosyllabic.

'Good. I bloody well saw you, though. I must have beat off four times just looking at you stood here like this and when Jim started fucking you, good God.' He shook his head in mock disbelief. 'Was Angela getting a bit carried away? I thought she might.'

'Really.' I felt the feeling slowly return in my limbs.

'Oh, she jumped at the chance to do it, you know. She was always pretty keen on me when we were kids – I reckon she was delighted to be able to get one over on you for stealing her man.'

'Oh.'

'And as for Jim, he couldn't wait to do it. Good grief, he was mad for it, a bit of a worry, but . . .' He tailed off, as if realising something. 'So was it all right, babe? Was it what you wanted?'

'Oh, Ted, it was perfect.' I shivered with delight at the thought.

Ted reached out and undid the padlock, which held the two halves of the pillory together. He lifted the top half and I slid out stiffly. Smiling, he picked me up like a baby and carried me to the car.

'What about Angela and Jim?' I asked as we pulled away.

'Oh they'll make their own way.'

He reached over and undid the glove compartment in

front of me. 'Here, you might want this back,' he said, as a few handwritten pages fell out into my lap. I picked up the first one. It was my handwriting and the piece was entitled 'The Pillory'. It was my favourite sexual fantasy. I had written it all down for Ted after reading in a magazine article that shared fantasies helped to enliven a relationship. I had been nervous about being so honest with Ted, but now I was so glad I had been. On the pages I had described what had just happened, almost complete to every detail.

'Angela did a good bit of improv with the glass of piss,' I said.

'God, was that all right? I was so worried you'd choke or something. That's why I stepped in a bit early.'

'No, it was fine; it was good.'

I looked over at him, silently guiding the car through the deserted country roads. How many men would go to this much trouble to fulfil a girlfriend's sexual fantasy? I thought. How could I dream of going to London without him? I wondered if it had been the threat of me leaving him that had spurred him on to plan this whole thing. If so, it had definitely worked.

I smiled as I remembered his fantasy, which he had shyly written down for me when we had swapped them. It featured him in traction and a very strict matron. I started to wonder what favours I could call in to make his dream come true.

Frustration

Lois Pheonix

Frustration

It was going to be another hot day in London. The city was ill-equipped for a heatwave but Cathy was lucky; the cool marble and stone of the museum where she worked provided blessed relief.

She thought of Josh, the archaeology graduate who had started work in the museum a week before, and smiled to herself. Already she had him sussed: uptight and sexually suppressed, living only for his research. Trouble was, he had Cathy down as a kindred spirit in matters academic, focused only on their discovery of a possibly Roman sarcophagus. She was focused on it too, up to a point. He wouldn't guess that he was her current sexual fantasy, though, and remained annoyingly oblivious to the way her nipples sprang to attention each time she smelled his musky aftershave anywhere near.

Running a hand over one taut nipple, Cathy rolled sideways in her clean, rumpled sheets. God, she'd like to teach him how to fuck. She thought of his dark head bent over the stone coffin, diligently brushing away the ancient debris, and crossed her legs, her clit beginning its slow, early-morning thrum. Cathy pictured the way Josh's shirt stretched across his broad back. Such a waste, a man of that build burying himself away with the long-dead. She held on to her fantasy and squeezed her thigh muscles hard, pushing against her swollen clit.

The first day Josh had started at the museum, Cathy had invited him back for supper. Their joint passion for archaeology meant the evening had sped by. Midnight came and when Josh had left, politely thanking her for a lovely evening, Cathy had pressed herself against the door, totally frustrated by his inability to pick up on the sexual tension in the air.

This morning, she played the night out differently, imagining his dark curls buried between her spread thighs, his hands kneading her breasts as he lapped and probed at her secret places.

With a shrill beep, Cathy's alarm clock sprang to life, shattering the fantasy. If she didn't find some satisfaction soon, she thought she would burst. Suppressing a groan, she rolled out of bed and headed for a quick, extremely cold shower.

A little later, dressed in a tan, raw silk skirt, a white sleeveless blouse and the most impractical sandals she could find, Cathy strode up Nantes Avenue towards the museum. A waiter, leaning on the door frame of a cafe, smoking his first cigarette of the day, leered at her breasts, bouncing beneath the white blouse, and gave a low whistle. Cathy forced back a smile and threw him a challenging look as she passed.

Reaching the museum, she was dismayed to find its exterior smothered by ugly scaffolding that had sprung up over the weekend. Stepping into the road to avoid a pile of chippings, Cathy looked up at the sound of a shout to see a row of workmen grinning down at her. Four rough-looking faces, their hard hats cocked at various angles, smirked at her.

'Gorgeous tits,' one of them called.

Shocked, Cathy stared back, feeling cross. One of them

grabbed the front of his filthy work jeans and yelled, 'You can have me any time, darling.'

Pulling herself together, she called up to him, 'I'd be too much for you to handle, sweetheart.' Riled, she forced herself to march on. She could hear the workman's mates laughing and ribbing him as she strode away, praying that her heels wouldn't catch in a paving stone and trip her up.

Balancing precariously on the makeshift gangway, Cathy walked smack into another workman.

'Whoa there, darling, take it easy.' Two burly arms clutched her elbows and steadied her as her bags fell to the ground. Mortified, Cathy found herself clutching on to two rock-hard biceps in a bid not to go tumbling after them.

'Hey, I know I'm irresistible.' The workman grinned, pulling her gently under the scaffolding away from his jeering mates. Cathy had no choice but to follow, and inwardly cursed her choice in shoes. She felt her face burn with embarrassment and pulled away, trying desperately not to notice his straight white teeth or his earring or his mocking blue eyes.

'OK now?' he asked. He smelled of Marlboros and coffee.

'Perfectly, thank you.' Cathy jerked her arms away, horrified that her sexuality had suddenly sprung into life.

As he bent to retrieve her briefcase and handbag, work jeans stretching over an incredibly tight ass, Cathy snarled, 'And don't try telling me you're any different from your mates. You're only being polite because you're separated from the pack!'

He straightened, lifting her bags, and let his gaze travel slowly from her ankles to her breasts, making no attempt to disguise the fact that he was admiring them. Cathy's nipples stuck out like organ stops, then a pulse began thudding violently in her chest and dropped straight to her crotch. She instantly regretted her waspishness and made a grab for her bags.

The workman held on to them and dragged his eyes from her tits to her face. 'I don't need to be surrounded by the pack to tell you that I could screw the arse off you, right here, right now.' His eyes glinted dangerously.

She pulled her bags free but remained rooted to the spot. The workman took a step closer, holding her gaze with his own.

'And what's more,' he drawled, 'I know you'd like it.' To Cathy's shock, he reached up and stroked her nipples with the backs of his huge hands. She bit her lip, not quite able to move away from him, her quim growing heavy and moist with lust. He leaned forward and whispered in her ear, his breath warm on her neck. 'I could ram it up you good and hard without anyone even knowing, sweetheart. Get that lovely white blouse good and dirty in the process.'

Cathy's eyelids began to droop as she took in the smell of fresh sweat on him. She gave a tiny moan and heard the workman chuckle.

'Bastard,' she hissed, appalled at herself. She forced herself to walk away, her legs trembling with the exertion of not wrapping them around his waist and thrusting herself against the rough denim of his fly. As she reached the steps, Cathy turned to see him watching her, tight-lipped and stern, the front of his jeans pushed out by a large, uncomfortable-looking erection.

Shakily, she entered the building, calming herself in the cool dark interior for a moment before making her way to her office, her footfalls echoing loudly on the marble floor.

She flung her bags on to her desk and drew huge breaths, the pulse in her groin still beating furiously. She paced the quiet room, trying to take her mind off the workman by concentrating on the laborious task of investigating the sarcophagus downstairs inch by precious inch. But unwanted images of herself spreadeagled on the cold stone kept interrupting her train of thought. She imagined a crowd of archaeologists, dressed in white coats, exploring her naked flesh with tiny soft brushes, presuming her dead and tantalising her with their soft, unsatisfactory explorations as she lay, frustrated, in the ancient coffin.

Cathy lowered herself into a chair. She could feel her panties damp against her sex, the lace riding up. Pushing her hips forward she forced the lace tighter against her clit. She hoped the bastard's erection was killing him.

'Cathy?'

Cathy jolted upright, a flush creeping up her neck. Josh stood in the doorway, eyeing her quizzically.

'Heavy weekend? You look as if you were half asleep.'

'I'm fine.' Cathy shuffled maps and sketches into piles on her desk. 'You?'

'Fantastic.' Oblivious to her discomfort, Josh perched on the edge of her desk, his knees inches from her face. Cathy willed herself not to look at his crotch. 'Apparently,' Josh continued, his eyes bright with excitement, 'a similar coffin was discovered in 1986. I thought we could check it out before proceeding with ours. If that's all right with you.'

Cathy watched him as he rambled on, enthused by his weekend research. She let his words soothe her, taking a deep breath as she crossed her legs, her skirt riding up a long expanse of thigh. What the hell, Josh would only notice her if she'd been dead for a thousand years and lay in a lead-lined coffin. Josh ran a hand through his soft curls and faltered.

'I think you're right,' Cathy urged. 'This one is far too rare for us to go at it like a bull at a gate. I'm quite happy to do more research first.' And it'll keep you here a bit longer, she thought, leaning back in her chair and placing her hands behind her head. She felt two buttons on her blouse pop open but ignored them, watching Josh as he talked, admiring the straight line of his nose, his young body beneath his shirt and the dark hairs on his arms where he had rolled his shirt sleeves up.

Josh suddenly jumped to his feet. 'Let's hit the library then,' he said.

Cathy followed him to the museum library, grinning at his unkempt hair and skew-whiff tie as he raced ahead of her. She placed a hand on his arm and he jumped.

'I know this is your first big project, Josh, but calm down.' Cathy smiled up at him. 'We've got plenty of time.'

She wondered, fleetingly, if he rushed sex. God, it would be such a let down if he rammed it in like a schoolboy and came straightaway. But what did it matter? She would probably never get to find out.

Cathy loved the library; it was dark and silent, filled with research literature. She felt a rush to her bowels as she smelled the musty secrets that lay in their hundreds on the shelves. Josh led the way to the relevant section and pulled the ladder along the runner when he realised that the shelf he was after was six foot up. He placed a foot on the bottom rung, testing his weight. Cathy gently pulled him away. 'I'll go. These ladders are pretty rickety.'

'If you're sure.' A nerve throbbed in his temple.

We picked him well, Cathy mused; he can't wait to get at the documents.

Tentatively, she climbed the ladder, balancing precariously on the rungs thanks to her quirky choice of shoes that morning. Her skirt impeded her and she pushed it higher up her legs to help her climb.

'Hey, down there,' Cathy called. 'Hold me steady; I don't feel very safe.'

Josh hesitated, unsure where to put his hands. Eventually, he chose to hold each side of the ladder and Cathy fought an urge to press her backside into his face. She found the documents and handed them down to Josh, who placed them gingerly on the floor, the paper quivering as his hands trembled with the excitement of finding them.

As Cathy reached for the final document, her sandal slipped on a rung and she toppled, clinging to the ladder for support. A tiny yell sprang from her lips and, despite himself, Josh grabbed her calves to steady her. His hands were hot and smooth.

'I nearly went then.' Cathy giggled nervously.

'Are you safe?' Josh asked.

'Don't let go. I've got a foot caught.' Cathy wrestled with her sandal. 'OK, I'm free, but you'll have to help me down.' Slowly, Cathy inched her way back down the ladder, rung by rung, biting her lip as she felt Josh's hands slide up her legs. She could feel his breath on the backs of her knees.

'I'm afraid I might fall,' she whimpered.

'I've got you.'

Cathy grinned to herself. She had him now. As her backside lowered towards him, Josh, ever the gentleman and determined not to let her fall, climbed two rungs and inadvertently let his hands slip up underneath her skirt in his bid to keep her steady.

Cathy shut her eyes and proceeded down towards him. His hands slipped up her thighs and her skirt rode towards her waist. She heard Josh's sharp intake of breath as his face was pressed against her smooth buttocks, the lace of her panties now wedged between them and tugging up against her clit.

The library was silent save for their heavy breathing, both pretending that Cathy might fall and that they weren't deeply aroused.

'I think if I turn, it may be easier,' Cathy ventured, wondering how far she could take the pretence, short of sitting on his face and demanding that he tongue her. She waited for his reply.

'I think that would be a good idea,' Josh replied breathlessly.

Slowly, carefully, blouse buttons straining, skirt rucked around her waist, Cathy turned. Josh gripped her thighs, rotating her like a ballerina. At last, she faced him and Josh groaned, his face an inch from her swollen sex lips, the lace riding high between them and pushing them apart. Spreading his hands, Josh moved his thumb towards them, pulling the lace to one side. Cathy gasped, smelling her own scent, which wafted around them. Her legs wobbled on the ladder, her knees weak with lust. Tentatively, Josh edged nearer and ran his tongue between her lips, just nudging her clit. Cathy braced herself, waiting for his tongue to fill her but he pulled away.

'Come on, I've got you,' he whispered instead, and Cathy wanted to wail in frustration. She edged downward, gratified only by the feel of his hands all over her, squeezing her breasts as they drew level with his face. She hovered, desperate for his touch, and he nipped at a hard nipple through her blouse. Cathy edged down quicker, determined to free his cock from his trousers, but as her feet hit the floor, Josh backed off, ashen faced and shaking.

'Christ, Cathy, I'm sorry,' he muttered, and fled from the library.

Cathy leaned on the ladder in shock, half crazed with unsated lust, her legs splayed, skirt riding her waist, breasts heaving beneath her crumpled blouse, as she watched him run away. It took her several minutes to realise what she must look like and that she and Josh were not the only ones to use the library. Smoothing down her skirt and picking up the documents, Cathy marched back to her office, biting her lip in a bid not to scream with frustration.

Dumping the documents on her desk, Cathy shook with humiliation for the second time that day. What was Josh's problem? The lure of the mysterious had always held a strong attraction for her but it was now beginning to seriously piss her off. Perhaps some fresh air would cool her down.

Grabbing an emergency packet of cigarettes, Cathy stalked towards the back of the building. Ignoring the puzzled looks of the curators and straggling bunches of school children, she slammed open the fire doors and headed for the privacy of the museum's back yard.

Arms folded tightly around her chest and pulling on her cigarette, Cathy put as much distance as she could between herself and the oppressive building. In her agitated state of mind she did not see the workman from that morning, who was loading bricks on to a trailer at the entrance to the yard. She was almost upon him before she realised what she was doing.

'Changed your mind?' he drawled, wiping sweat from his forehead with the back of a forearm.

'Piss off!' Cathy snapped, in no mood for his games.

The workman wore thick gloves and had removed his T-shirt in the heat, exposing a tattoo of a Celtic cross on his bicep. A trickle of sweat ran from his neck and disappeared into the hair on his chest.

'Don't pretend you haven't been thinking of me all morning.' He faced her down and Cathy's heart thundered despite his arrogance.

She took a final pull on her cigarette, then threw it to the ground and stamped on it before spinning back towards the fire doors. The workman was too quick for her; in a flash he had her round the waist, slapped one glove over her mouth and dragged her back behind a stack of packing crates. Cathy bit down hard but her teeth made no impression on the thick gloves.

'Time someone taught dirty girls like you a lesson,' he grunted, his grip only growing tighter. 'Parading around in tiny skirts and see-through blouses, then complaining when men take notice.'

Cathy struggled, her weight no match for his tough, work-honed body. The blood pounded in her ears and panic rose in her throat. She drove a heel down hard on to his foot, but the tiny spike didn't even dent the steel toecap of his work boot. Then, just as quickly as he had grabbed her, he released her. Cathy slumped, limp as a rag doll over a packing case.

'Don't worry, I've never forced myself on anyone.' He sounded breathless. 'I just wanted to ruffle your feathers a bit, that's all.'

'What the hell was that for?' Cathy glared at him.

The workman removed his gloves and ran a hand through his close-cropped hair. 'You really pissed me off this morning.'

'So?'

'Look, lady, I was only trying to help you and you treated me like scum.'

He was trying hard not to gaze at her breasts and failing miserably; lust lurched through Cathy's groin again.

The workman pointed a finger at her blouse. 'You might want to do those up.'

She looked down at her boobs, which were spilling out of her blouse. Her nipples grazed the tops of her bra cups. The workman raised an arm to wipe his forehead again, exposing his dark underarm hair. She caught a faint whiff of his male scent as he looked away, embarrassed now, and shuffled his work boots in the grit beneath his feet.

Her frustration leaped to new heights; she wasn't going to go unsatisfied this time.

'If you were a real gentleman,' she said, 'you'd do them back up for me.'

The workman's head snapped up, his eyes questioning. Cathy shot him a defiant look and stuck her breasts out further. 'Well?' she challenged. 'Can't those rough workman's fingers handle flimsy little buttons?'

The workman hesitated, confused by Cathy's apparent change of heart and reluctant to advance. The semi-erection, which he had nursed since their encounter this morning, now nudged painfully into life. He wanted to walk away, not certain he could let her go a second time if she goaded him any further. Cathy's hair had tumbled into disarray and her dark nipples enticed him from beneath their flimsy covering.

Cathy sensed his confusion. The packing case dug into her backside. Her pussy felt swollen and heavy with lust. The air hung hot and still around them. The museum was light years away and all she could think of was satisfying her craving.

'I get it,' Cathy sneered. 'All mouth and no trousers.'

The workman edged nearer, fists clenched at his side.

Cathy goaded him on, half afraid yet too aroused to back off. 'No wonder women like me treat you like dirt when all you do is sniff around like a dog looking for a leg to jerk on.'

He stood in front of her now, breathing heavily, and she looked him straight in the eye.

His voice was low and gravelly. 'Little wonder when stuck-up tarts like you are parading around like bitches on heat.' As he spoke he traced one callused finger from her jaw down to the cleft between her breasts.

Cathy could barely speak. 'I bet all that big talk is just to make up for the fact that you have such a small dick.'

He tugged at the remaining buttons of her blouse and separated it excruciatingly slowly, his eyes riveted on her nipples. 'You've got a filthy mouth for such a classy piece,' he murmured. 'I'm going to have to ram my cock in there to shut you up – it won't seem so small then.' He hooked his thumbs beneath her bra and pulled it upwards, exposing her breasts to the warm air. 'Christ,' he gasped. 'You're beautiful.'

Cathy moaned with desire, but she didn't want soft caresses; she wanted to push him further. Before he could bend to nuzzle her breasts she caught him a hefty whack on the side of his face. 'Bastard,' she hissed.

Stunned for a second, the workman reeled, then,

realising the game, he grabbed her arms and held them tightly with one hand. His strength aroused her further.

'You're going to be sorry you pissed me off, you foul-mouthed little tart,' he grunted, trying to ram his tongue into her mouth. Cathy twisted her head away and the workman lowered his head, biting her nipples roughly, his stubble chaffing the smoothness of her skin. Cathy struggled to break free, wanting to grab his head and pull it closer, but he wouldn't let go.

'No fucking way,' he growled. 'I'm in charge now.' He ran a rough hand up between her legs, pushing her skirt up around her waist. He found her expensive panties and jerked them down to her knees. Cathy heard the lace rip as huge fingers pulled at them. She yelled in protest and felt her arms freed, but one hand slapped over her mouth.

'Shut the fuck up,' he panted, pressing her hard against the packing crate. The other hand probed her opening and Cathy spread her legs wider to let him enter, her delicate sandals skidding on the ground. He stuck one finger up deep inside her. 'You're soaking,' the workman leered. 'I'm doing you a favour, sweetheart; you must be gagging for it.'

Cathy bit into his hand in ecstasy, splaying her legs wider in a bid for satisfaction.

'Oh, yes,' he murmured, slipping another finger inside and pushing them up high.

Cathy gasped and arched backwards, raising one leg around his waist and pressing her throbbing clit against the ball of his hand. He released her mouth, eager to hear her moans and ran his hand through her thick hair, grabbing a handful to hold her head back.

'Not such a bastard now, am I?' he goaded, easing in another finger and massaging her clit with his thumb. 'Go on,' he whispered against her throat. 'Beg me for it.'

'Fuck you,' Cathy spat, and he stopped his deft fingering, slowly withdrawing his hand. She couldn't bear it and, grabbing his wrist with her own hand, she pushed his fingers back up her. 'Harder,' she murmured. 'Please.'

Easing his fingers as high as they would go, he began to finger-fuck her as fast he could. Cathy dropped back on to the crate, legs splayed wide open and called out in sheer ecstasy.

'Quiet, or you'll have the whole fucking museum out here watching.'

Cathy bit her lip, throwing her head from side to side in a bid to control her moans.

'Perhaps you'd like that, would you?' Sensing her muscles begin to contract, he withdrew his hand. 'Not yet, posh totty. You don't get it that easy. You can do something for me first.'

Cathy watched him through half-closed eyes as he withdrew a little. Forcing herself up on to her elbows she watched him unfasten his tool belt. He let it drop to the ground with a thud, his gaze focused on her spread pussy, juice stuck to the insides of her brown thighs. He sucked his fingers clean.

'You taste good,' he said. 'Now you can taste me.' He unhooked the metal buttons of his fly and pushed his jeans down over his buttocks to mid thigh. Cathy watched as his thick cock sprang out, the head swollen purple, pre-come glistening on its tip. 'On your knees,' he commanded. 'And you better be good or you won't get anything else.'

Cathy complied, despite the sharp stones beneath her knees. She ran her hands over the rough hair on his sturdy thighs and reached behind to grab his buttocks, which were taut with anticipation.

'Oh, yes,' he muttered, grabbing her head and guiding her mouth on to his shaft.

Cathy licked the tip, tasting his salt, and slowly took the length of him deep into her mouth. He gasped, and, spurred on by his moans, she dug her fingers deep into his buttocks, working her mouth faster up and down the thick stem. All too quickly, she felt the tell-tale pulse of his impending orgasm and he pulled her head away. Cathy looked up at him. His eyes were glazed with barely controlled abandon. He was fighting for control and Cathy grinned.

'Better than I even imagined,' he whispered. 'But I don't want to come yet.' Lifting her up, he sat her on the crate. 'I've only one problem with you, baby,' he continued. 'I don't know how to stick it to you first.'

'Just give it to me,' Cathy pleaded, desperate to have him inside her.

'Oh, I will, baby, I will.' Grabbing her arms, he turned her roughly over, forced her torso on to the crate and pulled her backside towards him. Cathy felt the rough wood on her cheek and stretched her arms out, searching for something to hold on to. She grabbed hold of the sides of the crate, for want of something better, and braced herself. Fleetingly, she thought she saw a figure, possibly Josh, watching from an upstairs window, but was too far gone to care.

'Give it to me,' she called out. 'Fuck me!'

'I knew I'd have you begging for it,' the workman gasped.

'Oi, Paul, where are ya? You getting this load shifted, or what?' An angry, authoritative voice rang out across the museum yard.

'Jeez-us!' The workman came dangerously close to slicing his cock in two as he struggled to get it back into his trousers.

'Shit!' Cathy pulled her clothes together and watched as an angry site manager paced up and down the courtyard.

The workman was strapping on his tool belt with shaking hands. 'I could get the sack if the guv'nor catches me slacking again.'

Cathy felt that she would have quite happily taken the

risk, had it been her. 'Best you get back to your work then.' She smiled and stalked back towards the museum.

She ducked into a staff toilet and splashed herself with cold water; her face, her neck, her arms, until the heat of the workman had left her and she shivered slightly. Struggling for composure, Cathy held her head up high and took the spiralling stone steps down towards the basement. It was cool here and silent. She moved between two pillars and leaned her head against the cold stone of the sarcophagus, letting her breathing slow and the strength return to her shaking knees.

'Cathy?' She heard her name as a whisper and looked up at Josh's troubled face.

'Sssh.' He placed a finger on her lips. 'I saw you, outside.' He ran the finger across her mouth and down along her jaw. 'It's very frustrating when you don't get what you want.' The finger was smoothing an eyebrow now, his voice low and hypnotic. 'It can be hard to tell people what you want . . . what you need.' The finger was tracing the arch of her throat.

Cathy examined his young, pale face and hardly dared breathe, afraid of breaking the spell. 'Tell me,' she murmured.

Josh was smoothing her hair away from her face with trembling hands. 'Such beautiful bones,' he whispered. 'Can I see you?'

Cathy tipped her head only slightly, sensing that her stillness encouraged him. Every nerve ending was electrified by him, waiting for his touch. Slowly, Josh undressed her. Cathy had never seen such concentration on a man's face. As each garment fell – her blouse, her bra, her skirt – he slowly ran his fingertips along the skin underneath, tracing the outline of her collarbone, her ribcage and, as her panties slid towards her ankles, her hip bones.

'Will you lie for me, Cathy?' He held a hand out to lead the way to the marble slab, which they used to lay out the artefacts, and helped her on.

Cathy's skin rippled with goosebumps as she lay on the slab, naked except for her sandals. His shaking fingers closed her eyelids and crossed her arms over her chest, smoothing her hardened nipples as he did so. She felt a sheet flutter over her, sensual against her bare skin.

'Be still now, it's only for a moment . . . for the anticipation.'

Cathy heard Josh's footsteps leave the room and the stillness buzzed in her head. The seconds stretched out in exquisite torture until finally Josh's footsteps returned and the scent of his musky aftershave filled the room again.

Cathy's senses strained towards Josh, trying to guess what his next move would be.

She sensed him standing over her for a while before the sheet was pulled slowly away. She felt Josh's breath on her shoulder, and she kept her eyes closed, willing her excited breathing to still. Then he began the exploration of her flesh with his small, soft brush, a procedure she had seen him perform countless times. She imagined his look of total concentration. She felt as if every hair on her body was standing on end. It took every ounce of will-power not to moan and writhe beneath his touch but Cathy remained silent and still, as she knew she should.

Josh was removing her sandals now, with infinite care. She felt his delicate touch magnified a thousand times. And then, bliss, her legs were drawn apart and her knees raised until her lips parted and her pussy was displayed for Josh to examine. She felt incredibly vulnerable and intensely aroused at the same time. The longer she sensed Josh examining her, the more aroused she became. The effort of breathing slowly was becoming almost impossible as the longing for penetration overwhelmed her. Josh ran a finger slowly over her clit, up and down, slowly, slower, slowest, until Cathy was sure that she would scream the place down and break the spell completely if she remained impassive one second longer.

Finally, as if sensing that he had tormented her long enough, Josh's long body was on top of her. He pushed her hands above her head, and his own were all over her now, hot and urgent. His tongue was on her breasts, her neck; his breath in her ear.

'Wake up for me, Cathy.' He reached down and she felt his fingers push deep inside her.

Cathy groaned.

'That's it, Cathy, come back to me.' Her neck was slick with his kisses and she smelled herself on his fingers as he held her still to penetrate her. Cathy moaned loudly against his mouth, relief and pleasure lapping her in great waves.

'Yes, Cathy, yes!' His cries were mingling with her own as he thrust deeper and harder, pulling her knees up to her chest as high as they would go.

She reached down to hold Josh into her as she pressed her clit hard against him. Then Josh reached beneath her and thrust one finger deep into her anus. Her body tensed and she came, hard.

Josh pumped into her, moaning into her ear, 'Cathy, I knew you'd come back to me!'

He threw his head back and, for the first time, looked her in the eye.

Cathy smiled; some things were definitely worth waiting, and waiting, and waiting for.

Teen Spirit

Louise James

Teen Spirit

I fell in lust with him the moment I weighed his balls. It was almost chucking-out time at the Sirens bar, and I had been watching him for an hour. The last time he looked I had held his gaze, but I now felt my chance closing on me like sliding doors. One more vodka and I would have the bollocks to do it, to behave like a teenager again.

When at last I was talking to him, I played with the pearlised buttons on his black silk shirt, which hung outside his trousers. His face was beautiful, all angles like a geometrical puzzle, but I *had* to find out the truth. My friends often said I could be cold and calculating. Well, what I was about to do was almost scientific in its execution: weighing his balls to calculate the length of his dick, like an executioner computing the weight of the condemned man by shaking his hand. And he thought he was just getting a lucky grope . . .

It couldn't be as simple as just taking the damn thing out. Leaning into him as he stood against the bar, so that nobody could see what I was doing, I worked my way down from the top to the bottom button of his shirt and cupped his balls in my right hand. In my left hand I held my glass, raised up to my face so that I would be able to see, from the corner of my eye, the reading in the vodka. His balls were as big as Fabergé eggs, and just as precious. The vodka in the glass swelled, as if a spirit were passing through water.

My lips unfolded into a broad smile; I pressed my face into his, and I drank a kiss from his mouth: a shot as neat as the spirit that had revealed him to me.

I was sitting behind the till at Where The Girls Are wondering why I had let my girlfriends drag me away from him. Always, I have been able to get whatever, whomever, I wanted – and this was one big catch. Perhaps the vodka which had inspired me also overpowered me; maybe the charge the spirit received, and the size of the cock I perceived, had got the better of me for once. I left, having only talked dirty to him. I said I wanted him to split me in fucking two with his rock-hard dick, and then I was somehow swept away in a huddle that staggered towards the nightclub.

Now, I was sitting in my shop watching women pawing at things, determined to soil the clothes on display and spoil my Quality Fantasy Time. I shuffled on my chair and felt my short skirt ride up my thighs, like a retracting foreskin. Finding myself in a vague strop, I stood up to straighten a rail of marked-down dresses, and imagined him adjusting his cock. It would be changing position in his trousers right now, as he thought about me. The water in my glass on the counter rippled. Yes, there it went. Where was he? In what stupid situation was his burgeoning erection being wasted? In a lift, perhaps? In his car? In bed with his partner? Whatever. It was *me* who had got his blood pumping, infusing every little capillary that collectively engorged that stunning shaft.

There was a woman in the shop who looked like shit,

and she was ransacking my stock. A burglar could not have treated it with as much disrespect.

'Can I try these on?' she said, and I knew she had no intention of buying the trousers which she had thrust at me. My fanny was sticky.

'No, you can't,' I said. 'Now get the fuck out of my shop.'

I bundled her out of the door as if I were putting out a bag of rubbish, turned the sign to CLOSED, and disappeared into the fitting room to have a lie down and a quick wank.

It was a good'un, a two-minute shiver. I reckoned I could soon be beating men in the time required to reach a climax. Admiring myself in the fitting room mirror, I straightened my clothes, rubbed away a streak of lipstick that a stray hair had lashed across my cheek, checked my tights for snags, drew back the curtain and entered the shop again, a new woman – for the next few minutes, at least. It was then, as I was turning back the door sign from CLOSED to OPEN, that it happened.

It was him. His fathomless black eyes stared straight at me, pinning me against my subconscious like a double-barrelled big dick. I was stunned. He had disorientated me, and the swimming sensation swept me back to my teens. All right, so I was only twenty-five but it felt like a long time ago to little melodramatic me.

I opened the door and let him in. He walked around my New Season room, looking at the winter coats, and then stepped up on to the platform on which the till counter was raised like a DJ's booth on a small, provincial nightclub dancefloor. I withdrew behind it. The water in the glass was swelling close to the brim.

This was the Sale room. He looked at every item, feeling the material, checking the price tags and the garment care labels. So, he knew about clothes. The bitch for whom he was buying should appreciate that. And him. Oh yes, The Cock That Was Not Mine . . . yet. He picked out a three-quarter-length camel coat, size 18. I allowed myself a nasty smile.

'Can I exchange this if the size is wrong?' he asked.

'That's the biggest we do,' I said with glee, 'but do call back for a full refund if she can't get in it.'

A cloud of moisture darkened my crotch.

What the hell was happening here? The fact that the object of my lust was married, or entwined with a partner of some description, had never stopped me before. And I had let him slip from my grasp twice now. Moreover, why had he come to my shop? It was too much of a coincidence.

Then I remembered. Before I had left Sirens that night, I had given him my card. Not very romantic, granted, but it could have been worse: I could have given him the clap. But he had chosen to ignore my mobile number, which I had written on the back, and instead decided to call on me at work. Was he trying to make me jealous by flaunting the fact that there was a woman in his life? Well, if that was the case he had picked the wrong woman to rile and, anyway, I had already guessed: all the best ones are in relationships.

That evening, I treated myself to a facial, an aromatherapy massage and a bikini line wax: if he was to come in to the shop the next day, I was going to be ready, physically and mentally. Oh, yes, I also got myself a new bottle of vodka and some cheap perfume from the market – a quick squirt of any old nasty scent and men would think you smelled great. Losing him the first time was a mistake; the second time seemed like carelessness, but a third would be fucking unforgivable.

So, there I was the next day, politely serving the dribs and drabs who ducked in and out of my little empire, despite the fact that I had to keep nipping in to the back to check if the red spots around my pussy – from the waxing, of course – had disappeared yet.

The witching hour, when the toddlers were unleashed from school and were dragged in to the shop by their mothers, passed, and still my man had not arrived. But I knew he would. He probably picked up that coat because he could think of nothing else to do; it would not have been intended for anyone. Yes, he would be here soon, explaining how he was terribly sorry and he should have checked what size she was and could he fuck me senseless please? Why certainly, sir . . .

He was probably waiting until after four-thirty, when the shop would be quieter. It was sensible, although he could have arrived at midday amidst a shopful of nuns and I would have cleared them out for him. At about four, a woman, mercifully bereft of children, entered the shop as the last of the mothers was leaving.

She was better dressed than anyone who had been in all day, and she clearly wanted me to notice this, undoing her coat with a flourish as she came in. Her clothes were understated and classy, but I could not help focusing on her legs, which flowed long and effortlessly from her short A-line skirt as if she and it were one. And for a tall, well-built woman, she had magically thin ankles, although I suppose that could have been a trick of her hosiery. I always thought I had the best legs in the world, but now I had met a challenger. And the cow was showing them off like a flasher.

Then I recognised the three-quarter-length coat. Oh God, it was her! His wife, his partner, his other half, his whore, or whoever she was. The coat was a perfect fit, and she carried her size with grace. She bent down to examine the hem of a dress, and her shrinking skirt revealed more of her beautiful legs. To my surprise I felt my pussy lips poke out a quick tongue of lust. But her mannerisms were almost theatrical – they were not the movements of a woman behaving normally. She knew I was watching her.

I folded my arms and sulked behind the till on the upper floor. Soon she was stepping up towards me, and I made a point of not looking at her. Now it was me who was being showy, filing my nails like a flaming drag queen. She walked straight past me with a daring, very short beaded party dress and disappeared into the corridor towards the fitting room.

She had been in there for some time, so I emerged from behind the till and called down the corridor: 'Do shout if you need any help, won't you?'

Behind me, my glass of vodka wobbled. Had I caught it as I stood up? I could not remember doing so, but it had definitely been disturbed. Drops of liquid had been sprayed around the counter, as if a penny had been dropped into it.

'Could you just help me with this zip?' she said. She sounded nervous, her voice broken.

I pulled back the curtain and looked up her long legs, which shimmered in black Lycra-laced nylon like knife blades caught by sunlight. Then I tried to focus on her back. The zip fastened easily. I pulled it up slowly, and as it reached her neck she pulled her hair to one side. This made me look over her shoulder at her face in the mirror. Her black eyes bored in to me. God, how narcissistic was *he*? He was with somebody who looked like him in drag.

There was a smashing sound from the other room. The vodka had swelled, and the glass shattered. The eyes in the mirror held me captive, and a hand reached round to grab mine. I watched it being placed on the front of the dress, and felt the impression of a huge cock beneath it. I looked at it in the mirror: the frock looked as if a sleek animal was shinning up it.

I pulled away and ran from the fitting room. God, I had never been taken in like this before! The glass was broken but there was still plenty of vodka in the bottle. I took a large shot of it. Just admit it, I told myself: he's fucking gorgeous, even in drag. Or, *especially* in drag. I turned the door sign to CLOSED and when I turned back around, he was standing on the floor in front of the till, tossing the long black tresses of his wig behind his shoulders. That little dress only came to the tops of his thighs.

I walked over to him and put my arms around him, as if we were about to smooch on a dancefloor. As I fondled his firm buttocks beneath the flimsy material, I felt his dick pressing into my stomach. We sat down on the sofa by the window and I put my hand on his knees, and when he crossed his right leg over his left, I ran my nails up his thigh until my hand disappeared beneath the hem of his dress. The clothes were like a second skin on him, and it was not until he bent down his face to kiss me that I remembered he was a man in drag.

What was I doing? I stood up, swiped the bottle from the counter and disappeared into the stock room. I took a huge swig of vodka, hoping it would tell me what to do. Then I heard the click of his heels advancing towards the door.

I retreated into the back of the room, hiding amongst the rails and boxes and old kettles. Old kettles? Whatever, I didn't have time to be puzzled. The door creaked open and the clicking become louder. It wasn't as if I could hide successfully. And as the vodka infused my spirit I began to realise that I didn't want to hide. The perfume, I felt, was rising from me in visible form, like heat. I wanted to be hunted out by him, and found, and fucked.

I took a fake fur out of its cellophane shroud and spread it on the floor, stepped out of my clothes and laid on my back with my legs spread as wide as possible. I dipped in a finger, testing the water, and touched my clit. My lust went off like a flare, letting him know exactly where I was. I knew he was stalking me through the rails of clothing which he probably wanted to wear and, God, yes – I would dress him up in every damn one and do his make-up and treat him like a woman, but only after he had taken me like a brute. Would he still do that? Would he just want to sit down and talk about knickers?

I need not have worried. As the heel clicks got closer they began to slow. On my left and right were two rails of clothes, and I saw the fat head of a rampant cock nudge out from the side of a hanging fur, like a beast nosing through a jungle, sniffing me out.

Oh, he'd got it out; it was leading him to the Holy Water of my pussy, and I so badly wanted him to dive in and splash my lust all over us as liberally as cheap aftershave. The cock shaft began to appear, at a forty-five degree angle, inch after inch, revealing its breathtaking length, its exciting girth, slowly, powerfully.

His appearance when he came into the shop had been the most feminine of any of my customers, but his clothes only served to emphasise the power of his rampant maleness. When he came into view fully, he was holding the little dress above his waist, and his dick stood out at me like the gun on a tank. The glare of the sun from the back window highlighted, as if with the dash of a marker pen, his stockings and the big, thick vein on the underside of his cock.

I parted my lips and my cunt opened like the mouth of a big cat. My naked body was soon being crushed into the fur beneath me by the weight of his big but elegant body. And then I felt the dilation of my pussy, the first plunge, and the slap of his balls against me – those precious eggs that I had weighed in the bar that night.

I stretched out one of my arms and knocked over the empty vodka bottle, making it spin on the floor as madly as my head was swimming. Facing him, his eyes pinned me down, and his dick drilled into me: I could not have been more in his grasp if he had shackled me. And I knew this was only the start.

He pressed his face into my neck.

'You smell fantastic,' he said.

His cock plunged into me again, and it felt as though the head was going to pop out of my mouth like a plum. 'And you feel fantastic.'

His voice was not faltering now. I pulled his head towards me and sniffed his skin.

'What's that you're ... Oh *Jesus* ... What's that you're wearing?' I breathed. 'It smells like ...'

'Teen Spirit,' he grunted, ramming me hard, as if he was telling me to shut the fuck up.

I had found it. My quest was over. I was eighteen again, and I was being fucked like I had never been fucked before.

The Lesson

Catherine Miller

The Lesson

It was happening again. My mind was wandering in a lazy, daydreaming dance away from the content of the lecture on French Revolution history, attuned instead to the music of his voice. I knew where this was headed. To a failing grade on the exam scheduled for next week.

It had been like this all semester. I had no problem studying the textbook at home, but the lecture material escaped me, not because it was difficult, but because Professor Matthews himself was far more intriguing.

I was older than the other students, 32, having taken a long break for travel, marriage and divorce between my first and second years of college. At this rate, I felt I would be confirming the stereotype of older, returning students as dilettantes or intellectually past their prime. Thankfully, I was acing all of my other courses. And given the way my body responded sitting in class with Professor Matthews, I was sure I was just coming into my prime.

How can I explain the attraction? He was no movie star, although I often suspected there were muscles lurking under his clothes, waiting to be admired and stroked by soft, feminine fingers. He had a bit of a stomach, but I liked it. It made him look vulnerable, like some kind of Achilles heel. Besides, almost all men his age had some padding there. His age, right. To be honest, he was old enough to be my father. But who was counting?

As class ended, the usual din of 50 students getting up from desks took over. I was about to join them, and the usual reluctance to leave the room and Professor Matthews behind fluttered in my stomach like the flapping wings of a thousand tiny birds.

'Ms Anderson. I'd like to speak to you for a minute.'

The voice I'd come to know and love came from close behind me and reverberated through me. I turned around to face him, trying to compose myself. I knew I was blushing.

'Please . . . sit down.' He motioned to a chair in the first row. I stumbled into it ungracefully.

'I've noticed that your exam performance has been spotty. You seem to have a good grasp of the material on parts of the exam, and then to be completely in the dark on other parts. Often on the same topic, which is hard to figure. Look, if there's anything I can do to help you, I'd like to try. As you know the exam next week counts as forty per cent of your grade for the semester. And judging from your previous exam scores,' he said, glancing at his grade book gravely, 'you cannot afford to fail this one.'

Was there anything he could do? He wanted to help me. I smiled weakly. Short of meeting me before class and screwing me silly, I thought, I was beyond help. And I knew he wasn't offering me that kind of assistance.

'I've been a little distracted lately,' I stammered, being as truthful as I dared.

'Well, I don't want to pry into your personal life and I suppose there's nothing I can do about your being distracted . . .'

If only you knew, I thought, wryly, you're the only one who can do anything about my being distracted. I tuned back in as he was saying, '. . . but I'm willing to stay for a while now and go over some of the questions you may have.'

It was Friday and 4.30pm. Classes were over for the week. One last clang of the building door resounded and then all was silent. Everyone else was headed back to the dorms or home to start the weekend. Why wasn't he? Wasn't there someone eagerly waiting for him? There had to be. But there we were, alone, and he was looking at me, searching my face quizzically.

'Are there any areas that you feel particularly shaky on that I could review for you?'

Yes, my whole body is shaking, I wanted to say, but didn't. I was suddenly more aware of feeling aroused than usual. Being alone with him and the way he was focusing his attention on me was rendering me speechless. Not wanting him to leave, or think I was a hopeless case, I searched my mind for some intelligent question to ask.

'I'm uncertain about the stages of government which followed the French Revolution,' I finally said. Actually, I'm uncertain whether I can keep up this pretence, I thought to myself.

'Very well.' He turned to the blackboard and started writing an outline. The clicking sound of the chalk as it struck the board mixed with the sight of his large hands moving across it. I felt hypnotised.

'Let's start with Robespierre. What was his role?' he asked me cheerfully, in his kindness apparently trying to ask me something he thought I would know to build my confidence.

'I know he was the . . . actually I'm not sure,' I admitted.

He looked a little worried on my behalf, then turned back to the board. I took off my sweater and laid it on the seat next to me. It's getting very hot in here, I thought.

'Robespierre was . . .'

It was no use. I didn't hear anything he said. I was

watching the way the seat of his pants cradled his ass, an ass worthy of a Michelangelo sculpture, the way it strained against the fabric of his khakis when he walked as he did now from one side of the blackboard to the other, pointing to parts of the outline.

'Does that help?' he asked.

'Yes,' I said, telling a white lie, meaning the glimpse of the shape of his ass I had just had.

'And what about the Revolutionary Council? Do you understand what their role was?' he asked me, trying to involve me actively in the lesson.

'I have to admit, I'm not clear on their role either,' I heard myself saying, as though from a distance. I regretted this. I wished he could see how bright I was. But there was nothing I could do about that.

He turned back to the board, his arms folded across his chest, apparently pondering how to best illustrate the role of the Revolutionary Council to the slowest student he'd ever met. His shirt strained across his back and I saw for the first time how big it was. How I wanted to sneak up behind him and press my breasts against it.

Instead, I took off my blouse. And how, you may ask, did I justify this at the time? It felt like a strange sort of truth-telling, taking off an item of clothing for each answer I did not have, exposing my ignorance of the material and my desire for him in this very direct, physical way that mirrored how I felt inside.

I wasn't kidding myself. I knew I'd probably be put on academic suspension for this. But it was worth it, I decided, especially when he turned around and I saw the look on his face as he took in the white skin on my neck and shoulders, followed the curve of my breastbone to my breasts in their sheer bra that had a sheen that made them look like they'd been sprinkled with stardust. His look was part shock, part disbelief, and several parts desire in a measure that told me there was no woman waiting for him at home.

He turned back to the board, feebly trying to go on with the lesson. Did he think I would put my blouse back on or that this would never have happened when he turned back again? While his back was turned, I unhooked and removed my bra, letting my breasts spill out and bounce under the florescent overhead lights.

'So, when the Revolutionary Council made the decision to . . .' he trailed off and turned to look at me again, at my pink nipples, now rosebuds, erect and pointing at him unmistakably, my shoulders shaking ever so slightly with the cool classroom air and the desire to at last be seen and touched.

He came towards me tentatively. I could smell the scent of chalk mixed faintly with the aftershave he must have sprinkled on that morning. His large hands reached for me through the air, but he seemed rooted to the spot on which he stood. Unable to wait, I stood and moved in his direction, unzipping my skirt as I stepped towards him and slipping out of it with more grace than I'd ever had before. All that separated me from him was my thong, which was soaked with my juices and pressed against my pussy and ass the way I longed for him to.

I reached him in a few short steps and pressed myself against him. It was intoxicating to finally be touching him, to feel all of his body against mine. I loved how exposed I was, wearing almost nothing while he still had all of his clothing on. I felt both powerful and powerless at the same time.

I watched his face change, confidence and calm replaced by uncertainty and desire. His features seemed to have changed as well, once laid out on his face in perfect order, now contorted, lips trembling, eyes moist and shining. A tiny whimper escaped from his lips from somewhere deep inside him. I loved being ogled like forbidden fruit, and I savoured the struggle in which he was engaged. At last, we were on equal footing.

The stiff fabric of his chambray shirt scraped gently

against my nipples, making them tingle. The warmth of his body was a welcome change from the cool air of the classroom, from the solitude of my many nights spent between too cool sheets in an empty bed. His hands surrounded my face, dwarfing me with delight, then moved over my shoulders and down to my breasts, cupping them in apparent awe. The French Revolution may have been old news to him. I, on the other hand, was an entirely new discovery.

I unbuttoned his shirt, peeled it off of his sturdy shoulders and arms and tossed it into the sphere of space that surrounded us, but which was now a blur. Nothing else existed but the feeling of being against him, smelling him, feeling at last the hard curves of those muscles – and there were more than I could possibly have seen through his clothing – pressing into my soft cushioned flesh.

Our lips found each other like magnets; tongues met and snaked around each other. My knees nearly buckled with the aroma and flavour of his mouth. His cock pointed urgently at me and I brushed my pubic bone against it, making it leap and him shudder.

At last I could no longer take anything separating us and I watched my determined hands fiercely unbuckling his belt, unzipping his pants and dropping them to floor. He didn't help me. It was as though if I undressed him, was the one to reach for him, then it would all be my responsibility. Or perhaps being seduced by a sexually aggressive young woman in his classroom was as much a fantasy of his as seducing him was mine. I did not have long to wait for an answer to this question.

'I have stayed after class with many students in my time,' he whispered, his hands still on my breasts, 'but never with one as promising as you or who takes such initiative.'

His briefs clung to the curves of his ass and thighs, accentuating their size and muscle. My mouth watered as I slipped my fingertips inside the rim of the band and pulled them slowly down over his ass, pausing to watch as his hard cock, redder than the skin elsewhere, popped out and up, and blanched the white fabric of the briefs by contrast.

His large fingers stroked my ass cheeks gently, tic-klingly, sending wave after wave of excitement coursing through my pussy. He gently ran one delicious finger across the wet fabric of my thong. The tease was so exciting and left me longing for so much more that I moaned, and pulled down my thong to reveal myself completely to him, to invite him to touch me unrestrained by any barrier.

Much as I enjoyed watching his thighs straining against what was left of his briefs, his cock and balls hanging like tempting ripe fruit over the waistband, I wanted them gone. I was impatient for our bodies to be free completely, to explore each other. I pulled them down and he stepped awkwardly out of them. I silently bid them farewell, tossing them to some unknown part of the classroom, my eyes never leaving his delectable body.

'I've been watching you all semester,' I breathed. 'But I never dreamed that you would be this glorious under-neath your khakis.'

'And I thought the problem was that you weren't paying attention in class.' He smiled, exposing a row of perfect, white teeth.

I could have drowned in that smile. My fingers traced his chest, shoulders and neck and my lips moistly fol-lowed, lighting on his nipples, tonguing them. His body trembled faintly and I could feel again how much he wanted me. But he made no move to take me, which maddened me and increased my hunger. Despite his seductive smile and banter, did he think it was wrong to indulge in enjoying me fully? Of course, it *was* wrong. But I would have him anyway.

I took his hand and pressed it against my pussy. My pelvis thrusted pleadingly at his fingertips and he moved them ever so slightly, so teasingly against my lips. I wiggled against them, starving for more stimulation.

Gradually he increased the pressure and movement slightly, and I continued to press and writhe against them, until my legs felt like Jell-O and I was on the verge of coming, my moaning getting louder and louder, my skin tingling everywhere from the full body contact with him.

My upper thigh felt his cock pressing against it and his pubic hair tickled my skin. A drop of pre-come had slithered from his cock on to my thigh, making the feel of him against me delightfully sticky. I could smell me and smell him, and there was so much to enjoy that, like a kite climbing ever higher into the sky, I soared into a powerful climax, leaning my head against his chest as I came, my grateful voice echoing through the halls of the empty building, my thrusts towards his hand diminishing as the joyous contractions in my cunt gradually subsided.

I wanted him inside me like I wanted to live another day. I knew he wanted it too; his cock was harder and redder and wetter than it had been before. It was now or never. I led him by the hand to the large desk at the front of the class, pushed my body against his until he was lying with his back across the desk and hovered over him, my body full of promise of pleasures yet to come. I heard a thud as the grade book he had been so gravely consulting earlier on my behalf, long forgotten, fell off the desk and on to the classroom floor.

I reached down and, with feathery touches, tickled and teased his inner thighs, his sweet puckered hole, and his balls, their sac now tight and ridged with built-up tension. He wiggled and moaned until I knew neither of us could wait any longer. His sounds and his movements drove me wild. I lowered my body on to his, my nerve endings exploding with the pleasure and relief of his finally being inside me.

He cried out with pleasure as I enveloped him and moved up and down in unmeasured strokes. I had no more patience left. Every time I rose up and he slipped part way out of me, I couldn't wait to feel him inside again and plunged down over him quickly. He expanded further, stretching me deliciously. In his excitement, he put one huge hand on each hip of mine and bucked up to meet my cunt. I smiled inwardly, silently enjoyed his loss of control, his yielding to the overwhelming desire to take an active role in our lustful union.

'How am I doing now, Professor Matthews?' I whispered teasingly in his ear, pausing to wait for his answer.

'A+,' he sputtered, his eyes pleading with me to continue.

His breaths came faster and faster, his chest heaved, pectorals dancing under the taut skin of a much younger man, from his fevered clutching of my hips and ass. I was overwhelmed with the visual feast before me. I was sure I had never seen a more beautiful masculine sight.

'Mona . . .' he cried, using my first name, which sent shivers down my spine. He had always addressed me formally in class.

He began to lift me up with his hips and thighs each time he bucked up at me, like a bronco at the rodeo. If I wasn't so determined to hang on, I might have been thrown off.

I loved watching him lose control. I was no longer 'Ms Anderson', and he was no longer the composed professor. Whatever he had once been before, he was now a wild man, unleashing passions that went far beyond the intellectual. It no longer mattered whether someone else from the college came into the room unexpectedly. There was nothing to be done to stop us. It was all too compelling.

When he came, with a long, baritone groan, I shook with satisfaction, and the jerks of his body with each wave of his climax pressed against me like staccato notes in a symphony.

I lay down on top of him, enjoying the scent of fresh

sweat, manoeuvreing my nostrils under his arm to breathe it in more deeply as he leaned his head against the desk. I smiled with the joy of one who has quenched a long-burning fire.

And then it came rushing back to me: the facts about the French Revolution that had been eluding me all semester while my lust for Professor Matthews had gone unsatisfied.

'I think I remember now who Robespierre was!' I declared, with more excitement perhaps than such a memory normally warranted.

'Robespierre who?' he answered groggily, his voice thick with the remnants of passion.

That's when I lost it. It started as a giggle, bubbling up from somewhere deep inside me but, before I knew it, I was in the throes of an unending series of full-throated belly laughs. It was contagious. Soon, my dear professor and I were laughing so hard, we almost fell off his desk.

We had left the French Revolution behind.

Or perhaps not. *Liberté, égalité, fraternité*. Oh, I knew that this was not exactly what the designers of the Revolution had in mind. But the freedom I'd felt, fraternising on equal terms with this man I was forbidden to have, gave these three words new meaning. And it was a lesson I doubted either of us would forget for a long time to come.

A Matter of Interest

Rosetta Stone

A Matter of Interest

He knew something was wrong as soon as he woke and blinked to clear his muzzy head, but it was only when he tried to stretch that he realised how wrong it was. He, who prided himself on always being in control, was naked, chained and as helpless as it was possible to be. He was also being watched.

'What the hell?' he demanded, staring at his three slaves.

'Hell?' He stared at the diminutive blonde whose smile set new records for vindictiveness, wondering why he'd been stupid enough to think that fragility meant the same as lack of strength. 'This isn't hell, Master.' The intonation she gave the final word made it clear that he was the one who'd been mastered now. 'Hell was what you've put us through; as you're going to find out.'

'You asked me to. You said you wanted to be mine.'

He protested, tugging against the cuffs that held him, not surprised when they didn't creak, let alone break. Hadn't he had them made to his exact specifications to ensure none of his captives could escape? It was useless, so he lay back and assessed his surroundings, fighting back growing terror. He was chained to a Y-shaped frame that had swung from the ceiling on long strong chains as he struggled. His legs were spread wide, fastened to the arms of the 'Y', not just with ankle cuffs, but with long lengths of silky rope that made any movement impossible and escape the stuff of his wildest fantasies. They could do anything they liked to him now; anything at all. They could even . . . His mind rejected the implications, panic growing steadily. Not that. Never that.

'Let me go.' He tried to put the normal snap of authority into his voice, but held back on the threats that would usually have enforced obedience.

'No.' Zoe must have been elected spokesperson, but the other two were just as terrifying.

Miranda looked taller and more statuesque than ever in the black leather costume that he'd insisted she wore on the memorable night when he'd first shown her the delights of the frame he was now fastened to. Lesbian Miranda, who'd cried so bitterly when he'd first used her. She'd cried harder still when she'd come; as if he'd wrecked her world by proving that she could enjoy a man. There'd be no mercy there, so he wouldn't demean himself by asking for any.

And beautiful blond James, with his wide, fawn-like eyes and the little-boy-lost expression that seemed to invite abuse. James, who he'd kept in bondage for hours; sometimes even days. He'd been blindfolded and helpless, continually penetrated while he waited for his master to bring pleasure or pain, denial or release. James with the sulky mouth and clever tongue; whose bisexuality had made him such a fascinating challenge.

Tonight that little-boy-lost look had been replaced by grim resolve, and the master began to tremble, biting his lip to stop himself pleading. It had been such a normal night; at the start of an equally normal weekend. His three 'slaves' had arrived, as they did every other Friday night. As usual, they'd stripped naked in the hallway, handing him their clothes to be locked away as a symbol of their willing subjugation. Then he'd given them their costumes. There'd been a black leather bodysuit for Miranda, with an array of zips that allowed him to bare her lush body gradually, prolonging the torturous pleasure of bringing her to orgasm after unwanted orgasm.

He'd left James naked except for a cock harness, but he too was wearing black leather now. As the master looked down he realised that same cock harness was fastened around his limp penis, the leather straps as loose as the metal rings. Zoe, who he'd left naked; beautiful, wanton, hedonistic Zoe, who prided herself on being able to enjoy anything, was still naked. She smiled as he looked at her, and he realised how he'd been trapped.

He'd ordered her to fetch him a drink, then kneel beside him, her back arched to act as his table. He'd sipped from the glass he'd left ready in the fridge, putting it down between each mouthful, revelling in her trembles as the icy tumbler met warm flesh. Occasionally he'd caressed one heavy pendulous breast or stroked her moistness, feeling her struggling not to react to him. Now he was as helpless as he'd ever made any of them, and Zoe was moving closer.

'Tonight,' she murmured, licking her finger in a gesture that brought back a million memories of that full, passionate mouth sucking his cock. He felt the moisture as she stroked his chest, then traced a gentle line over his flaccid cock. 'Tonight we'll show you what it feels like to be used, and don't think we'll let you off gently. You owe us; with interest.'

'But you wanted it,' he protested, as she kneeled astride him with her back to him as if he weren't worth looking at. The frame swung perilously under the added weight, then steadied as she leaned forward, the full globes of her bare arse swaying as she took him into her mouth.

'We didn't have a choice.'

He couldn't remember hearing Miranda laugh before,

and he'd never heard her sound so triumphant. She moved closer, standing by his head, stroking his face as if he were a pet; just as he'd once touched her. He could smell leather and sweat, and, overlaying it all, the scent of an aroused woman. He closed his eyes, knowing that whatever lay ahead for him wouldn't be good. Miranda loved to be in control, and he'd taken such pleasure in taking it away from her that she'd revel in turning the tables now.

'Any more than you do now.' She rubbed his nipples with a gentleness that he wasn't fool enough to believe would last.

He winced as she nibbled the soft skin at the base of his throat, fear turning to unwilling lust as the women worked on his body. Zoe's mouth was warm and insistent on his cock, her hands gently massaging his balls. Miranda's tongue was just as clever, her hands on his nipples just as persistent, and he groaned as his erection grew.

He didn't want this, but there was nothing he could do to stop them, and Miranda wasn't the only one who hated losing control. He'd always been able to buy anything he wanted, just as these three once had. But this loss of control was as different, and tinged with unwanted pleasure, as their lives had become when he'd lent them the money that he knew they couldn't afford. Then, when they'd admitted that they couldn't repay him, he'd given them a stark choice. Either they faced the scandal of bankruptcy, or they could work off their debts by becoming his slaves.

'There's nothing you can do to stop us.' Until now, James had seemed content to watch. Now he moved closer, standing by his captive's waist. 'All you can do is take it.'

'You can't make me vanish,' the master blustered. 'All hell will break loose if I'm not in my office on Monday.'

'Don't worry, you'll be there,' James said with a worryingly placid smile. 'But this is Friday night. A lot can happen in a weekend, as you showed us.'

He opened the hand that had been clenched by his side, made one rapid movement, and the captive screamed. He'd used the nipple clamps on the women, particularly Miranda with her small, incredibly sensitive breasts, but he'd never experienced them himself. He tried to writhe away from the relentless pressure that left him feeling as if his nipples were about to explode, but all he could do was watch as James snapped the second clasp under his nose.

'You'll like it in the end,' he cooed, in hideous mimicry of the words the master had so often used to his slaves. 'In the end, you'll beg me for it.'

'Like hell I will!' The captive groaned as the second clamp snapped into place, and Zoe's teeth nipped his cock. 'I'll waive the debt.' He gambled, swearing that once he got free they'd suffer in a way that would show them how generous he'd been before.

'We know you will, but that isn't all we want.' Miranda abandoned her licking, sucking exploration of his body and tugged at one of the multitude of zips that adorned her bodysuit. It slid over the satin lining beneath, revealing one shockingly white breast. She eased it free, cupping it in her hands, caressing it as he'd so often done. As he remembered those happier times his cock sprang erect, growing painfully hard as he savoured the contrast between tight black leather and abundant female flesh. The straps and metal rings bit into his swollen cock, making his second groan one of pain rather than pleasure. He bit back a third one when Miranda smiled.

'You're starting to understand now, and to want. But we're not finished yet. You've given us such wonderful ideas, Master.' She put an emphasis on that last word that made it clear that the master had been mastered and he began to tremble.

'What are you going to do with me?' He might have

sworn never to plead or beg for anything, but this was different. These three people were set on vengeance, and the more he remembered the 'games' they'd played, the more certain he was that their vengeance would be slow and painful.

'Get our debt repaid; with interest, of course. And it will be interesting.' She tweaked one clamped nipple, reawakening the pain that had died to a bearable throb. 'I've always wondered how it would feel to watch you lose control; to see you beg and plead; first for me to stop, then for me to go on. The others feel the same, don't you?'

Zoe was too busy licking his captive cock, tasting and tormenting him until he found it hard to think of anything except the urge to bury himself deep in that supple body to answer, but James nodded.

'And more,' he said simply, and stroked Zoe's buttocks, first parting them, then sliding a finger along that glistening, hairless cleft. The prisoner watched, wondering whether James would fuck Zoe as she kneeled astride him, leaving him achingly unsatisfied. Then he realised that voyeurism was the least of his punishments. Zoe grunted, deep and content in her throat as two fingers slid into her cunt. She worked her body against the invaders, encouraging them, riding them, taking all the pleasure he wanted so badly.

'Poor dear,' Miranda cooed, as she too began to caress Zoe. Her hands were white against Zoe's tanned breasts, the black leather an erotic counterpoint to Zoe's mass of blonde hair.

Their erstwhile master groaned and closed his eyes, trying to block out this new torture. Miranda had been stroking her fellow slave with slow, gentle movements, just as he'd had her do so often while he'd forced Zoe to wait for the climaxes she needed so desperately. Tonight he was being forced to wait; and that wasn't all. He opened his eyes as he felt the pressure, shivering as his worst fears were confirmed. James's fingers were no longer buried to the knuckle in that sticky, welcoming pussy. Instead, he stood between the master's wide-stretched legs and was parting his buttocks.

'No! Please!' He'd used James that way, revelling in his silent resistance, but this was one experience he'd never had; and never wanted to.

'You'll like it once you get used to it.' James's angelic smile was a serene counterpoint to the moist finger that pressed against the tight ring of the master's anus. The master clenched his muscles, fighting the invidious attack, but James didn't force his way inside. Instead, he worked Zoe's secretions into the skin around that dark, tight, virgin entrance.

'Let me go,' the master whimpered, his assertiveness vanished, but James ignored him and opened the leather-bound chest that stood in the corner. The master looked up, wondering what lay ahead, and what he saw made his ordeal ten times worse.

One of Miranda's long, slender hands still caressed Zoe's large heavy breasts, but the other was reaching down to caress the tight bud of her clit. Still, Zoe's mouth worked relentlessly on his cock, countering the fear that might otherwise have unmanned him.

'We mustn't hurt him, must we?' Miranda cooed. 'That wasn't in the bargain. Of course, it's interesting to define hurt. Hurt pride doesn't count, does it? Does it?' she repeated when he didn't answer, twisting the nipple clamps until he gabbled.

'You agreed. You signed.'

'We had no choice. You'd have had us bankrupted if we didn't do what you wanted. Then we'd have been fired, with no hope of any other jobs. And you'd have kept us like this forever, so we changed the rules.'

He'd always been sure his three slaves disliked each other; that he was safe because they'd never work together against him. After everything he'd had them do they shouldn't have been able to bear the sight of each other, but tonight they moved as a smooth, practised team. As smooth, he thought numbly, as the lubricating gel that James had just taken from the chest. He held it up, as if to make sure his victim understood the implications of that apparently innocent tube, then burrowed again, producing a long, slender tube with a plunger like a syringe but without a needle.

'I'm being kinder to you than you were to me,' he murmured as he filled the tube with gel. The master clenched his buttocks together, hating every second of what was being done to him as his erstwhile slave wandered across the room.

'I want him to really feel this,' James said, as he took up position between the master's straddled legs and Zoe obediently scrambled off the prone body. The loss of those smooth, warm, tantalising lips around his painfully swollen cock was a relief so intense as to be almost pleasure in itself. Then the cool nozzle pushed against his anus, and he began to shake with fear.

'Any minute now,' James murmured, savouring the words as much as the actions.

The master tried to heave his body upwards, but the bindings held firm, and the gesture was his undoing. He howled rage and pain, but it was too late. The nozzle slid through his sphincter muscle, replacing fear with red, raw pain.

'Stop! Please! Stop!' He screamed; pride abandoned. Academically he knew the tube was only half an inch across, and the pain would soon pass if he relaxed, but how could he relax when he was so helpless, so penetrated?

Humiliation piled on humiliation. His cock, red and engorged after so long inside Zoe's clever mouth, was jerking convulsively, as if he welcomed what was being done to him, and he knew this was only the start.

'Please stop.'

He whimpered, but he wasn't surprised when James shook his head then, achingly slowly, depressed the plunger. Cool gel flooded the master's back passage, leaving him sticky and terrified. He fought his bonds until the cuffs bit into his wrists, but he knew they wouldn't give way. He'd designed them that way; just as he'd had this playroom soundproofed at such vast expense and made sure that no one would disturb him. No one would find him or rescue him, and it was only Friday night. A whole helpless weekend lay ahead of him and there was nothing he could do to stop it. All his money, all his power counted for nothing now.

This should have been the ultimate humiliation for the control freak he'd always been sure that he was. Yet, as James eased the syringe into him, there was a strange sort of pleasure too. For once in his highly organised life nothing was expected of him except to react. There was no need to think, or plan, or control. All he had to do was feel; and what he felt was new pain and humiliation as the syringe was replaced by first one firm finger, then another.

The master howled as James scissored his fingers apart inside his arse, working the gel into the sensitive inner tissues. He embraced the discomfort, hoping it would ease the pressure on his over-aroused cock, but Zoe crouched beside him again. As her tongue ran lasciviously up and down him, his whimpers became continuous, just as his slave's protests so often had. And seeing Miranda taking the same pleasure in his abasement that he once had in hers made the unwanted pleasure more humiliating still.

The fingers withdrew briefly, then re-entered, this time joined by a third finger. They were laced together, the knuckles feeling knobbly inside him and the pain was joined by a dark, viscid, intense pleasure. If it hadn't been for the cock harness, he'd have climaxed, and realising that he was all the things he'd despised James for being caused the loudest howl yet.

'You understand now,' Miranda murmured. He began to hope that his ordeal was almost over, then realised that it had barely begun. His tormentors withdrew from their invasions of his body, but only for a second, and what they were doing was worse.

He heard a tearing sound, as if of foil. Then James was standing beside his head, his erection red and hard. He'd never realised how long and firm it was before, never cared as he'd taken his own pleasure in that boyish arse. Now all he could do was stare numbly at it, knowing that he too would soon be penetrated; taken, abused. Zoe had taken up James's old position, standing between his knees, and he groaned as he felt himself ensleeved in soft, yielding latex.

'Let me go and I'll tear up the documents and destroy all the pictures.'

He began to hope when Miranda paused, frowning. She was a lawyer; bright and savvy. A lesbian like her would have no interest in his body, so she was his best hope; maybe his only hope. 'You won't owe me another penny,' he swore, and he'd never meant anything more sincerely.

'Right.' Miranda turned on her heel and stalked out, leaving James and Zoe to watch their prisoner. He lay still, determined not to provoke them to new excesses, swearing that some day, somehow, he'd have his revenge. There were pictures they didn't know about; taken with the cameras that were hidden in the ceiling; those same cameras that would be running now, triggered by movement. He glanced up involuntarily, and Zoe smiled.

'We'll take the film from those cameras with us. Just in case you change your mind, you see.' She kissed him with unexpected tenderness, her tongue entwining with his, and his cock, which had begun to relax, jerked erect again. 'But once the debt's cleared, you'll never have to see us again.'

He couldn't answer, couldn't fight, couldn't do anything except watch the door, longing for Miranda's return and his freedom. At last she returned, the black leather briefcase incongruously co-ordinating with her catsuit, the single bare white breast seeming to taunt him. She put the briefcase down on the frame beside his head, unlocked the combinations and took out a document, holding it where he could read it. As he'd expected, it was a full and final release from all their debts. He'd lose a lot of money, but for once the cash didn't matter.

'You'll sign it?' she asked when he nodded to signify that he'd finished reading. He nodded again, flexing his fingers gratefully when she undid the cuffs and strap and let him sit up. He signed, then waited for her to release him. Instead she reached for the cuffs again.

'No! That wasn't in the deal.'

He began to struggle, then stopped dead. He'd been so engrossed in the cleverly drafted document, he hadn't realised that James was standing between his legs. As he'd begun to fight, James had eased his cock against his captive's hole and begun to push, slowly, steadily, relentlessly. The master screamed and struggled as the pain intensified, but each girl grasped one of his wrists, pulling him flat. Gradually, with James savouring each movement, he was penetrated.

'Lie still,' Zoe ordered.

The master shook his head, writhing to try to unseat the intruder. James's cock slid free, and for a second he thought he'd won. Then it was back; this time in one brutal thrust that felt as if it would tear him apart.

'I warned you,' Zoe cooed. 'Now lie still.'

'We had a deal. I let you off; you let me go!'

'And we will, but there's still the interest to consider. The interest on our pain and fear and humiliation, and, worst of all, the pleasure. The pleasure your mind doesn't want, but your body's desperate for. The pleasure that's almost worse than pain, because it's addictive. Only you don't know that yet, do you? And teaching you that will be the worst punishment of all.'

Images flashed behind the master's eyes, piling fear upon fear. Miranda sobbing bitterly. James's eyes, so expressive as he flinched away from the touch that would bring such reluctant pleasure. Even Zoe, who refused nothing, crying and pleading as he took her to orgasm after orgasm until pain and pleasure mingled with exhaustion. Zoe, who now watched him steadily; whose hands now gripped his wrists.

'Make it easy for yourself,' Miranda said, just as he'd said to her that first time, and he gave a long, humiliated sobbing sigh.

There was nothing he could do except endure, and maybe co-operation would end the ordeal more quickly. He tried to deny the tiny part of him that wanted to co-operate and experience those wrackingly intense orgasms that he'd become such an expert in inducing. But he couldn't, and knowing he wasn't entirely unwilling doubled the pain. He still had some pride left, so he lay still while the cuffs and straps were refastened, staring at the man who penetrated him. Once he was sheathed in the master's arse, James leaned forward, taking his weight on his arms as his cock throbbed inside his ex-master's arse. Then Zoe moved into position, facing her prisoner as she eased her wet, greedy cunt over his erection. He moaned as he was taken, but her warm wetness eased his sore cock, and the extra sensation was a welcome distraction from the pressure in his arse. Finally, Miranda joined the tableau, tugging at the long zip that ran along her groin till she was bare from the base of her belly to the cleft of her buttocks.

'You're going to make us all come,' she said, crouching astride his face, pressing her open cunt against his unwilling lips. 'You're good at it. You enjoy it.'

Normally he was, and did, but this was different. Between the pressure of her weight on his chest and the terror he could hardly breathe. All he could see was her belly, but he could smell her and feel her juices dripping on to his chin. His world contracted to his pinioned body, his overfull rear passage, the heady feeling of Zoe's pussy contracting around his cock. She gave a soft, pleasure-filled moan, and he didn't need sight to know Miranda would be caressing her again.

'If you don't obey us, I'll whip you,' she said conversationally.

He began to lick frantically, insinuating his tongue first deep inside her, then sliding it forward to caress her clit. She moaned and ground herself down on his face, her hips jerking as she rode him. Nor was she the only one taking pleasure. Zoe had begun to move, raising and lowering herself on his cock, giving the little whimpers he knew only too well.

Soon they'd climax, but he wasn't stupid enough to think they'd let him come yet. James hadn't moved at all and, as the captive strained to listen, he could hear him panting as he fought for control. His cock seemed to swell within the master's arse, adding sensation to sensation until his ability to think was replaced by the overwhelming need to come.

The women used him relentlessly, emitting soft sighs and moans of pleasure; as careless of his need as he'd once been of theirs. He panted hard, redoubling his efforts, wishing he could raise his hips enough to encourage Zoe that last tiny step to orgasm, but Zoe needed no encouragement. Her body convulsed, her moans turning to a long, keening wail as she climaxed. As if her orgasm was a trigger, Miranda's sex tightened round his probing tongue as she came and came as he'd never known her come before. Then they both slumped forward, making it harder still for him to breathe, and that wasn't just from terror.

Two of his erstwhile slaves had taken their pleasure from him, but James's cock still pulsed within his arse. And his former master had trained him to postpone orgasm for hours, so this punishment could have only just begun.

'Unfasten him.' James's voice was harsh with lust, and the master closed his eyes as the women climbed off him and stepped back, still entwined in a sapphic embrace.

He'd always prided himself on his ability to control, but they'd forced him to do the one thing he'd always sworn that he could never enjoy, and they weren't finished with him yet. Soft fingers eased the cock harness away from his sticky swollen flesh, taking the condom with it. He almost came then, but Zoe was too clever for him. Her fingers nipped his balls until his erection began to subside; lust replaced by fear of what lay ahead.

'Not yet. We want to see you come when James buggers you!' she ordered. He sobbed, just once, then closed his eyes as she added the final refinement. 'And we want the film of it from the camera.'

He should have expected that. Hadn't he trained his slaves in exactly the same way, pushing them so close to orgasm that the very perversion they most dreaded became their trigger? And hadn't they learned well? And wasn't James beginning to move at last? His cock slid gently inside the naster's slick arse, and the master held his breath, praying he wouldn't withdraw now. He was so swollen, so tight, the pleasure/pain so entwined that it was hard to tell where one ended and the other began. But James did not withdraw. Slowly, carefully, almost lovingly, he began to thrust in and out of the trembling body, smiling as he bent to kiss away the tears that were trickling down his captive's face.

'You know you like it really,' he murmured, using the master's own words against him as he removed the nipple clamps. After so long constricted, the pain of returning circulation had him jerking upwards, as if he wanted to meet the thrusts. In a horrifying moment of self-knowledge he knew that he did.

He wanted the total loss of control, the smooth movement in his newly opened passage, the slick sliding up his well-greased arse that set his cock jerking in time to the movements. Even knowing he was being watched by the cameras' dispassionate eyes, and the girls he'd once subjugated, magnified the sensations. He gave a single howl of mingled rage, pleasure and relief as he climaxed, his cock spurting thick white spunk into the air as James emptied himself inside him. He was lost, taken, beaten, and knowing the depths he'd plumbed only added to the pleasure, taking him higher, further, deeper than he'd ever been before.

The orgasm seemed to last forever, leaving him so exhausted that all he could do was close his eyes and drift into sleep. He was unaware of James withdrawing, or them unfastening him with surprising gentleness and shifting him to the mattress that lay on the floor.

When he woke, he was alone, and for a second he hoped it had all been a dream. Then he saw the note and the set of pictures taped to his wrist that wrecked that hope as surely as they'd wrecked his pride.

'The debt is repaid, with interest,' he read; then he swallowed. 'And we won't be back, unless you want us to be.'

At first, he couldn't think of anything he wanted less. Then he remembered the sweetness of that long-delayed climax, and the sense of power that came from total helplessness. James's powerful warmth, Zoe's deliciously evil inventiveness, even Miranda's anger would haunt him forever, but he was too proud to ask for the sensations he'd crave for the rest of his life. And knowing that only his own egotism was stopping him was a punishment that even he had never been cruel enough to inflict.

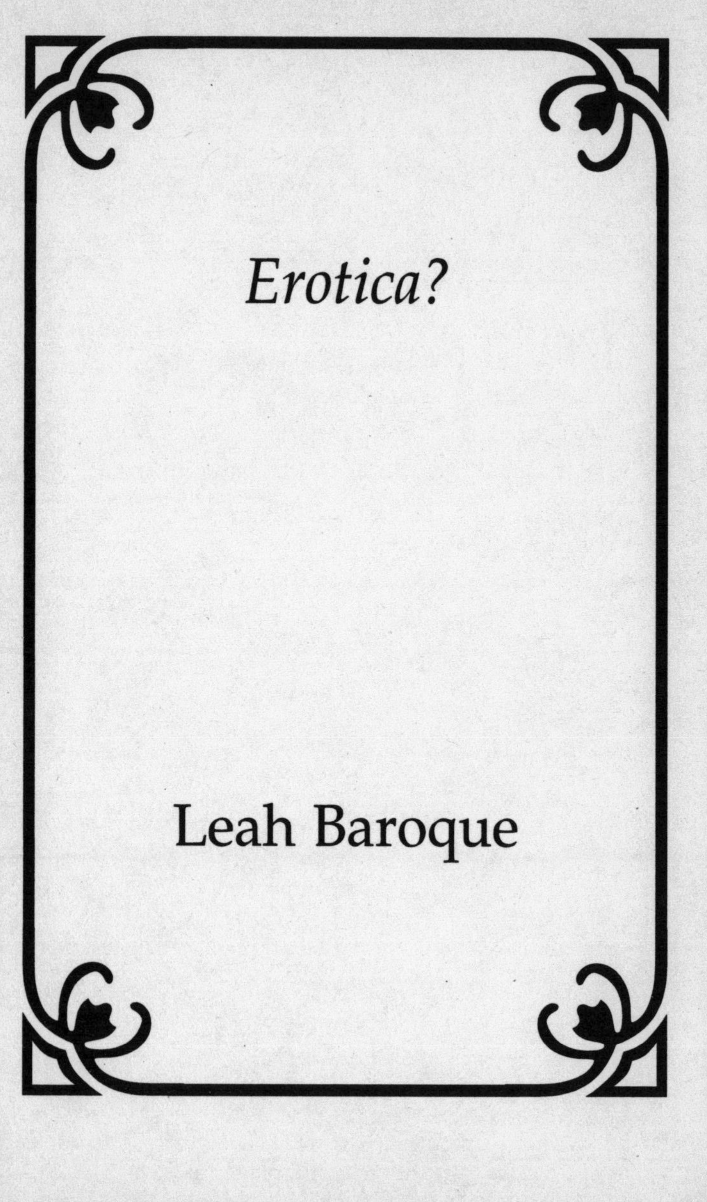
Erotica?
Leah Baroque

Erotica?

'Gotta surf sluts!' Jake called out excitedly from behind his porn-filled computer screen.

'Oh you're such a Sensitive New Age Guy.' Sarcasm may be the lowest form of wit, but that didn't stop me from regularly employing it.

'Hey, it's not that I personally view them as sluts, it's just the way they're promoted. Like this ad here, 'Hot and Horny Sluts'. It's a marketing thing.' He pointed to his computer screen, which was a mass of blonde hair, tits and pink bits.

'You're such a pervert,' I retorted, sitting on the couch and reading my favourite monthly women's magazine. It features centrefolds of naked men. Some of the photo shoots are in nature, at the beach or in tropical rain forest. Some of the photo shoots like to tease, with the model starting in his jeans and white shirt. As the photos progress he soon gets down to his Y-fronts, and then ... nothing at all. But I read it for the articles, of course.

'And you're a hypocrite if you think you're not a pervert too, Ali.' I looked up as Jake was saving another image to his hard drive. It was another blonde, maybe the same blonde; they all looked pretty similar to me. But this blonde was wearing miniscule denim shorts, quite tasteful compared to his usual fare. He might use this one as wallpaper for his computer screen, or perhaps add it to the many images that made up his pornographic screen saver collection. Once saved, he continued his mission of searching for more naked women in provocative positions.

'Do you see me downloading jpegs of naked women or mpegs of blow-jobs?'

'Ha, not exactly, but I see you doing the female equivalent. You're sitting there reading a magazine that has naked men in it . . .'

'I read it for the articles!' I'm always quick to defend myself.

'Well, the men are still in there, whether you're buying it to see them or not.'

'Yeah, but you're downloading pictures, only pictures, no words or anything.'

'You mean no pretence of words or articles to hide behind. Isn't honesty a virtue any more?' I find it funny how Jake rationalises being sleazy in front of me as part of the virtue of honesty.

'Depends on the circumstances; everything is relative, Jake.' I don't like Jake challenging my beliefs. Especially not on my day off. He wasn't even supposed to be here today. I'd been looking forward to a day by myself, after a busy week in the office. I'd planned to pamper myself with croissants, a bubble bath, erotica, and whatever delicious pleasures were to follow. But Jake's fishing trip had fallen through, so here he was, invading my private time. Not that Jake and I were having any problems. Well, no serious problems. We were still in love and had been together for the past two years. We'd only been living together for the past three months, though, and I was still adjusting to seeing him every day. It was nice to fall asleep with him, wake up with him, and having sex available whenever I felt like it was a definite bonus. But all of this familiarity had taken a little of the heat out of our sex life. Which is why I'd been looking forward to exploring my own fantasies, alone, today. Well, he might physically be here, but I wasn't going to let his presence cancel all my plans for the day.

I tried to imagine a large barrier between us. One that his comments couldn't penetrate so that I could read my erotica in peace. After finishing all of the erotica in that magazine I put it down, and picked up some I'd printed out from the Internet a few days before. The first story was a romance, completely vanilla. A few months ago it would have been enough to have my juices flowing, my pussy filling with need and my fingers fulfilling that need. But not any more; my fantasies had progressed. My desires had grown deeper, dirtier, a little more taboo. A vision of a happy couple having a candlelit dinner and making love on a bed of rose petals did very little to me now. I put the story aside without finishing it and looked over at Jake. He was still engrossed in his computer screen, another woman naked save for her little white socks, no doubt, or perhaps one with pink high heels and a spread, air-brushed cunt. Pathetic, I thought. He enjoys the mainstream and clichéd porn. I really don't understand that; it reinforces the notion that people's fantasies and desires are straightforward – uniform in fact.

I've always considered desires and fantasies to be highly individual. Sure, fantasies could certainly share some similar themes; there are always the classic ones that a great deal of people share, but then there are others, the more private and personal hidden desires. Perhaps Jake preferred to swim in the shallow end of his fantasies, only skimming the surface of the 'safe' ones that were shared by the majority. I often wondered if his mind harboured some of the more deviant desires that I was just discovering. But I was letting Jake invade my thoughts again. Instead of a day of relaxation and arousal, it was turning into a day of analysing the way my sexual psyche works. I think some things are better unanalysed; left to be enjoyed as a mystery. So I became engrossed in another story instead.

The next story I read was S&M, illustrated with black and white photographs of one woman spanking another who was tied up. The story connected loosely to the photographs, featuring two women playing with the roles of dominant and submissive.

In the story the dominant woman was paddling the submissive woman's arse, but the photographs only showed spanking by hand. I imagined what the sub's arse would look like as the wooden paddle hit it; how the flesh would wobble and quiver from the shock, like a pool of water after a stone has been thrown into its centre. I wanted to see the strap-on the story talked about: a big black double one with a dildo to fill her cunt and another smaller one to penetrate her arse. The descriptions of the slippery cunt and the tight clenching arsehole were delicious but I wanted to see it, in a photograph, or even in a film. Yes I wanted to see the action in real time.

'I said, if you're listening, I'm going down to the shop. Do you want anything?'

'Oh, the shop?' Jake had brought my thoughts out of the gutter and back to our lounge.

'Yes, for the third time, do you want anything?'

'Yeah. Milk, and some oranges. Thanks.'

'Reading porn are you?'

'Uh . . . it's erotica.' I held the pages closer to me so that Jake couldn't read any of the words or see any of the photographs.

'Yeah, "erotica" is just women's language for the porn they like. Whereas men's porn is called "porn".'

I held the pages a little looser, trying to appear more casual, like I didn't mind if he saw them or not. He laughed at me, saying he'd be about half an hour. As soon as Jake had left I went to get my vibrator and dildo from the bottom drawer in our bedroom, and jumped on to his computer, which he'd left connected to the Internet. A search engine soon delivered a list of promising sites.

Ah, a disclaimer, click on the button that says I'm over eighteen and I'm in. But it's a paysite and the sample stories break off halfway through, long before any climax . . . Back to the search engine, click on the button that says I'm over twenty-one. Agree to the disclaimer, which asks if my state and country laws allow me to view this kind of material. Well, actually they don't, but who is going to know, right? Click on the button that says my community is not offended by such material, although I'm sure Mrs Cruikshank down the road would be offended by it, and I'm in. Exactly what I was looking for: free fetish sites with illustrated stories.

I was already wet from the stories I'd been reading and the images on the screen sent bursts of electricity straight to my clit. A woman was squatting before a man, her hands on her hips, her thighs stretched wide and a dark stain spread over the crotch of her trousers. In following photographs the pee was soaking through and running on to the floor. The words 'she's never more beautiful than when she's wetting her knickers' jumped out at me from the screen. My cunt clenched a little, almost asking for something like a cock or a toy to grip. The thought of wetting myself in front of someone was shocking – a nightmare of humiliation – but today, seeing these pictures and reading about a man who loved wanking off to seeing women piss themselves, who revelled in it, playing the 'let's pretend I've been really bad' game, somehow this made me tingle and throb between my thighs. I imagined myself as the woman, standing or squatting before a man and telling him I had to please do it, honestly I did, and if he didn't let me use his bathroom I would have an accident. He'd be really wicked and not give in to me, and all the time he'd be rubbing himself, knowing that I was desperately holding on. Then I'd let loose, pissing through my panties and tight trousers, splashing on to the floor. I'd giggle at the stream, growing ever more aroused, watching him wank faster but staying hard so he could fuck me like I needed.

I was positively dripping, having been rubbing myself against the chair a little while reading the story. I removed my underwear, keeping my skirt on, and put the dildo on to the chair, then slowly lowered myself on to it. It slipped easily inside me, spreading my lips and making my clit bulge out around the width. My clit was throbbing and begging for attention from a finger or a tongue, a vibrator – anything to stroke it. As I lowered myself on to the dildo a second time, I imagined it wasn't a plastic cock but a real one. Yes, it was a stranger's cock I was slowly riding up and down on. He was leaning back on the chair and instructing my movements, telling me when to rise and when to sink back down. I clicked the mouse to load another story to the screen. It was another illustrated one featuring two men and a woman. Perfect: the woman was riding one man's cock, just as I rode my dildo, and the other man had his cock just inches from her hungry mouth. In the next photograph the cock was in her mouth, deeply down her throat, her lips around the base, with the other cock still in her. I longed for a cock to suck myself and started to suck and lick the vibrator a little.

I read some of the words; the woman was a naughty wife/slut. She had been cheating on her husband, Bill, and he'd caught her in the act with his best friend Steve, no less. Rather than call his lawyer to organise a divorce, Bill had unzipped his pants and put his cock in her face. Being the slut that she was, she'd hungrily sucked at her husband. But he didn't want her to have a good time; she was cheating on him, after all, so he was thrusting into her mouth, deeply, all the way. A slut could take such treatment, he reasoned. She gagged a little, but didn't dare complain because she was enjoying herself far too much. The husband soon tired of this, wanting to punish her properly. He instructed his stunned friend to take the slutty wife off his cock. He manoeuvred her around so that she was sucking her own juices from Steve's cock. Bill, her husband, started slapping her. Of course, she'd be moaning in pleasure at the painful heat spreading over her flesh.

My muscles spasmed at the vivid descriptions, imagining my own arse flesh glowing red as I was spanked by one man while sucking another's cock. The husband then thrust his cock in and out of his slutty wife's wet pussy several times before resting it at her tightly clenched arsehole. I moved a little faster on the dildo while looking at the pictures of the cock waiting to enter the tight hole. With some spit as lubrication, the head of the cock entered the wife/slut's arsehole. My fingers went to my own crack and moved around the satiny ring. When I saw the next few photographs, of the husband's cock buried in his slutty wife's arse while his friend lay on the ground, manoeuvring his cock into her cunt, I couldn't help myself. I took my vibrator, covered the tip in some lube and pressed it to the entrance. Slowly I eased the tip in, my arsehole clenching at the unfamiliar sensation of a foreign object entering it. When the spasms had subsided I eased myself down on to the vibrator, both orifices full of phallic plastic. I moaned loudly, never having felt so filled and at least a little surprised that my body could handle both at once. With both orifices filled, I rocked back and forth, the vibrator slipping a little out of my arse as the dildo fully penetrated my cunt, pressing against my clit, and then the dildo slipped a little from my pussy as the vibrator pressed deeper into my arse.

The plastic phalluses became real cocks in my mind's eye; one may belong to Jake – that detail didn't occur to me; in my fantasy I couldn't see whose cock was buried in my arse, and the cock in my cunt was a stranger's. But they were manhandling me, whoever they were. The guy underneath me with his cock working in and out of my previously virgin arsehole slapped my thighs and buttocks. The man fucking my cunt called me a slut for letting two strangers do this to me. I started moaning to myself about being 'a cock-hungry whore', and 'a little horny slut'. Especially to be fucking myself in both my cunt and my arse with plastic cocks.

'You slut, you dirty fucking disgusting slut . . .' I started muttering to myself as I was close to coming. The sound of the door slamming shut broke my erotic spell. I turned around to see Jake standing in the doorway. The shopping bags had dropped to his feet and a look of astonishment was glued to his face. My own face flushed red in embarrassment, but there was no hiding what I was up to. So I did the only thing possible and turned back to the computer screen, acting like this was perfectly natural. Jake came up behind me, kissing my neck and rubbing his hands over my shirt, undoing several of the buttons to free my breasts and pinch my nipples. I moaned at his attentions, my embarrassment subsiding slightly, much weaker than my desire. Jake helped me up, the dildo falling from my pussy, but his hand ensured the vibrator didn't fall out of my arse. He moved the chair away from the desk, bending me over it and undoing his jeans as he read the words on the screen out loud.

'"To his disbelief his wife was happily riding his best friend's cock, and on the leather sofa he'd bought her as a present last Christmas, no less. Bill couldn't believe his eyes; how could his wife do this to him? How could his best friend do this to him? His pain turned to lust at the vision before him; he undid his pants and released his cock. His wife looked up at him and opened her mouth. She didn't even look guilty or ashamed, only happy to have another cock to play with . . ."' He read on in silence, turning the vibrator on to a low setting, and my anus gripped at it, vibrating strongly. I gasped at the sensations, never having felt them before.

'A spanking for the slutty wife, huh? Do you know

who else gets spanked? Naughty girls get spanked, Ali. You've been sitting here fucking yourself with plastic cocks, reading pornography on the Internet. I think that's very naughty, Ali.' I held my breath, there was no point in denying it, this was porn; the mask of erotica wouldn't hold with Jake. I had to admit it, as humiliating as it was, I was a hypocrite.

'Isn't it, Ali? It's porn. And that makes you a pervert, more of a pervert than me, in fact. I don't read stories of double penetrations. What else have you been reading while I've been out?' He rubbed one palm around one of my buttocks, holding the vibrator inside me as he humiliated me further.

'Yes, it could probably be classed as porn . . . And I've been reading spanking stories . . . and pissing stories, but that's all.' He pushed my face against the bench. My buttocks rose up in the air, exposing my glistening lips beneath the vibrator that was still buzzing away.

'No, that's not all, Ali; you've been fucking yourself, and not just in your cunt but up your arse too.' He started moving the vibrator in and out of my arse, just to illustrate the point that I was enjoying such a dirty thing. I couldn't help but moan at the situation: I was bent over a computer desk; my boyfriend had busted me looking at porn and was now fucking my arse with a vibrator I'd put there.

'Yeah, that's it, baby, show me how naughty you are. Even now you're enjoying this, aren't you?' He slapped my arse with his spare hand and it turned into a wobbling mass of flesh. I gasped at the shock; it's what I'd been fantasising about but I hadn't expected Jake to be the one to initiate it. He slapped again at the other cheek and it too wobbled from the force. I imagined how delicious I must look, bent over with a vibrator stuck up my arse and my flesh wobbling around it, growing redder with every slap.

'How long has your deviant little mind been imagining

such things, Ali? How long have you been fantasising about having something up your arse, or having your buttocks spanked?' His spare hand pulled at my nipples, knowing that arousal was the best way to get confessions out of me.

'Only recently . . .' I was ashamed to tell him that over the last few months, during sex, I'd been imagining all kinds of filthy things. Like when he'd been fucking me doggie style I'd been imagining his cock was actually fucking my arse rather than my cunt.

'Only recently?' Well, I don't believe that for a second.' He released my hard nipples and started slapping my arse harder than before, believing that I'd told him a blatant lie. I moaned and gasped with the shock, trying to control my reactions, fearing that if I made too much noise he might stop. And I didn't want him to stop. My pleasure was building from the buzzing vibrator and the stinging slaps on my arse. With just the briefest touch to my clit I knew I could have come instantly.

'Oh, don't you dare do that. Don't you dare come, you horny little thing. You'll do as you're told, and I'm telling you not to come yet, OK?'

'OK.' I was amazed that he was enjoying this role of being the dominant punisher as much as I was enjoying being the naughty and submissive girl, busted looking at and doing filthy things.

He took his cock out of his jeans and rubbed it around my lips and clit. I moaned, pushing back against him. He started reading out the story, following it like a script.

'"Bill positioned his slutty wife over his friend's cock and she happily lowered herself on to the cock she'd previously been sucking. She started to ride him, up and down, bucking her hips to rub her clit against him. But Bill had other ideas; he didn't want to watch her pathetic show, she'd obviously been having too much fun without him lately and didn't deserve any more. He pushed her forward so that she was leaning over his friend; her tight little arsehole was in perfect view, twitching innocently."' Jake took the vibrator out of my arse and slowly pushed his cock into my pussy. I moaned deeply, loving the heat of his flesh in contrast to the cool plastic dildo. '"Bill positioned the head of his cock against his slutty wife's anus." Mmm, do you like the feel of this vibrator against your anus again, Ali?' Jake asked, his cock deep in me. The vibrator was hard and slippery against my anus. He must have put some more lube on it – how sweet. '"Bill slipped the head of his cock into his slutty wife's arse. She gasped a little at the full feeling of two cocks in her body at the same time."' Jake slipped the vibrator back into my arse as he read that – I was the slutty wife at that point in time. '"Bill wasn't sure if his wife had had anal sex before. He'd certainly never done it with her before now, but she didn't seem shocked that his cock was sinking deeply into her secret hole. His mind raced with the possibilities . . . perhaps his best friend had taken his wife's anal virginity, or any of the neighbours. Christ, it could have been anyone for all he knew. He started to move his cock in and out of her arse as the other cock moved in and out of her cunt."' Jake started moving the vibrator in and out in alternative thrusts to his cock.

I felt deliciously dirty, bent over the computer desk with my boyfriend fucking my cunt and penetrating my arse with a vibrator. Jake turned the vibrator on to a medium setting and held it firmly in place as he fucked my cunt harder. The vibrations spread out from my anus to my pussy and even my clit. It must have felt delicious for Jake, moving his cock in and out of my vibrating body. '"As both cocks sped up their thrusts in and out of her body she started to come."' Jake played with my clit, rubbing my juices around it, tapping it and squeezing lightly. And just as the story said, I started to come. The orgasm started in my arse, my pussy and my clit, and exploded into waves of pleasure which rocked through my body from toe to head and back again. As I continued to squirm on top of the desk, Jake removed the vibrator from my arse so that his cock could thrust more deeply inside me. In a few more thrusts I felt his come melting my insides, splashing against my muscles, which were still in spasm.

'"And as her body clenched around their cocks they both came deep inside her."' Jake read the last line of the story and collapsed on top of me, his torso wet with sweat and sticking to my back as we both caught our breath. In my post-orgasmic state I had a revelation: call it erotica, softcore pornography, hardcore pornography, hardcore erotica, literary pornography, or just plain porn – I loved it!

Visit the *Black Lace* website at

www.blacklace-books.co.uk

Find out the latest information and take advantage of our fantastic **free** book offer! Also visit the site for . . .

- All *Black Lace* titles currently available and how to order online
- Great new offers
- Writers' guidelines
- Author interviews
- An erotica newsletter
- Features
- Cool links

Black Lace – the leading imprint of women's sexy fiction.

Taking your erotic reading pleasure to new horizons

BLACK LACE NEW BOOKS

Published in September

GAME FOR ANYTHING

Lyn Wood

£6.99

Fiona finds herself on a word-games holidays with her best pal. At first it seems like a boring way to spend a week away. Then she realises it's a treasure hunt with a difference. Solving the riddles embroils her in a series of erotic situations as the clues get ever more outrageous.

Another fun sexy story from the author of *Intense Blue*.

ISBN 0 352 33639 0

CHEAP TRICK

Astrid Fox

£6.99

Tesser Roget is a girl who takes no prisoners. An American slacker, living in London, she dresses in funky charity-shop clothes and wears blue fishnets. She looks hot and she knows it. She likes to have sex, and she frequently does. Life on the fringe is very good indeed, but when she meets artist Jamie Desmond things take a sudden swerve into the weird.

Hold on for one hot, horny, jet-propelled ride through contemporary London.

ISBN 0 352 33640 4

FORBIDDEN FRUIT

Susie Raymond

£6.99

When thirty-something divorcee Beth realises someone is spying on her in the work changing room, she is both shocked and excited. When she finds out it's sixteen-year-old shop assistant Jonathan she cannot believe her eyes. Try as she might, she cannot get the thought of his fit young body out of her mind. Although she knows she shouldn't encourage him, the temptation is irresistible.

This story of forbidden lusts is a Black Lace special reprint.

ISBN 0 352 33306 5

Published in October

ALL THE TRIMMINGS

Tesni Morgan

£6.99

Cheryl and Laura, two fast friends, have recently become divorced. When the women find out that each secretly harbours a desire to be a whorehouse madam, there's nothing to stop them. On the surface their establishment is a five-star hotel, but to a select clientele it's a bawdy fun house for both sexes, where fantasies – from the mild to the increasingly perverse – are indulged.

Humorous and sexy, this is a fabulous yarn of women behaving badly and loving it!

ISBN 0 352 33641 2

WICKED WORDS 5

A Black Lace short story collection

£6.99

Black Lace short story collections are a showcase of the finest contemporary women's erotica anywhere in the world. With contributions from the UK, USA and Australia, the settings and stories are deliciously daring. Fresh, cheeky and upbeat, only the most arousing fiction makes it into a *Wicked Words* anthology.

By popular demand, another cutting-edge Black Lace anthology.

ISBN 0 352 33642 0

PLEASURE'S DAUGHTER

Sedalia Johnson

£6.99

It's 1750. Orphaned Amelia, headstrong and voluptuous, goes to live with wealthy relatives. During the journey she meets the exciting, untrustworthy Marquis of Beechwood. She manages to escape his clutches only to find he is a good friend of her aunt and uncle. Although aroused by him, she flees his relentless pursuit, taking up residence in a Covent Garden establishment dedicated to pleasure. When the marquis catches up with her, Amelia is only too happy to demonstrate her new-found disciplinary skills.

Find out what our naughty ancestors got up to in this Black Lace special reprint.

ISBN 0 352 33237 9

Published in November

THE ORDER
Dee Kelly
£6.99

Margaret Dempsey is an Irish Catholic girl who discovers sexual freedom in London but is racked with guilt – until, with the help of Richard Darcy, a failed priest, she sets up The Compassionate Order for Relief – where sexual pleasure is seen as Heaven-sent. Through sharing their fantasies they learn to shed their inhibitions, and to dispense their alms to those in sexual need. Through the Order, Margaret learns that the only sin is self-denial, and that to err is divine!

An unusual and highly entertaining story of forbidden lusts and religious transgressions.

ISBN 0 352 33652 8

PLAYING WITH STARS
Jan Hunter
£6.99

Mariella, like her father before her, is an astrologer. Before she can inherit his fortune, she must fulfil the terms of his will. He wants her to write a *very* true-to-life book about the male sexual habits of the twelve star signs. Mariella's only too happy to oblige, but she has her work cut out: she has only one year to complete the book and must sleep with each sign during the month of their birth. As she sets about her task with enthusiastic abandon, which sign will she rate the highest?

A sizzling, fun story of astrology and sexual adventure.

ISBN 0 352 33653 6

THE GIFT OF SHAME
Sara Hope-Walker
£6.99

Jeffery is no more than a stranger to Helen when he tells her to do things no other man has even hinted at. He likes to play games of master and servant. In the secrecy of a London apartment, in the debauched opulence of a Parisian retreat, they become partners in obsession, given to the pleasures of perversity and shame.

This is a Black Lace special reprint of a sophisticated erotic novel of extreme desires and shameful secrets.

ISBN 0 352 32935 1

To find out the latest information about Black Lace titles, check out the website: www.blacklace-books.co.uk or send a stamped addressed envelope to:

Black Lace, Thames Wharf Studios,
Rainville Road, London W6 9HA

Please note only British stamps are valid.

BLACK LACE BOOKLIST

Information is correct at time of printing. To avoid disappointment check availability before ordering. Go to www.blacklace-books.co.uk

All books are priced £5.99 unless another price is given.

Black Lace books with a contemporary setting

THE TOP OF HER GAME	Emma Holly ISBN 0 352 33337 5	☐
IN THE FLESH	Emma Holly ISBN 0 352 33498 3	☐
SHAMELESS	Stella Black ISBN 0 352 33485 1	☐
TONGUE IN CHEEK	Tabitha Flyte ISBN 0 352 33484 3	☐
SAUCE FOR THE GOOSE	Mary Rose Maxwell ISBN 0 352 33492 4	☐
INTENSE BLUE	Lyn Wood ISBN 0 352 33496 7	☐
THE NAKED TRUTH	Natasha Rostova ISBN 0 352 33497 5	☐
A SPORTING CHANCE	Susie Raymond ISBN 0 352 33501 7	☐
TAKING LIBERTIES	Susie Raymond ISBN 0 352 33357 X	☐
A SCANDALOUS AFFAIR	Holly Graham ISBN 0 352 33523 8	☐
THE NAKED FLAME	Crystalle Valentino ISBN 0 352 33528 9	☐
CRASH COURSE	Juliet Hastings ISBN 0 352 33018 X	☐
ON THE EDGE	Laura Hamilton ISBN 0 352 33534 3	☐
LURED BY LUST	Tania Picarda ISBN 0 352 33533 5	☐
LEARNING TO LOVE IT	Alison Tyler ISBN 0 352 33535 1	☐

THE HOTTEST PLACE	Tabitha Flyte ISBN 0 352 33536 X	☐
THE NINETY DAYS OF GENEVIEVE	Lucinda Carrington ISBN 0 352 33070 8	☐
EARTHY DELIGHTS	Tesni Morgan ISBN 0 352 33548 3	☐
MAN HUNT £6.99	Cathleen Ross ISBN 0 352 33583 1	☐
MÉNAGE £6.99	Emma Holly ISBN 0 352 33231 X	☐
DREAMING SPIRES £6.99	Juliet Hastings ISBN 0 352 33584 X	☐
THE TRANSFORMATION £6.99	Natasha Rostova ISBN 0 352 33311 1	☐
STELLA DOES HOLLYWOOD £6.99	Stella Black ISBN 0 352 33588 2	☐
UP TO NO GOOD £6.99	Karen S. Smith ISBN 0 352 33589 0	☐
SIN.NET £6.99	Helena Ravenscroft ISBN 0 352 33598 X	☐
HOTBED £6.99	Portia Da Costa ISBN 0 352 33614 5	☐
TWO WEEKS IN TANGIER £6.99	Annabel Lee ISBN 0 352 33599 8	☐
HIGHLAND FLING £6.99	Jane Justine ISBN 0 352 33616 1	☐
PLAYING HARD £6.99	Tina Troy ISBN 0 352 33617 X	☐
SYMPHONY X £6.99	Jasmine Stone ISBN 0 352 33629 3	☐
STRICTLY CONFIDENTIAL £6.99	Alison Tyler ISBN 0 352 33624 2	☐
SUMMER FEVER £6.99	Anna Ricci ISBN 0 352 33625 0	☐
CONTINUUM £6.99	Portia Da Costa ISBN 0 352 33120 8	☐
OPENING ACTS £6.99	Suki Cunningham ISBN 0 352 33630 7	☐
FULL STEAM AHEAD £6.99	Tabitha Flyte ISBN 0 352 33637 4	☐
A SECRET PLACE £6.99	Ella Broussard ISBN 0 352 33307 3	☐
GAME FOR ANYTHING £6.99	Lyn Wood ISBN 0 352 33639 0	☐

FORBIDDEN FRUIT
£6.99
Susie Raymond
ISBN 0 352 33306 5 ☐

CHEAP TRICK
£6.99
Astrid Fox
ISBN 0 352 33640 4 ☐

THE ORDER
£6.99
Dee Kelly
ISBN 0 352 33652 8 ☐

PLAYING WITH STARS
£6.99
Jan Hunter
ISBN 0 352 33653 6 ☐

THE GIFT OF SHAME
£6.99
Sara Hope-Walker
ISBN 0 352 32935 1 ☐

Black Lace books with an historical setting

PRIMAL SKIN
Leona Benkt Rhys
ISBN 0 352 33500 9 ☐

DEVIL'S FIRE
Melissa MacNeal
ISBN 0 352 33527 0 ☐

WILD KINGDOM
Deanna Ashford
ISBN 0 352 33549 1 ☐

DARKER THAN LOVE
Kristina Lloyd
ISBN 0 352 33279 4 ☐

STAND AND DELIVER
Helena Ravenscroft
ISBN 0 352 33340 5 ☐

THE CAPTIVATION
£6.99
Natasha Rostova
ISBN 0 352 33234 4 ☐

CIRCO EROTICA
£6.99
Mercedes Kelley
ISBN 0 352 33257 3 ☐

MINX
£6.99
Megan Blythe
ISBN 0 352 33638 2 ☐

PLEASURE'S DAUGHTER
£6.99
Sedalia Johnson
ISBN 0 352 33237 9 ☐

Black Lace anthologies

CRUEL ENCHANTMENT
Erotic Fairy Stories
Janine Ashbless
ISBN 0 352 33483 5 ☐

MORE WICKED WORDS
Various
ISBN 0 352 33487 8 ☐

WICKED WORDS 4
Various
ISBN 0 352 33603 X ☐

Black Lace non-fiction

THE BLACK LACE BOOK OF WOMEN'S SEXUAL FANTASIES
Ed. Kerri Sharp
ISBN 0 352 33346 4 ☐

- - - - - - ✂ - - - - - - - - - - - - - - - - - -

Please send me the books I have ticked above.

Name ....

Address ....

....

....

.... Post Code ....

Send to: **Cash Sales, Black Lace Books, Thames Wharf Studios, Rainville Road, London W6 9HA.**

US customers: for prices and details of how to order books for delivery by mail, call 1-800-805-1083.

Please enclose a cheque or postal order, made payable to **Virgin Publishing Ltd**, to the value of the books you have ordered plus postage and packing costs as follows:

UK and BFPO – £1.00 for the first book, 50p for each subsequent book.

Overseas (including Republic of Ireland) – £2.00 for the first book, £1.00 for each subsequent book.

If you would prefer to pay by VISA, ACCESS/MASTERCARD, DINERS CLUB, AMEX or SWITCH, please write your card number and expiry date here:

....

Please allow up to 28 days for delivery.

Signature ....

- - - - - - ✂ - - - - - - - - - - - - - - - - - -